GENESIS OF WOOD

The Elementals Book 3

Jennifer L. Kelly

Library of Congress PCN: 2017900504

BoxerBull Books

Cleveland, OH

ISBN-10: 0-99-77764-5-5
ISBN-13: 978-0-9977764-5-4

*TO ANYONE WHO'S EVER WONDERED WHO AM
I? OR WHY AM I HERE? OR IF PERHAPS YOU'RE
STILL TRYING TO WORK THAT BIT OUT.*
-J.L.K.

OTHER BOOKS BY JENNIFER L. KELLY

THE ELEMENTALS

ARMY OF FIRE
THE EARTH KEY

THE LUCIA CHRONICLES

THE PROPHECY
THE DISSENTIENT
THE BEACON
THE GIRL WHO WASN'T LOVED (NOVELLA)

STAND ALONE FICTION

THE FRACTURED LIFE OF JENNY MCCLAIN

PROLOGUE

There once was a naive, young woman named Novea. She was fascinated with mankind. Sure, she looked like she was human, except for the radiant skin and silky, chestnut-colored hair. Only she wasn't human; she was a daughter of the Universe, one of the five goddesses birthed of Raj and Katayun. The entire Universe was at her fingertips, until the Imminent Darkness, disguised as a codger, tricked Novea and her four sisters. He separated the sisters, drawing a wedge between them. As a result Raj created a Land for each one of his daughters: one each of Fire, Earth, Wood, Metal, and Water. Novea ruled the planet Earth, until her sister Celosia played a trick on her, gifting her the sun to create life, but then cruelly taking it away, for as we now know, the sun was a star. And eventually stars die.

Xon 9 is where mankind went to live before the Earth

disappeared in a fiery inferno. That's where things get interesting. Novea was intrigued by humankind, specifically their ability to feel so deeply and passionately. She would wear her golden cloak and wander the streets, sticking to the shadows, until one day she was noticed by a handsome young man named Absalom. Novea didn't intend to fall in love with Absalom, but soon she found herself wanting to stay with the mortal man. Raj and Katayun gave their blessing, under the condition that Novea would have to become mortal. If she returned at any time to her home, the Land of Earth, she would never be able to return to Xon 9. If she returned, she would die. All of time and space, given up in the name of love. She agreed.

They were married and eventually had a child, a half-immortal, half-mortal daughter. A seemingly impossible hybrid. Absalom knew Novea was a daughter of the Universe and he knew his daughter was bestowed with powerful gifts from each of the Elemental Goddesses upon her birth. But sometimes things don't go quite as planned. The daughter's birth created an imbalance in the Universe, a balance that had persisted since time itself began.

Now their daughter is grown and the Imminent Darkness has returned to restore what has been lost.

But not if I can help it. Who am I?

I'm the granddaughter of Raj and Katayun.

I'm the daughter of Novea and Absalom.

I am the Impossible Girl.

I am Ka.

CHAPTER 1

The familiar, constant breeze has gone still. I have blisters on the soles of both my feet and they rub uncomfortably against my boots. The palms of my hands are caked with dirt and dry blood. Somehow the surrounding mountains have blocked the breeze. The air here is humid and so thick you could cut it with a knife. Sloan and I pause to take a drink and swallow some nutrient pills. It's only been about two days' time and already his face has taken on a more angular appearance, his sea green eyes alert in the shadows of his face. The gills that line the right side of his face wiggle thankfully as his water equilibrium is restored.

"Don't look at me like that," he says replacing the cap on the bottle of nutrient pills and tossing it back to me

"Like what?" I ask slipping the bottle inside my messenger bag. It drops with a clunk beside my jacket, more bottles of water, a couple flashlights, an empty glass jar and the burlap sack Bina gave me. All that's left in the sack is a speckled feather, a pack of matches from the Old Tavern and the Sea, and a small crystal.

"Like I'm some alien just landed from outer space."

I push myself off the mountainside which I had been leaning against. "We are in outer space."

We're colonists on Xon 9. Not the original colonists, that was some years ago. But we are the descendants: the Elementals. The scientists discovered Xon 9 when they went out searching for other habitable planets since Earth was about to become toast, thanks to the dying of the sun. Xon 9 was good enough. Its two moons provided enough gravitational pull, the red sun never setting past the horizon, casting the planet forever in an eerie glow of pinks and reds. There's no surface water on Xon 9, but there is plenty in the planet's inner layers, nothing a state-of-the-art drill can't extract. Animals and crops from home are raised in storehouses run by the Earth Elementals from the Agricultural Department.

The only thing the original colonists hadn't accounted for once they set up shop on Xon 9 and decided to call it home, was the unique physiological affects the planet's Elements would have on our fragile human bodies. I guess these things can be overlooked when you're running against the clock of a supernova. There are five Elements: Earth, Fire, Wood, Water, and Metal. Over time, the colonists came to harness the unique gifts of each of these Elements. Earth is wise. Fire is passionate. Wood is steadfast. Water is nurturing. And Metal is strong. Which was all fine and dandy until they also realized the whole yin and yang of it all. If one is not careful, the Element can take over, and cause one to become Unbalanced. Earth can become stubborn, Fire impulsive. Wood can turn unyielding and Water unrelenting. And Metals can become aggressive. The Elements have a fine balance and it is up to the individual to harness and control it. Only, it's not that simple.

"Is that it?" I ask squinting and pointing a short distance up the path. Sloan turns and peers in the direction which I'm pointing.

"I don't think so. Remember Bina said Old Earth-cactus style. Those just look like bushes." We keep walking, the thickness of the air pressing on us from either side. I'd always taken the constant 67-degree Fahrenheit temperature and ever-present breeze of Xon 9 for granted. I make a silent vow to be more appreciative.

What I mean when I say that it's not that simple is really that none of it makes any sense. All of the Elements affect each one of us, yet at the end of our schooling, as we near our eighteenth moon, we're forced to choose one Element. Choosing an Element is a Pronouncement and a lifelong label. I had the worst time deciding. I didn't feel connected to any of the Elements. I felt like nothing. Hollow almost, like an empty shell.

And that's because I *was* empty. But now I am becoming filled. Filled with each of the Elements. All of the Elements. I am the Impossible Girl of Legend. I am born of the goddess Novea and her mortal lover Absalom. I am the only grandchild of the Universe itself. Because of this, upon my birth, I was bestowed with many gifts. In fact, I was given one gift from each of my mother's sisters: the gifts of each of the Elements. Unfortunately, my aunts' generosity threw the Universe off-kilter and now the Imminent Darkness is out to restore the balance that was lost. And not necessarily in my favor.

When I was young my mother saw my propensity for each Element and was afraid the ID (Imminent Darkness) would come for me. So in order to protect me she consulted a Seer, a Metal woman named Bina, who also happens to be Sloan's mother (more on that in a minute). The Metal woman told my mother that in order to protect me she had to throw five stones—one for each Element—into the Elemental Abyss, deep in the mountains of Xon 9, and as I now know, not short on enchantments and obstacles. My mother did as she was told. With each stone trapped inside the Elemental Abyss, so too was that Elemental part of my personality, thus explaining the emptiness. Retrieve and destroy the stones, restore my fractured personality. Sounds simple.

Only the Imminent Darkness grows stronger as I grow stronger. And now with both my mother and father in the Land of Earth, I have to rely on Sloan. I watch his lithe form as he hikes up the trail in front of me, periodically pausing and scanning the rocky landscape for a bright red flower atop a plant with poisonous thorns. Sloan was my teacher and is now my boyfriend. Now before you get all weirded out, he's only about three years older than me. After Pronouncement, new Elementals attend the University Complex to become more familiar with their Element and to induce the Transition Phase. Even weirder still (I know, really, does it get much weirder? Yes, in fact it does.) Sloan is my protector. Not that I can't protect myself, because I totally can with my ability to conjure Fire energy and my newest trick: green vines that shoot out from the inside of my wrists. I turn over my hand, inspecting the green tinge my veins have taken on. Normally, an Elemental develops the telltale signs on the right side of the face: a clear indication of your forever affiliation. Apparently, being half-goddess, and half-mortal manifests the Elements in a completely different way. But back to Sloan.

Before he'd even met me or even knew who I was, his mother had told him about her visions, about the Impossible Girl who would be coming to save the colonists (and possibly the Universe) from the deception and darkness of the ID. Sloan has some of his mother's gifts, like he can dream walk, and send these sort of weird messages, but he's also like his father, Finn. He's got a fierce allegiance to the truth, sometimes to a fault. While my mother was tossing stones into the Elemental Abyss, Sloan made an Everlasting Vow by the light of the twin moons, to protect the Impossible Girl no matter the cost, not so much *for* me but because *of* me. Because I may have all the Elements in my blood, but so too does every colonist of Xon 9. The notion that we must choose is a farce. We are all one.

Sweat drips down the back of my neck. I rub the droplets away, feeling the smoothness of my tattooed skin juxtaposed against the Fire filigree and tubular green Earth vines that now bulge beneath my fingers. My Elemental Star. With each acquisition of a stone, my tattoo seems to morph in response. Two down, three more to go. Only first...

"There!" I call out, seeing the glint of red just past Sloan's right shoulder.

"I see it!" He starts to jog toward it, veering off the path and heading into a small alcove. There's a cluster of three sturdy-looking green plants. They kind of resemble people with a head in the middle and arms held up in an awkward surrender posture. White spines poke out from the plant everywhere and nestled in the top, where I imagine a face would be, is a large red blossom.

"Ignis Flos," I breathe.

"The fire flower." Sloan takes a step closer inspecting the plant. He's about to reach out and touch one of the white spines, but I put a hand out to stop him.

"Bina said they're poisonous, remember?" The red flower seems to taunt us, its beauty protected by the poisonous spines surrounding it.

He nods and pulls a small knife from the pocket of his cargo pants. I reach up carefully, gently pulling the red, silken petals out of the way, avoiding the spines that surround the plant.

"And what about you? What if you get pricked?" He asks as he tries to maneuver around the numerous poisonous spines to get to the plant itself, which is nestled around an intrusive cluster.

"Half-immortal," I reason.

"Tsk. Half-mortal," he corrects. "That's the kind of thinking that will get you killed, Ka Waylon."

Ever so delicately he takes the blade and slices at the base of the flower which I pluck off the cactus. The blade of his knife slices through some of the nearby spines and a black substance oozes along the blade, dripping to the red dirt at our feet.

I pull out the empty glass jar and place the bloom inside it, careful to avoid the base of the plant in case there's any lingering poison.

"*Ignis flos to appease the beast in the chasm*," I recite the words from my mother's hand-written notes.

"At the very least, I hope it's appreciative," Sloan says dumping some water on the blade of his knife. He closes the knife and drops it back into his pocket, taking another long drink of water. "So, where to now Ka, Warrior Princess?"

I pull out the tattered map with my mother's notes, trying to orient myself. We need to get back to the cavern with the enchanted lake. I look up, and point in the opposite direction. "The Elemental Abyss is that way."

Chapter 2

It's as if the mountains themselves had been holding their breath. We round a corner and the wind begins to pick up, whipping my short ponytail and tossing bits of dirt that sting my cheeks. The path has opened up and we're walking along a ledge about two meters wide. To my right is a jagged red wall of rock and to my left is nothing but air. Straight down to the red earth below or straight up to the red sky.

The warm breeze caresses my sweat-moistened skin and the atmosphere seems to release, the heaviness evaporating. I pause at the ledge, peering off into the landscape. I know there are stars in the sky, outer space has stars after all, our red blazing sun being one of them. But I cannot see any of the others because our own shines so bright. In the distance I can see the tiny flickers of lights, little golden dots on the horizon. Home. So small, so seemingly insignificant. How is it that Xon 9 appears so vast, yet what we've come to inhabit is so small? The Imminent Darkness is what some would say. I'm not sure what I believe anymore.

My mother is a goddess and my father is a mortal. My mother lived in the colony as an Earth Elemental, working in the Agricultural Department. She studied food shortages, one of the downfalls of Old Earth society before the dying sun had other ideas in mind. My father was a Liege to the Leadership Council, a group of four male and one female Wood Elementals. Woods are the natural leaders, although not charismatic like Fire, they are steadfast and yielding when in balance. Their roots are planted firmly in the ground and yet they have the ability to reach toward the stars for advancement. Only we haven't advanced. *Divide et impera.* The motto of the University Complex drifts into my mind. It isn't the first time I've heard the peculiar phrase. I've heard it one other time in a story. The story of how the Imminent Darkness disguised itself as a codger and tricked the five goddesses, my mother included. Divide and conquer. If you divide the whole into smaller parts it is easier to conquer is how I've come to view the phrase, knowing what I now know.

The Imminent Darkness is as old as time. It is an ancient, formless energy and can take on any form that it pleases: a wolf, a mummy, a young girl, almost anything. Sloan comes to stand beside me, also peering off into the distance. The ID could even take his form and I would never know the difference. The ID drains the energy of all those around it. That's how I'll hopefully know. An ancient darkness out to claim a debt to be repaid. I guess I'm the debt in this scenario. But I don't plan on paying it back so easily. Somehow the ID has infiltrated the ranks of our Leadership Council. A mysterious group of citizen law enforcers formed, only it wasn't the laws of Xon 9 that they were enforcing. Anyone who spoke against the Imminent Darkness, and called out the dark force for what it truly was, was taken away. Sloan's dad Finn Braden, my own father, and countless others. The Imminent Darkness somehow reaches into the darkest, tiniest recesses of the hearts of those it infests, like a plague.

But why? I'm still trying to make sense of it all. I can't believe that people are just inherently evil. But neither can I believe that they are simply inherently good either. If the Imminent Darkness were to kill me, would the Universe go back to the way it was supposed to be? Would my fellow colonists live in a thriving, expanding metropolis? Or would they continue to live in their small, almost quarantined part of the planet?

"It seems so small." Sloan's voice is soft, barely above a whisper. He's never been up here in the mountains of Xon 9. This isn't my first trip. Each one stranger than the last.

"I know. It's odd, isn't it? This whole planet." I gesture as if I could encompass the expanse of desert beneath us. "And that's it."

"Maybe you're right. Maybe the Council somehow has something to do with the Imminent Darkness."

"But what?" That's the feeling that's been nagging at me since my last trip to the Elemental Abyss. I feel like I'm missing something important, a key of some sort to solving the puzzle.

"It will reveal itself in due course."

"You sound like Bina. Cryptic and not making any sense."

"Ah, but she always makes sense in the end." He kneels and then sits on the ground, his feet dangling precariously over the edge, brown hair tousled by the wind. He pats the ground beside him. "Sit. Rest."

As much as I want to head into the cavern that I know is just around another bend, I oblige and sit down on the rough ground beside him. He's right. The journey will be exhausting. Even once we get past the enchanted lake and over the fiery chasm, we will head into a portal to another Land where time is altered. Who knows when the next chance to truly—and safely—rest may be. He scoops up my hand and I can feel the callouses that have formed since our journey into the mountains began.

"Tell me about the Land of Fire again." He closes his eyes.

"Fiery inferno. Black sky, volcanoes, rivers of lava, very unpleasant."

He opens one eye. "For some reason when grading your Universal History papers I found you to be much more eloquent."

"You were just blinded by love."

"Something like that." He grins. "Tell me about the Land of Earth."

Images come flooding to my mind amid the recollection. There are so many details: so many colors and sounds. How can you describe something so beautiful with mere words? "A forest with birds chirping and insects buzzing. A bubbling creek rushing down from a beautiful, purple mountain. Lush green grass and flowers of every color you could imagine. Furry creatures rambling about. A sandy beach with crystalline blue water." He smiles at this. "A pyramid with a gold tip shining into the cyan blue sky, and a golden orb hanging in the horizon that can turn the sky curious shades of purple, pink, and orange." I shake my head. "My words don't do it justice."

"That's okay. I can still see it."

I nudge him. "You know I hate when you do that."

"You said so yourself words don't do it justice. Besides, I don't always do it. Mostly only when I sense that you're in danger." You think being in a relationship is tough? Try having a boyfriend who can walk right into your dreams and who can read your mind. Puts the whole trust thing on another level. "Do you feel better?"

"Huh?"

"You were nervous."

"How do you know?"

"Ka, really." I raise an eyebrow. "Well, if you must know, no, I wasn't peering into your mind. Whenever you're nervous you bite your bottom lip. Do you know how many times I called on you in class or noticed you do that while taking an exam?"

"You noticed?" Despite everything I still find it amazing that someone as handsome and smart as Sloan noticed me. Sometimes I think he noticed me before I even noticed myself.

"Of course I did. You're kind of hard not to notice. Now more than ever." He wraps a hand around the back of my neck so that his palm is flush against my tattoo and pulls my mouth toward his. He pulls away too soon leaving me breathless, my heart fluttering in my chest like the wings of a tiny bird.

"We should get going." I push myself to my feet. And Sloan follows me down the path, leaving the dotted lights of our colony even farther in the distance. The twin moons hang high in the sky flanked against the low sun. Nighttime. Even so, there's still plenty of light. We reach the opening to the cavern, dark and ominous. I pull out the two flashlights from my messenger bag and hand one to Sloan.

He shines it into the darkness. The white beam of light catches the dewy stalagmites and stalactites. The stalagmites emerge from the floor of the cavern reaching up like knobby fingers toward the stalactites' jagged edges. Some of the stalagmites and stalactites have met in the middle forming a sort of column. Water drips down their sides. In the distance I can hear the crush of the enchanted waterfall as it pours into the lake. Luckily, we're still too far away to be affected by its charms.

"It's like another world in here," Sloan says, still sweeping his light this way and that taking in the enormity of the cavern.

"A world within a world within a world."

We begin to head down the path which slopes down and to the right. The nearer we get to the lake, the crush of the waterfall grows louder. "Here," I say stopping. I flip open my messenger bag and pull out the glass jar labeled Medeis Seaweed. It looks disgusting. It's greenish-brown water with brown-green chunks floating in its murkiness. We're supposed to stick it into our ears to block out the sound of the waterfall's enchantment. As I know all too well, the waterfall lures you to sleep, taking you to your chosen place of comfort. Once you're asleep there are only two ways to break the enchantment. One, is to get far enough away that you can no longer hear the pounding of the waterfall. Easier said than done if you and everyone else is in the Land of Nod. Two, is to die. Yeah, I know, right? If you die in the dream, you wake up alive and in one piece in the real world. That is if you can trust that you aren't really dying, despite your entire body telling you otherwise.

I unscrew the lid and close my eyes, thrusting my hand into the nastiness of the jar. It's even worse because the liquid is temperate. I try not to gag as I pull out a handful of chunks and hand them to Sloan. He makes a face, and if I do say, turns a little green around the gills. Come on, he's a Water Elemental. Seaweed can't bother him all that much.

"When it's been sitting on a shelf in my mother's kitchen for who knows how long, yeah, it bothers me." I pull out another small handful. We got this from Bina, but if we run out we'll need to buy more in the Black Bazaar. The Black Bazaar is the market of the Underground. It's a haven for Unbalanced Metals who sell forbidden treats to the uninitiated. I take a deep breath and press the seaweed into my ear cavity, careful not to push it too far down. The seaweed is damp and slimy, but much to my surprise it seems to expand and solidify when it enters into my ear. Not solid like a piece of wood or something, but more like a spongey material. I can no longer hear the crush of the waterfall. I screw the cap back on the jar with the remaining Medeis Seaweed and toss it back into my bag. When I look up, Sloan's mouth is moving but no sound is coming out.

I shrug and shake my head no. He points to his ears and rolls his eyes. He forgot. This time he's careful to annunciate each of his words so I can read his lips. "Are you ready?"

I nod. Together we round the corner leading us to the enchanted lake.

. . .

Sloan comes to a stop. He's never been here before. The first time I came here my now friend Doran came with me. The second time I took a bit of a detour and only returned by way of the Elemental Abyss. It's quite magnificent. A beautiful, cerulean lake is before us. On the other side of the lake is a gigantic, manmade waterfall that glows luminously, almost as though it is lit from within. The top disappears into the jagged stalactites above. The shoreline is small and dirt packed. A lone wooden rowboat rocks idly in the shallow water. A frayed rope tethers it to a wooden stake.

I nudge past Sloan and begin untethering the rope. More likely than not I was the last one here. I look up. It's as if Sloan is frozen to the spot. I know the seaweed is working because I can't hear a thing, the resounding crush of the waterfall is blocked out. I wave my hand in front of his face and he snaps to and begins to help me climb inside the boat. I do a mental head slap. Sloan is a Water. I've been in the Water Building at the University Complex. There's a beautiful pool of water in its lowest levels where Waters can truly immerse themselves in their Element. But even that was manmade. Sloan's probably never seen anything quite like this waterfall, tucked deep inside an unsuspecting cavern.

We sit across from each other. The boat is down an oar from one of my previous visits. Sloan takes the remaining oar and begins to rhythmically paddle us across the lake, heading directly toward the waterfall. The portals are located on the other side, behind the waterfall. His green eyes dart around, taking in the surroundings. If I hadn't traveled myself to other worlds—the Land of Fire and the Land of Earth—I'd think we'd already entered one. But this is only the beginning of our journey.

Suddenly, there's a *plunk* and a splash of water, cool droplets kiss my forearm. The boat rocks. Sloan's eyes go black, but I shake my head. This time I know better. It's not a threat. A reptilian face breaches the surface. The face has scales like Sloan, but where his softly line one side of his face, this face is entirely covered with them. Pale green eyes peer back at me. Thick, fleshy lips peel back revealing sharp pointy teeth. But I know this creature isn't here to devour us. It's my friend, Brooks. And, yes, that's really his name. I totally get it with the whole Water thing.

"Hey, Princess."

I point to my ears and shake my head to indicate I can't hear him, only I realize that I *can* hear him. "Hey, wait. How'd you do that?"

He raises an eyebrow and it disappears into his shaggy green-black hairline. "What can I say? I'm gifted." I roll my eyes. "Okay, okay. The Medeis Seaweed comes from this lake. It's like, I don't know, that I'm one with the seaweed."

Sloan nods. "It's true all ecosystems are interrelated. I wouldn't be surprised that the creatures were in tune with the environmental vibrations of the plants and other species." Reading his lips I think I get about every other word.

"Who's the smarty pants?" Brooks asks.

"That's my boyfriend, Sloan. Sloan, this is Brooks. I've already told him all about you."

"Only the good things I hope." Brooks grins, but instead of having a warm, fuzzy affect, it looks more like a snarl.

Sloan has stopped paddling and we're drifting in the middle of the lake. In the past, Brooks has only shown up as I've drifted off to sleep. He's saved my life more than once, not that he'd let me forget it. But since neither of us has drifted off to the land of enchantment thanks to the Medeis Seaweed, I'm wondering why he's here. And I don't think it's just to say hello.

He swims closer to the boat and his webbed fingers grip the sides. "It's been here." His voice is barely above a whisper.

"Who?"

His eyes widen. "You know. It."

"You mean the Immin—"

He stretches out a hand and presses a finger to my lips, dripping water into my lap. "Shhh! Don't say it. It will upset the others." I haven't interacted with any other creatures in the lake, but I know that they're here. I've felt them even if I haven't seen them. "We were put here by Raj and Katayun, given a home here in order to protect the Elemental Abyss. But it's been here." His eyes are clouded with worry. He removes his finger from my lips, leaving a cold film that I want to wipe away on my t-shirt, but don't want to be rude. "We don't know how."

"It's tricky. It can take on almost any form."

"True. But we're creatures of magic. We have more acute senses and capacities."

Then a new piece of insight dawns on me. "Wait. That must be why I saw it in the Land of Earth. It must have snuck into the portal."

"If it even needs the portal," Sloan points out.

"It does," Brooks objects. "It may be ancient and formless, but those portals, those other worlds were created by Raj and Katayun; who are infinitely more powerful than the—well, you know. Therefore, it must enter and exit in the same manner as everyone else. If it is as you say, and it can take on virtually any form, there are infinite possibilities. It could have taken the form of the smallest of insects or microbes."

"I don't understand though. When I saw the Immi—the ID in the Land of Earth it took two forms: a wolf and a mummy. But when I went to the Land of Fire I don't remember seeing it."

"The breach has not been recent, Princess. Perhaps, you didn't know what to look for."

My eyes widen. "The volcano. I thought it was my Aunt Celosia, but maybe I was wrong. Why else would it have erupted on Doran and me?"

Brooks nods. "It is possible." He leans in closer. "But the reason I tell you is not to scare you or your friend. But to prepare you. The closer you get to retrieving all five of the stones, the angrier it gets and it will not rest until you are destroyed."

"Gee, thanks."

"It is the truth." There's a splash a ways behind him. He turns and looks, then when nothing breaks the surface, he turns back around. "One last thing. The energy here. It has shifted. And not necessarily for the better." He glances behind him once again. Is it fear that I sense this time? "I am your friend, Princess. And any friend of yours is a friend of mine. But you need to know not everyone is as loyal."

The words are ominous. How could anyone turn against Raj and Katayun? They created the entire Universe out of their love. Who would side with something dark and evil? Tristen. Eoin. Countless others of my fellow colonists. People side with the perceived power, whether or not it's the ethical side.

"I have to go. Good luck, Ka." It's the first time he's used my actual name.

I reach out a hand, cupping his scaly webbed one in mine. "Thank you, Brooks." He nods and smiles, but the worry never leaves his eyes. The clouds of concern are the last thing I remember before he dives beneath the surface and is gone.

...

We're silent as Sloan continues to paddle. It seems we cross the second half of the lake faster than we did the first. Sloan eases the boat behind the waterfall which butts up against the edge of the shoreline. Once the boat is almost ashore, I climb out and begin tethering the rope to the stake on this side.

Together we head down the passageway which I know opens up on the actual Elemental Abyss. When we're a safe enough distance away to no longer hear the crush of the waterfall, we pull out the Medeis Seaweed, tossing it to the ground. "Ah, that is so much better," I say sticking the hem of my t-shirt into my ear and trying to wipe out the remaining sludge. "That stuff is disgusting."

"Brooks seems like a nice guy."

"He is, as far as Unbalanced Waters go."

"Should I be insulted by that?"

"No, I'm just saying that as nice as he is I still try to exercise some caution. The Imminent Darkness could even have taken Brooks' form. That could have been ancient, evil Brooks." I drop the hem of my shirt.

"He seemed frightened." I nod my agreement. It's true. He definitely wasn't up to his normal flirty, bravado-filled self like he was the last time. "You should be frightened too, but you're not. You and your mother, you are powerful. But the Imminent Darkness is infinitely more powerful. It's as old as, or older than the Universe itself. It's every bad, evil, sinister thing you can think of all rolled into one. It can be anyone or anything at any time. That should frighten you."

I consider this. "Determined yes, but no, I'm not frightened. As odd as it may sound I feel that I was almost meant for this, that defeating the ID is exactly what I was created to do," I continue. "But if you think I should be frightened, then what about you? We're now on this journey together, so shouldn't you be frightened too?"

He frowns slightly. "That's just it. I am. And the fact that you aren't is what frightens me the most."

CHAPTER 3

The actual Elemental Abyss consists of five doors. The doors are painted black and are labeled in calligraphy with the words for each corresponding Element: Fire, Water, Earth, Metal and Wood. An eerie white glow emits from three of the five doors; no light peeks out from around the doors labeled Fire and Earth. Once I've opened and then closed the portal there is no going back. To the right of the doors is a sleek, metallic pedestal. Atop the pedestal is a glass sphere that glows blue, casting ominous shadows on the walls of the cavern. I touched it once and the sensation was as if my hand was melting into the glass and the sphere accessed my memories. No doubt another safety feature from Raj and Katayun. The cavern itself has smooth walls as if someone painstakingly dug out the area. Who knows, maybe they did. But before we can reach the doors, we have to cross the chasm of fire.

Sloan eyeballs the fiery schism. It's about two meters wide, which really isn't all that wide when you think about it, except that on the other side are stone battlements. "You mean to tell me we need to get to the other side of this?"

"Yes. I told you all about it. Why do you seem so surprised?"

He peers down into the chasm. Flames jump and lick the sides, illuminating his face in a wash of orangey-gold. "I guess I thought you were maybe exaggerating."

"I don't exaggerate."

"Okay, was hoping. So how do we get across?"

Finally, one time where I'm the expert. Sloan knew all about me before I even had a clue about my true identity. It's good to finally be the one with the upper hand.

"Ignis Flos." I reach into my bag and pull out the glass jar with the red bloom. The chasm contains a beast. The beast is born of smoke and fire. In the past, it has been summoned by blood and saliva, the DNA of a Fire to another Fire. But truth be told, I'm not only a Fire. I am all of the Elements. At least I will be. My mother used Ignis Flos, even though she is a goddess, one of the conditions of living amongst the humans was to do things the human way. Or rather, the hard way.

I unscrew the lid of the jar and pinch a few petals off the bloom. I don't know why, ceremonial precedence maybe, but I close my eyes. "Beast of the chasm, I summon your help in crossing. I offer you petals from the Flower of Fire." I open my eyes and sprinkle the petals into the chasm. Sloan and I watch as they float down slowly, as if suspended in time. To my surprise they don't whither or curl up and burn. Instead they just sort of dissolve into the fire.

"Now what?"

"Just give it a second," I whisper. We continue to watch as the fire below seems to writhe and move. The crackling grows louder and then there's a whoosh of warm wind as a plume of dark gray smoke comes rushing out of the gorge, sending us both reeling back from the ledge. The smoke churns and twists as it morphs into a golem with glowing eyes of fire. "That's new," I whisper. "Look."

Sloan's eyes find where mine had already landed. The red petals of the Ignis Flos have coalesced and formed into a miniature pinwheel right where a human heart would be, or where the heart of the smoke beast would be if it had one. That's why the petals didn't burn. They give life to the beast quite literally. The smoke golem towers above us, peering down, fiery eyes blinking.

"Please," I say. "We wish to cross to the other side."

The eyes blink back and at first I think that this time might be different. That it doesn't understand me or remember who I am. That it won't let us cross. But the beast places a smoky limbed hand over its Ignis Flos heart and I swear a look of appreciation crosses its shadowy features. I feel a pang in my chest where my own heart resides. Why didn't I see it before? The beast is yet another Unbalanced Elemental. Fire, the only Element that can be consumed alive by its own passion and desire.

The beast begins to twist and stretch until it forms a bridge of hazy vapor across the chasm. Sloan looks at me. "You're kidding."

I shake my head. "It's solid. Just get out of your head and into your heart. Trust." I take a step forward. And then another until I make my way across the rift and step through the space in between the battlements. I turn. Sloan still stands on the other side, a weary expression on his face. "Come on. You've asked me to trust you. Now, I'm asking you to do the same."

I can see his shoulders sink in a sigh, the sound swallowed up by the crackle of the fire below. He closes his eyes and takes a step. And then another and another until he finally crosses through the battlements. No sooner does his foot hit the other side then the bridge begins to evaporate and the smoky beast disappears deep inside the chasm. I whisper a silent *thank you.*

"See? That wasn't so bad," I say to Sloan.

"Speak for yourself." We turn and look at the doors, hovering slightly above the ground. "These creatures…"

"Are Unbalanced Elementals."

"I'm not so sure."

"They have to be. They're not creatures conjured from Raj and Katayun, so they have to come from somewhere."

"Okay, say they are Unbalanced Elementals. Why did Raj only put the Waters and Fires here? Why would the Unbalanced Metals be allowed to stay in the Underground, but the Fires and Waters are put here?"

"Because Metal becomes Unbalanced too easily. There would be too many. An Unbalanced Water or Fire, it's rarer."

He considers this. "Okay, but what about the Unbalanced

Woods and Earths?"

Now, he's got me because I don't have an answer for that. "Well, I've never…"

"Exactly. You've never seen one. Neither have I."

"But that's not even possible. Any Elemental can become Unbalanced."

"You're right. But then where are they kept?"

The possibilities unnerve me. Is there another prison like the one where my father had been kept? Deep beneath the Council Hall, cages where those who spoke against the Imminent Darkness were kept. Or are they put somewhere else? What happens to an Unbalanced Earth or Wood? Where do they go?

My eyes are drawn back to the doors. I didn't see any Unbalanced Earths in the Land of Earth. But that doesn't mean that they weren't there. Seeing isn't always believing. Sometimes believing is simply being willing to see. I twist the ring on my left index finger. It's a simple metal ring with a small broken piece of turquoise stone: the Earth Stone and my ticket back to my mother. I have a feeling if I find the answer to this question, I may not like it. Maybe finding out is part of the plan.

I walk over to the pedestal. "Be ready. The door only stays open for a few seconds." Sloan nods. I hesitate with my hand over the glass orb, the inside of which seems to ebb and flow as if it has a life—or a memory—of its own. Maybe it holds the memories of all who touch it. Are these my mother's memories swirling like clouds inside this blue sphere? I take a deep breath. I place my palm flush against the cool surface. Immediately, it's as if it is merging with my hand, glass and human skin becoming one. Then comes the pull, the pull of my memories, which swirl through my head in flashes. Faster and faster, as if it's sorting through to determine whether it should open the doors for me or not. I begin to feel dizzy.

The steady blue glow of the sphere morphs into a brilliant white light and then, and only then can I finally pull my hand away.

"Ka! Hurry!"

The door labeled Wood has clicked open and nothing but blackness peers back at us. I rush over as Sloan steps across the threshold, his hand closes around mine, pulling me inside. The door slams closed behind us.

. . .

No matter how many times, I still can't get used to the sensation. I can feel myself hurtling through time, only it's not linear-spatial time as we know it. It's all of time and space converging at once. There is no past, present, or future. There just *is*. That's it. I feel light as air, as if my body has temporarily disappeared and will meet me on the other side to resume our travels. Ah, that's it. The feeling is of consciousness. Pure conscious. No body to weigh me down. No time or space to box me in from either side.

There's no sensation of going up or going down, yet I know that I am moving. There is no light. There is no dark. There is nothingness. And yet there is everything too. Memories float past me as if they are being fast-forwarded on one of those old-fashioned movie reels. Glimpses of the parts that I didn't notice: Anuja's gray eyes watching me from beneath the hooded cloak, my father's pained expression when I returned from the Land of Earth alone; my best friend Li's tear-filled eyes as he angrily walks away from me…so many nuances that go unnoticed in daily living. I once had a teacher say that we are bombarded with so many billions of sensory data a day that our minds automatically sort it for us and expose us to only what it deems most vital. But what about the rest? I think the rest is here.

Images from Sloan's reel intermix with mine. Then I remember. And as I do I feel the sensation of his hand in mine even though our physical bodies are no longer present. It's as if I'm an outsider looking in: the sad look on his face as Diadona knocks my books to the floor as we leave Universal History class; the jealous look on Michaela's face as she peeks around the corner noticing Bina and Sloan practicing mind travel in the trailer's small living room; the horror on Bina's face while Sloan restrains her as her beloved Finn is taken away in restraints. I don't need sound to hear the howls of anguish that escape her lips. She jerks and thrusts against Sloan's lanky, teenage arms eventually going limp in his grasp.

The images flit by quicker and quicker. I'm overcome with the sensation that I am speeding up. The images are a blur now and I see a pinprick of light ahead of us. The pinprick rapidly grows, wider and wider, expanding to accommodate the return of our physical bodies. I want to warn Sloan that the landing is rough, but there are no voices where there are no bodies. The light continues to grow and the Universe seems to cough us up, out, and through.

CHAPTER 4

I'm falling downward, but my gaze is upward looking at a deep blue, cloudless sky. I feel a pinch, then a poke and a prick. Little burns clawing at my skin. The sound of ripping leaves rushes through my ears. Tree branches. I'm falling through trees. As I have the thought a canopy of green forms above my head, blocking out parts of the cerulean sky. How high are we falling from and, more importantly, how will we land without being killed?

I can't see Sloan, but I can hear the crashing of the tree branches and leaves alongside me. I use my thumb to twist my turquoise ring. Round and round my finger. I know it's not a communicator and only has the ability to send me home, but I whisper silently to my mother, to Raj and Katayun, to please not let me die here in the Land of Wood with my mission still in me.

My wishes must be fulfilled because there's a deafening squawk and I feel myself land on something soft and fleshy. I scramble right side up and get a glimpse down which I quickly regret. I can barely see the ground from this high up. The softness is feathers and the fleshiness belongs to a giant bird of some kind. Its head is covered in silky white feathers and the body is a mix of gold and lime green feathers. Its wings appear wide as a small house. My family must have heard my pleas for help. We nose dive down, its wings pressed near its side, and I lower my face in its neck, protected by its giant head and I dig my fingers into the feathers to better hold on.

Just when I think I can no longer keep my grip, we swoop back upward and there's a soft thud behind me. Sloan. The bird's flight becomes less pressing and it spreads its wings wide and makes a slow zig-zag back and forth amongst the trees. Sloan scrambles behind me to right himself and I feel his hands find my waist and his lips find my ear.

"How did it know where to find us?"

I smile, stroking the feathers of the giant bird's neck. "The Universe always knows."

"And I thought my family was strange."

His words are swallowed up in the rush of wind. I try to take in our surroundings as we descend. The dirt and moss-covered ground begins to come into focus. From this angle I can appreciate the magnitude of such sturdy trees with the thin, red-barked trunks. Surely, if we'd fallen all the way to the ground we'd both be dead right now. I bury my face in the giant bird's neck.

"Thank you," I whisper. As if it can understand, it lets out another gigantic squawk as we finally reach the ground.

The landing is a bit rough, but considering I've never actually flown—somehow always tumbling—through the air before I think it was pretty good. Sloan slides off first and then gives me a hand getting off the magnificent creature's back. We walk around to its head. Our hero and we haven't even seen its face.

Warm amber eyes look back at me on either side of a wide, hooked beak. I definitely wouldn't want to be bitten by that. As if reading my mind—I'm starting to wonder who isn't reading my mind—it nuzzles my cheek with its beak. And for a brief moment I have a sense of recognition. When we were in the Land of Earth my mother took the form of a dragonfly. I know this bird isn't my mother, but could it be one of the other goddesses?

"Constancia?" My mother's sister, the Elemental Goddess of the Land of Wood. The amber eyes sparkle and the bird gently pecks at my cheek again.

I rub the feathers at its neck, burying my fingers into the down.

"Who's Constancia?" Sloan asks.

"My mother's sister. My aunt, I guess you could say." I turn back toward the bird. "You saved our lives. Surely, we would have died if you hadn't come along." Constancia bows her head bashfully. She nudges me with her beak again. "I know that you mustn't interfere. And that I need to find the stone on my own, but I am so grateful for what you have done for us." She takes her beak and plucks the hem of my shirt between it, pulling me so that I'm facing the opposite direction.

Before us are two paths. *A path diverged in the woods*…Don't tell Sloan, but I much preferred Old Earth Literature to Universal History. One of the paths is overgrown and chaotic. The clusters of trees make it appear dark and ominous, not letting in any of the light from above. The other path, the one to my right, is well-maintained and clear. Sunlight filters in through the canopy above as if it's reaching for the path below. Colorful flowers bloom against the backdrop of green foliage. I look again at the path to my left. The hair on the back of my neck prickles in response. I reach deep down into my pocket and feel the smooth stone that I put there what seems ages ago now. I pull it out. The stone is a Heliotrope. It's green with red splotches that look like blood, hence the nickname Bloodstone.

"What's that?"

"It's a Bloodstone. My mother gave it to me to protect me. It can clear energy blocks." I turn to Constancia. "It's the Imminent Darkness, isn't it?"

She bows her head.

"You mean that dark path there?" Sloan asks.

I nod. "The Imminent Darkness is here. Or has been here. Look how the shadows seem to be creeping over closer to the other side." The Bloodstone is cool in my hand. When I hold it, it's as if I can feel the battle between the two paths. The negative energy of the shadowed path pushing against the positive energy of the light path.

"Which way do we go then?"

Constancia nudges me forward. Then she nudges me again,

pushing me toward the dark path.

I turn to face her. "But why?"

She doesn't answer. She can't. Her amber eyes are solemn. It's almost like she knows she's sending me on the tougher, more difficult path, but that she also knows I have to go that way for whatever reason.

"Are you sure?" I ask. She lets out a soft squawk and then nudges me toward the darker path yet again. "Okay, then. You saved us once already and I can't imagine you saved us only to lead us toward our death." I wrap my arms around her feathery neck and kiss what I assume is her cheek, if birds even have cheeks.

Sloan comes up and gently rubs his hand over her beak. "Thanks, Constancia." She lets out a melodious little trill and playfully snaps at his shoulder. Then she turns serious again and gives him a nudge toward the path.

We take a few steps, but then I turn around. "Will we see you again?" Constancia tilts her head, her right ear toward the ground. I take that as a *yes*. We turn back around. I slip the Bloodstone back into my pocket, a reminder of protection, a compass to guide me if my energy—or Sloan's—should somehow be compromised by the Imminent Darkness. Sloan wraps his fingers around mine and we head toward the dark shadows of the path to the left, leaving the light and lively buzz of the rest of the forest behind us.

. . .

This part of the forest isn't just dark. It's downright sinister. No sunlight filters in from the canopy. We stop a moment and I pull my zippered hoodie out of my messenger bag. A cool breeze drifts through the trees. No colorful flowers grow on this path. Rocks, dirt, some moss, and leaves that have shed. But not like the leaves at home. At home the foliage has a greenish-silvery tint to it, even the grass. Here, it is similar to the Land of Earth, and the living foliage is green, but the dead foliage is varying shades or red, orange, yellow, and brown. It smells damp and a bit musty, as if I can smell the decomposing leaves and whatever else. There is no buzz. No noise. Just an eerie silence.

"This is extremely creepy," Sloan finally says after walking in silence for some time.

"I don't like it."

"Why do you think she had us go this way?"

"Either the stone is this way…or she needed me to see something for myself. Or both."

"How will we know where the stone is located?"

"We won't. It's just dumb luck."

And it's true. There's no actual way to tell. For Doran and me it was in fact just luck. The Land of Fire is barren and the volcano was the only plausible place for the stone to be hidden. When I was with my mother she knew the location, but it took days to get to the pyramid on the beach. Both times, even though the stones were tossed into the Elemental Abyss, they were placed on pedestals and seemingly protected with enchantments. Which leads me to believe that my mother, in her mortal form, tossed them in, but it was my aunts—the sister goddesses—who received them and protected them until I could come to retrieve them.

So the legend goes, a girl would be born, an Impossible Girl, born to an immortal daughter of the Universe and a mortal man whose love knew no limits and was as vast as the Universe itself. The daughter would be born and bestowed with many gifts, but in order to protect her from the Imminent Darkness, who seeks to keep balance in the Universe, her mother would toss five ancient stones into the Elemental Abyss. Only when the daughter grew old enough to restore her fractured personality, would she have to travel to each Land in order to retrieve and destroy the stones to restore what is rightfully hers. Five sisters, five Elements, five stones.

"Destroy the stones, restore your gifts, and dissolve the barrier. You were created out of love, not just of your father and me, but also of my sisters, of the entire Universe. You were born simply to be loved." My mother's words drift back to me. *"With love there can be no division, and love is the antithesis of power. While power feeds on deception and greed, love is true and there is always enough."*

Not only will all of my gifts—magic Elemental powers—be restored, but the fate of Xon 9 will be determined. The Imminent Darkness, or ID as I've now come to call it, has shadowed the minds of the colonists, using its dark energy to influence people to turn on one another. That's what it does, it contorts and manipulates what's beautiful and true into something grotesque and evil. Like the path we now walk.

The trees are gnarled and twisting, bending overhead to form a sort of skeleton canopy above us. I reach into my pocket for the

Bloodstone, and run my thumb back and forth over its smooth surface. *"This stone will help protect you. It can clear energy blocks. Even you aren't completely insusceptible to the power of the Imminent Darkness, as long as the balance remains in its favor. Use the stone to clear the negative energy out. It's both a healing and protective stone. Keep it with you."*

I was never exceptionally close to my mother. I've always been closer to my father. Somehow, my mother always made me feel less than capable, doubting my decisions even up to and after my Pronouncement, when I chose Fire. The black box, this contraption we step into that essentially analyzes us from the inside-out, recommended Water. But, truth be told, I was afraid to Pronounce Water. I didn't yet know of Sloan's connection to me, and even though my heart yearned to be near him, my head was more protective. Besides, Diadona, the bully from Sloan's memory in the Abyss, Pronounced Water and I didn't think I could stand two more years in University with her around. Granted, choosing Fire was a mistake. Even though I now know there are no actual mistakes, even if that's how we perceive things at the time.

If I hadn't Pronounced Fire I never would have found out who I truly was. I never would have met Everly, an amazing woman who died in my—no, in her own—honor. I can't tarnish her memory with my selfishness. I never would have met Rhian, my first actual friend in Fire, nor would I have saved Doran from Tristen. Tristen was part of the Imminent Darkness and let's just say she makes the wicked witch in the fairy tales from childhood look like saints. We killed her. I think. According to my mother she's floating somewhere amongst the stars, but I'm not so sure. Someone like Tristen, especially with the ID's help, I don't think they die all that easily. Doran, his sister, Zora, and his mother, Mrs. Chatfield, have become dear friends to my family. Zora even did my Elemental Star tattoo. And Doran made my ring with the fragment of Earth Stone.

But. If I hadn't declared Fire, I wouldn't have almost killed one of my best friends. I have two best friends, twins named Ahna and Liwald. They've been my best friends since forever. We grew up in the same housing complex. Li declared Fire too. I can't say I was surprised. Li is passionate, fiery, and charismatic. Don't tell Sloan, although I'm pretty sure he already knows, but Li was my first kiss. Just for clarification when Li kissed me it was good, but when Sloan kisses me it's like the twin moons of Xon 9 rise just for me. Just to put it into some perspective.

Anyway, while I was off with Doran retrieving the Fire stone, Tristen decided to create what became known as the army of Fire to destroy the Council of Leaders. Her and her henchman, Eoin, gathered up all the newly initiated Fires and injected them with a serum to expedite the Change. When I returned home, I was greeted by a fireball-conjuring army of my newly made friends, and Li. He tried to get me to run away, but he was wired into some sort of collective consciousness. Besides, I couldn't run out on my best friend. Fortunately or unfortunately, I was able to save them, but almost at the cost of their lives. Now, Li is drained of all his Fire and left with a black tattoo along the right side of his face where the metallic filigree of Fire once marked his skin. Every time I look into

Li's eyes I see pain and I can't help but know that I'm the one who caused it. Despite all those things though, I don't regret choosing Fire. It helped me find out who I am and who I am meant to be.

Now my mother, she didn't want me to choose Fire. She would say to me, *"Head or heart, Kata?"* Looking back, she knew that if I followed my heart I'd be a Water with Sloan's protection, under his Everlasting Vow. Let's just say, I'm not one for listening. Turns out my mother isn't one for listening either, having gone and fallen in love with a mortal out of her sheer curiosity to experience humanity. I guess we aren't so different after all.

My mother had given up her immortality in order to be with my father, but in order to save our lives, she violated the arrangement with Katayun and Raj. She returned to the Land of Earth, eventually convincing my father to stay with her. Time is different in these Lands; it passes much slower. You'll think you're gone for several days' time only to go home and find barely any time has passed at all. My mother is immortal again. My father is not. At first, I thought my mother had made a great sacrifice in giving up her immortality in order to be with my father, but I now know that my father is the one with the greater sacrifice. He knew who my mother was and that she could take on other forms and other lives—the maiden, the mother, and the crone—because as a daughter of the Universe she could never truly die, even though her mortal form could. When my mother returned to her true home, my father refused to go back with me because he feared she wouldn't be the same person. But she is still the same person. Now, my mother remains young and beautiful back in her maiden form of Anuja, and my father will slowly age and eventually wither away and die. My father has sacrificed not only his heart, but his entire life to be with my mother. If that's not love, then I'm not sure what is.

"Did you hear that?" Sloan pauses ahead of me, putting out a protective arm.

"Hear what?" Lost in my own reverie, I haven't heard anything.

"I swear I heard—" He takes a step forward.

And that's when the ground beneath him gives out.

CHAPTER 5

All I hear is the yelp of surprise and the final thump of him hitting the earth below. I rush to the edge of the hole that had been packed over with dirt and leaves. I drop to my knees and lean over the edge. With the darkness above me and the darkness now below me I can't see much of anything but shadows. I lay on my stomach gripping the edge of the crater with white knuckles.

"Sloan! Sloan, are you all right? Can you hear me?"

No sound greets me.

"Sloan!"

Silence. The only sound is the pounding of my frantic heart. The cool breeze makes my hair stand on end. Was this some sort of trap? And if so who left it?

"SLOAN! Darn you, answer me!" I scream into the hole. This can't be happening. Doing this without Sloan, being anywhere without him, it just simply isn't an option. I fumble for one of the flashlights inside my messenger bag. Then ever so faintly, I hear a low, anguished groan. "Where are you?"

"I'm at the bottom of a freaking hole," comes the grumbled reply.

I want to both laugh and cry at the same time. "You big jerk. You're lucky you're down there and I'm up here." I can hear the half-moan, half-chuckle. He's not that far down. But how will I be able to get to him or get him out for that matter? "Are you hurt?"

"Mostly my pride."

I click on the flashlight and shine the beam into the hole. Sloan is sitting up and rubbing at his shoulder. He blinks as his eyes adjust to the beam of light. The hole is only about a meter wide, but more than two meters down. Possibly three. Whoever put it here had no intention of the person getting out. Not that there are any other people here that I've seen.

"How will we get you out of there?" He shakily pushes himself to his feet. "Are you sure you're okay?" I ask again.

"Fine. Just knocked the wind out of me." He rotates the shoulder he was rubbing forward then back. "You'll find that I'm pretty resilient. It helped that I clearly wasn't expecting it. It meant that my body was fairly relaxed and not tensed up which could have led to a more serious injury."

"Okay, Doctor Braden, but how do we get you out of there?"

"Dunno. It appears the sides of the hole are just dug out dirt. But there aren't any roots or anything to grab hold of. Maybe look for some vines you can tie together or something?"

"We're in a forest, not a jungle." I push myself up so that I'm kneeling and look around. Maybe there's a loose tree branch or something. The breeze tickles the back of my neck again and I rub my hand over my tattoo, finding comfort in the smooth, filigree flames and the bulging vines. Bulging vines. I peer back over the edge of the hole excitedly. "I think I know of a way!"

"Well, let's give it a shot then."

I haven't had much practice, okay I haven't had any. Just this one time and I didn't even try to conjure it. These green vines just sort of shot out of my wrists. I turn over my hands, inspecting the inside of my wrists, the green tinge of my veins and the almost invisible incision-like marks that only appeared after destroying the Earth stone. I close my eyes. Usually, it helps to think of the traits of any particular Element. It's like I'm tapping into that part of myself.

Earth. I think of Ahna. My best friend. She's an Earth. Actually, I could never imagine her as anything else. Her almond-shaped eyes, sand-colored skin, and thick black braid down her back. Ahna is smart, patient, and kind. You sort of have to be to put up with me. Grounded. No head in the clouds for Ahna, that was always my job. I close my eyes letting the sensation course through my body. Unlike Fire which burns when I conjure it to the surface, this brings a soft, sensual feeling. It's the same sort of feeling I've noticed the few times I've gone to the Earth Building at the University Complex. It's a soft, calming hum accompanied by a bit of awe, maybe even a nostalgia for a place that, even though we have been colonists on Xon 9 for hundreds of years now, still resides deep within us. A connection to a Home lost almost a millennia ago.

The inside of my wrists begin to pulsate. There you are. I hold out my hands palm up and thin, green rope-like vines begin to snake out, growing longer and longer. They continue to wind down into the hole below me. I wrap the slack around my wrists for extra support.

"What the..."

"Trust me." There are three incision marks on the inside of each wrist. "Braid them together to make it stronger. I-I don't know if they can hold human weight. But it's the best I can do. Braid them and then use them to help you walk up the side of the hole."

"Ka, this is crazy. You know this is crazy, right? What if they snap or what if you get hurt?" Even as he asks I can feel the gentle tug letting me know he's following the directions I gave him. "I'm at least thirty pounds heavier than you. How will your weight even be able to withstand it?"

I sit on the ground and dig my heels as best I can into the ground. "Did you know that spiders from Old Earth could produce a silk that was stronger than steel?" I feel the gentle tug on either arm. He's ready.

"You're not a spider. You're my girlfriend."

"I learned in Earth Science that Black Widow Spiders eat their mates. Close enough."

"Are you ready?"

"Yeah." I feel a yank and my butt slides across the dirt. I clench my teeth and dig my heels deeper into the moist dirt. The tugging gets harder as Sloan ascends and it's near impossible to not move without the use of my hands. Tug. Scoot. Tug. Scoot. Beads of sweat begin to form at my temples. *Please let this work.* If this doesn't work I don't know what else to do. The pain in my wrists is bordering on unbearable. The incision marks are red around the edges. In my previous attempt—or rather lack thereof—the vines just stopped on their own. I hope the strain of Sloan's weight doesn't cause them to break.

Just when I think I can't do it any longer, sweat coursing down my cheeks, dirty white knuckles appear, gripping the edge of the hole. I scooch closer and with my sigh of relief the vines seem to release and fall away into the darkness below. I grab Sloan by the hands and use all the energy I have left to yank him up and out over the edge.

He's covered in dirt and sweat too, and for a minute he just flops over there lying on his back staring at the gnarled canopy of branches and leaves above us. "That was not fun."

I rub the inside of my wrists and shake my head. "No, but you made it out and that's all that matters right now."

He reaches up and pulls me half-down to kiss me. I can feel the sparks of my Fire deep inside my belly. "Thanks to you." He looks back up. "It looks like it's getting darker. If that's even possible."

"What are we going to do?"

"We'll have to look for a hollowed tree trunk or some sort of cavern to sleep in. It's the only option. And hopefully one of the safer ones."

We don't waste any time. I pick up the flashlight and hand him the other one from my bag. We veer off the path and into the forest, leaves and twigs snapping beneath our feet. And he's right, quicker than a blink it's almost nightfall, the blue-blackness creeps across the forest like a fog rolling in. This Land also has a single moon, like the Land of Earth. What I can see of the sky, which isn't very much, is cloudy and there's a hazy halo around the moon.

"Here." Sloan stops. He squats down, moving some brush. There are some twisted up roots, pushing up out of the earth. The tree to which they belong has a shallow hollowed out area about half a meter tall and half a meter wide. He shines the light in. Empty. But deceptively deep, the hollow seems to go back at least a meter.

"Ladies, first."

I duck and step into the hollow. Sloan follows me in. There are some leaves and sticks inside. Perhaps another creature called this place home at one time. Although, I've yet to see a creature down this dark path. But I guess that doesn't mean that there never was.

I drop my messenger bag and flop to the floor. I didn't realize I was so exhausted. Actually, I'm not even sure the last time that I slept. I move some of the sticks and leaves near to the hollow's entrance, and then take out the pack of matches from *The Old Tavern and the Sea* and strike a match, tossing it into the kindling. I wiggle my fingertips above it until I feel the familiar zing of my Fire coaxing the small flame to grow. Sloan pulls his sweatshirt over his head and fluffs it like a pillow beside my messenger bag. He lays down and pulls me close beside him. He nuzzles the back of my neck.

"Do you think it's a bad idea to have made the fire?" I ask, watching the small flame flicker and dance in the dimness.

"If you're worried that it will draw attention or alert the Imminent Darkness to our whereabouts, then I'd say no. It—and anyone else—already knows we're here."

The exhaustion penetrates deep into my bones and the warmth perpetuates my drowsiness. Sloan's breath is slow and even behind me.

"How can you be so sure?"

"Because someone—or something—created that trap. And it's just a matter of time before we find who—or what—did."

CHAPTER 6

The sound of rustling leaves jolts me awake. Sloan is sleeping soundly beside me, the rise and fall of his chest slow and even. "Did you hear that?" I whisper, nudging him gently in the ribs. He has one arm slung across his eyes to block out the light.

"Hear what?" he mumbles.

"Obviously, the answer is no, you did not hear it."

"Everything's fine." His voice is soft and low. He reaches an arm to pull me back toward him.

"Have you forgotten where we are?"

He lets out a sigh, removing his arm from across his eyes. "No, but it would be nice to for maybe a minute."

"Very funny."

"I wasn't kidding." He pushes himself up, wincing.

"You're hurt."

"Uh, yeah I fell, what, like two meters onto solid ground yesterday."

I narrow my eyes. "I thought you said you were fine."

"I *am* fine. Just sore." Before he can stop me, I reach out and yank the collar of his t-shirt over to my right, exposing his left shoulder, which is a reddish-purple. His clavicle juts out slightly, forming a bump just beneath the skin.

"That's not sore," I accuse.

"Okay, so it's not just sore." He shrugs with his good shoulder and carefully pulls his shirt out of my fingertips.

"We need to go back."

His green eyes grow serious. "You know we can't do that. Once we go back, the portal is sealed. You'll never be able to retrieve the Wood stone. And then what?"

"We—we…You need to go to a hospital. What if you get a bone infection or something?"

"And what if your Wood is never restored? What then? I think a fractured collarbone is a drop in the bucket compared to saving the entire colony, possibly even the Universe, from the Imminent Darkness."

I'm torn because there are no right answers here. Sloan is right and so am I. If his bone is broken bacteria can get into the bones and cause an infection. At least the skin isn't punctured. And it's also true that if we leave, the portal is then sealed forever. There's no going back and that part of my personality will be missing. And so the legend goes, that after all of the Impossible Girl's personality is restored, *the world as we know it will come to an end because a decision will be made that cannot be undone.* I still haven't figured out what that all means yet, although I do know it's not a fixed point in my timeline. The vision can be changed; Bina's Sight doesn't give fixed points, more like possibilities.

"You're right," I concede finally. "But we need to find the stone that much sooner then."

There's another loud rustling of leaves. And this time there's no mistaking the sound. Sloan's eyes grow wide. He puts his finger to his lips, indicating that I should be quiet. Like I'm dumb enough to make a sound. My heart pounds in my chest.

He slips his sweatshirt over his head and crawls to the front of the hollowed out opening. The rustling continues. Stopping then starting again, then stopping. He glances back at me and indicates that I should follow him. But I shake my head, *no.* I'm going first. He knows it's pointless to argue. He may be my protector, but besides reading my mind and walking in my dreams, I'm the one with the real super powers, and the one who's half immortal. Still not sure what that even means. Do I live for like centuries, but not for eternity?

I sling my messenger bag across my shoulders and squat inside the opening. The darkness has faded, but the sun still doesn't filter through the trees. A fog has settled above the ground and what parts of the sky I can see are filled with angry gray clouds. There's a pile of leaves in front of the tree and I can see something moving, hidden among the reds and browns. It could be an animal. The Land of Earth had little mammals: squirrels and rabbits. Maybe that's what it is. The movement stops. And then continues back and forth. We could just step around it, go unnoticed. Then again the Imminent Darkness has clearly been here and can take on almost any form. Including whatever's beneath those leaves. It's a risk we can't afford to take.

I narrow my focus onto the little rounded mound that scurries back and forth. I wait for it to go still, not taking my eyes off of it. The vines shoot out before I can even summon them, entangling whatever's beneath the leaf pile. There's a high-pitched shriek and a tug. Before my vines can release, I pull the creature toward me. It's covered in my vines, which are brilliant green against the colors of the dying foliage.

The creature squirms and twists against the restraints. And then, before I can grab it and pick it up, a little head pops out. Only, it's not an animal head. It's a human head. A little-sized, human head, with pointy ears and brown hair that sticks every which way.

"Unhand me you, Giantess!" A little voice shrieks.

"It's a Wood nymph," Sloan says, coming out form the hollow and kneeling beside the wriggling form.

"A what?" I snap off the vines and the ends recede back into the underside of my wrists.

"A Wood nymph. My mother told me about them. You know collecting herbs and stuff, she knows a lot about the magical creatures of other worlds."

"Creatures! I'll show you a creature if you don't let me go!" The voice has a distinctly feminine quality.

"Are they nice?"

"From what I recall, they're fairly harmless. A bit temperamental, kind of narcissistic, but most magical creatures are."

"I'll show you temperamental, once I get out of here!" Sloan picks up the writhing body and it fits inside the palm of his hand. "I'll bite you, Giant!"

"Feisty, too," I say.

"Easy now," Sloan soothes. His voice is soft and calm. "We didn't know you were a Wood nymph."

"Yeah," I add. "You could just as easily have been the Imminent Darkness. It can be almost anything. In fact, how do we know you aren't and that this isn't a trap?" I narrow my eyes.

"If it were a trap," Sloan says, "I think it would have been set in motion by now."

The creature stops squirming and turns an eye to Sloan. Her eyes are large, taking up nearly a third of her face, and golden in color. They're kind of almond-shaped and are surrounded by long, dark lashes. Her mouth is like a tiny, pink button. Gold, metallic sparkles seem to emit from every pore of her body. She has a green leaf tucked behind one ear. "The Imminent Darkness is who I am hiding from. Although now you've ruined my hiding place and created a scene on top of it."

"If I untie you, will you talk to us? We're here to protect all the Lands from the Imminent Darkness, including our own," Sloan asks.

"Why should I help you?" the nymph scoffs. "You tied me up and all but man-handled me."

"We just had to be sure," I say. I'm not exactly feeling warm and fuzzy toward this creature, but she could prove an invaluable resource. Maybe she could even help us find the stone. And if there's one, surely there are others like her.

"Yes, I will help you. But only because it could help the others."

"There are others?" Sloan asks as he begins to carefully unwrap the vines with his free hand.

"Yes. Many. Except the Imminent Darkness is slowly destroying the forest. Most of the others have left. But a few of us have stayed behind to fight and protect what is ours." Once her hands are free she begins to help Sloan untangle the vines from her body.

"I thought you said you were hiding?" I ask.

"Oh, the Giantess, thinks she's a smart one," she smirks as she wriggles out of the cocoon of vines like a girl stepping out of a fancy dress. Her frame is petite and she appears to be wearing some kind of furry animal skin as a dress and has what looks like a flower and stem tied around her waist like a belt. She's barefoot and her feet are covered in dirt. "Ever hear of the element of surprise?"

"I think it would take more than hiding in a pile of leaves to surprise the Imminent Darkness, just saying."

She scrunches up her face and scowls at me.

"What's your name?" asks Sloan, slowly standing so that he's beside me. He raises his palm so that we are all eye-to-eye.

"My name is Hennie."

"I'm Sloan and this is Ka."

Suddenly her already large eyes grow round in her heart-shaped face, any haughtiness falling away.

"Oh my goodness. I beg your pardon," she says and curtsies, bowing her head so low that it almost kisses the thumb of Sloan's palm. We exchanged a confused glance.

"You know us?" Sloan finally asks.

Hennie rights herself. "You I have not heard of, but she…word travels to many worlds. Ka, girl whose name means Fire, and who is all Elements. Daughter of Anuja, the sister of my own Queen Constancia, and her mortal lover, Absalom, he who declared Wood." She smiles, revealing little pointed teeth. If a creature could be both beautiful and terrifying, Hennie is it. She turns toward me. "You are the Impossible Girl."

. . .

After helping Hennie find her quiver and bow—which quite literally was like looking for a needle in a haystack due to its small size—she directs us toward the location of the Wood nymphs' central command. Sloan drops her into his t-shirt pocket and she peers out the top, giving directions that lead us further from the path in the woods and deeper into the shadows and darkness.

According to Hennie, the Land of Wood is full of magical creatures: Wood nymphs and fairies of all sorts. "We Wood nymphs stick to the trees and such. The fairies take care of the flowers and whatnot. Not that we have much of those anymore." Her voice becomes hard.

"How long has the Imminent Darkness been here?" I ask. I know we may have gotten off on the wrong foot, but maybe it was just a matter of simple misunderstanding.

"Too long."

"What does it want?" Sloan asks.

"What doesn't it want? It's hungry. Insatiable. It's tainted the forest, that's what it's done." She balls up her little fist and shakes it at the air. "This entire forest was once lush and green, with beautiful flowers the color of the rainbow."

"What's a rainbow?" I ask. I don't recall learning about such a thing. "Is it magic too?"

I look at Sloan, but he shakes his head. He's never heard of it either.

Hennie's mouth gapes open. "You mean you have never seen a rainbow?" I shake my head. "Well, if I had to describe it, it's like, well, it's like ribbons of color woven across the sky."

I never saw much past the muted colors of Xon 9, at least not until I entered the Land of Earth, with its brilliant ocean and sky, crystalline river, and gemstone encrusted pyramid. It would not surprise me that there exists a Land where color can be woven out of the sky.

Hennie continues, "Typically, there are seven colors to a rainbow: red, orange, yellow, green, blue, indigo, and violet."

"How does it get there? Up in the sky?" I ask.

Hennie's face grows solemn. "They say that when our goddess, your aunt, Constancia, cries tears of joy from the heavens above they form the rainbow. The rainbow is the color of her tears."

"Wow. That sounds…magnificent."

"It is. Maybe you'll see one while you are here." Her face darkens and for someone so tiny she looks every bit a warrior. "If we can get the Imminent Darkness to leave, the forest can be healed, it can be restored. Then perhaps, Constancia will cry her glorious tears of joy."

We continue to walk in silence until Hennie points to a gigantic tree. It's easily the largest in the entire forest. Its trunk is gnarled and twisted, easily two meters wide and I have no idea how tall. It's peculiar because it stands among barren trees, yet it still has all of its leaves. Beautiful, almost silken green leaves that dot every branch.

"But how is that possible?"

"Nahele."

"Nahele?" Sloan asks.

"He is the leader of the Wood nymphs. He is very old, almost as old as Constancia. In fact, I believe Constancia is the one who planted the seed that gave birth to Nahele."

"I don't see anyone," I say.

"Because you look with human eyes. Look closer. Be still and you will see"

We're a few yards away still. I study the tree. There are two knotholes above which the tree bark seems to protrude from the trunk. Beneath the two knotholes is what appears to be a bulbous nose and a grim-lined mouth. A face. The chin seems to disappear into the ground with the roots. I no longer see ridges of bark, but ridges of time: with each ridge is a wrinkle. As my recognition seems to take place the giant face lets out a large yawn and the two knotholes blink open.

I know that by now I should come to expect the unexpected, but I'm still mesmerized by the greatness of the creature before me. I feel humbled, like I should drop to one knee and bow to simply show my gratitude for being in the presence of such a magical beast.

"I was getting worried about you, my little Hennie." The voice sounds rickety and old, yet harmonious at the same time. As he speaks the leaves towering above his head waver back and forth.

"I am alive, Nahele. No thanks to, or rather thanks to, these two humans. Nahele, this is the Impossible Girl of which you have spoken." Hennie struggles to climb outside of Sloan's pocket. He plucks her out and places her carefully onto the ground. "I know she doesn't look like much—"

"Hey!" I object.

"But she has superhuman powers. Vines that shoot out from beneath her skin."

"And fire," I add suddenly feeling very important. "I can conjure fire, well more like electrical charges."

Nahele chuckles. "Well, I don't think we'll be needing any of that."

Hennie turns and rolls her eyes. "He's made of Wood, you numb-nut."

I can feel my cheeks redden which only makes Nahele laugh harder, the sound the only thing alive besides Hennie that I've seen on this side of the forest.

"And you have come in search of the stone?"

"Yes, Sir, I have."

"And I'm sure you will find it. But what do you make of the Imminent Darkness?"

"I-I don't know what to make of it, Sir. It has permeated my home of Xon 9, and it has attacked my mother almost taking her life. It has imprisoned my father," I glance at Sloan. "And Sloan's father." I gesture around. "I was told that the ID had traveled to the Elemental Abyss and clearly it has been—is—here in the Land of Wood as well."

"But what do you *make* of it?"

"What is there to make, Sir? The Imminent Darkness is as old as, if not older than, all of time itself. It is ancient. It is both all forms and no forms. It creates only to destroy. It can turn one man against another in the blink of an eye. It casts a shadow over all that is right and true. It wants a debt to be repaid, but as far as I can tell no debt was ever made. Therefore, I would venture to say that the Imminent Darkness plays by its own rules, or no rules at all." I reach for my Bloodstone and run my thumb over its smooth surface. "What do I make of it, Sir? It appears to me, from looking around here, that the Imminent Darkness is the harbinger of death itself."

Nahele's mouth contorts into a smile. "Very good. Come inside, Children. There is much to discuss."

And with that the hollow that is Nahele's mouth opens wide forming some kind of entrance.

Hennie heads excitedly toward the trunk, like a long lost friend returning home. She stops and turns, gesturing. "Follow me."

CHAPTER 7

The opening closes behind us, like an old door that doesn't get used very often. We're in a darkened tunnel that heads downward. I reach into my messenger bag and pull out the flashlight. Hennie *tsks* in protest, but she lets me keep it on. The tunnel continues to wind downward. The walls are crumbling dirt with pieces of roots sticking out every which way. You'd think that it would feel suffocating, but somehow it has the opposite effect. I feel like the space is breathing with me. And considering we're inside a breathing and living creature, maybe it is.

We reach the bottom of the tunnel and there are two wooden doors. They have iron-ringed handles that remind me of the doors to the library in the Earth Building, except that the doors are about half my size.

"The iron handles keep the fairies out."

"Are fairies bad?" Sloan asks.

"Not bad exactly. More like mischievous."

"Hennie, I hate to be the bearer of bad news. But aren't Sloan and I a little, uh, large to fit inside those doors?"

A surprised expression washes over her tiny features. "Huh. I guess you are. Hadn't thought much about that. But Nahele, he knows what he's doing."

Sloan looks at me and I shrug. "Who am I to doubt the oldest tree in the entire Land and the King of the Wood nymphs?"

"Nymphs and elves," Hennie corrects.

"So, wait there are talking trees, Wood nymphs, fairies, *and* Wood elves?" I ask.

"You sound surprised," Sloan says.

"What are elves?"

Hennie gives me a sympathetic look. "They are our male counterparts in this Land. Surely, you know that nymphs can only be female?"

I nod slowly. "Uh, yeah. Of course. Ha-ha. Everyone knows that."

Sloan doesn't try to hide his smile.

"Now, if you don't mind. I'm famished. I never did catch anything, especially with you two dimwits."

"I thought you were hiding?"

"Protecting."

"But you just said hunting."

"I was both protecting and hunting."

Hennie pulls the door open and golden light falls across the dirt floor where we stand. Golden light with glittery particles floating in its beam. She steps into the beam and a dreamy smile plays across her lips. She lets out a contented sigh as she crosses the threshold. The door shuts with a thud behind her.

"Again. Ladies, first," Sloan says grabbing the iron-ringed handle and pulling the door back open.

I shrug. "At the very least we'll get a good meal out of this."

"They're just being hospitable. Maybe you'll meet an elf." He wiggles his eyebrows suggestively.

"Hennie's right, you are a dimwit."

"She was referring to both of us."

"Interpret it how you will."

The golden beam of light spills out across the floor. I close my eyes. Constancia wouldn't have sent us on this path if she thought it was too dangerous. Maybe she intended for us to run into the magical creatures of the Wood. I take a deep breath, duck my head, and step into the beam of light.

. . .

The sensation is unlike any I've ever felt before, a warmth so palpable that I can feel it all the way deep inside my bones. And something magical happens when I cross the threshold. I'm the same size. Or rather I'm the same size as everyone else. Something very peculiar has happened. Sloan enters behind me, the door closing with a soft thud.

We've entered into a sort of dining hall. There are chandeliers made from some sort of antlers with burning candles in glass jars hanging from the ceiling. I wonder if it's some kind of magic. There are long wooden tables that practically extend from one side of the room to the other. Benches run along either side of the tables and they're packed shoulder-to-shoulder with people. Well, nymphs and elves, I guess would be a more accurate term. The beauty in the room is almost nauseating. Everyone's skin seems to have the same luminescence as Hennie's, as if they are glowing from the inside out. The tables are overflowing with food: meats, vegetables, fruits, cakes, and glasses are filled with sparkling golden liquid. The atmosphere is inviting and that warmth that penetrated deep inside my bones hasn't dissipated. In fact, it seems to have deepened, almost having a drowsy effect on me.

"Do you feel that?" I ask Sloan.

"You mean that soft, warm feeling that tingles your body all over?"

"Yeah, that."

He grins. "Nope."

I roll my eyes. Hennie has disappeared and I can't place her in the crowd of people. Even though each elf and nymph has an almost indescribable beauty: perfect skin, large eyes, tiny, pert mouths and noses, long and lithe bodies—it almost makes it impossible to tell one from the other. I can't even recall what Hennie was wearing or what color her hair was, whether or not she wore it short or long.

A nymph wearing a dress fabricated from leaves woven together comes over to us. "You don't look familiar. You two must be new here." She has long red hair that flows in curls down her back. Her lips are a ruby red color and her eyes are large and green.

"Yes, we are. We're friends of Nahele's and Hennie's," Sloan offers.

The nymph scowls. "Oh, Hennie. She's always running off." She lowers her voice conspiratorially. "She thinks she's some sort of great warrior or something. But she's all talk."

"Somehow I think I sensed that," I reply.

"I'm Idaia. You must be half-starved." She leans in and whispers in my ear. "And no offense but you two are filthy."

"Yeah, we've come a long way."

"I'm right then. You are half-starved. Come on, there's room at my table for two more."

It's odd speaking to Idaia because we are eye to eye, unlike when talking to Hennie's petite form earlier. We must be the same size now, if I can find her. Probably off annoying someone else with her made-up tales of hunting and fighting the Imminent Darkness. Idaia stops at a table in the far corner and squeezes in between two elves. No one around here looks much older than a teenager. But, surely that can't be right.

"Qildor and Elephon, this is…I'm sorry I didn't quite catch your names?"

"I'm Ka and this is Sloan."

There aren't two seats beside each other so I squeeze in on the end beside Qildor and Sloan sits across from me beside another nymph, who's preoccupied in a conversation with the nymph on her other side.

"Help yourself to as much as you want. There's always enough here for everyone. They've traveled very far," Idaia says by way of explanation. She helps herself to a plate full of fruit. I do the same, taking a small piece of meat—not sure what it is considering we haven't seen any animals in this part of the forest—and some root vegetables.

Qildor eyes me. "You don't look like a nymph. What species are you?"

I glance at Sloan. I have no scales on the side of my face like he does. He could easily pass for a water creature of some kind. But I have no telltale sign of my Elements, besides my tattoo. I swallow down a bite of sweet potato.

"Um, human?"

Several of the creatures around us stop eating, forks and knives coming to a halt. There's a beat of awkward silence, then everyone resumes their eating and conversation.

"That explains you. And your friend, here, he's some kind of water creature?"

Sloan smiles. "Yep. Water creature, that's me." He shoves a piece of meat into his mouth.

"There are no humans in the Land of Wood. You really must have come from afar and for good reason to travel to this part of the forest given its condition," Qildor continues. His hair is shaggy and blonde, falling across deep brown eyes, and almost hiding his pointed ears. His nose is pointed and, like the nymphs, his mouth is small and round. He has a light spattering of freckles across his cheeks, but they don't detract from the glow of his skin. His shirt is some sort of natural, burlap-like fabric. He's handsome in an ethereal sort of way.

Idaia leans over. "They're friends of Nahele's and Hennie's."

"Did I hear my name?" Hennie suddenly appears. She looks down at me. "Oh, it's nice to see you in your right size. I dare say I didn't enjoy being so infinitesimally small earlier."

"How does that work by the way?" Sloan asks, waving a fork full of meat in the air. "The whole shrinking thing? Was it the doorway?"

Hennie smirks. "Who's to say you shrank? Maybe I just grew."

I practically choke on the pear that I just shoved in my mouth. I start to cough and Qildor slaps me on the back. I take the glass of sparkling golden liquid by my plate and down half the glass.

"Hennie, you know people don't respond well when you say such things," Qildor chastises.

"But it's fun to see their reactions," she grins her pointed teeth grin. That's when I notice Qildor also has pointed teeth.

"We can minimize when we go outside of Nahele. Nahele is our home. But we are free to wander wherever we please. However, it can be dangerous. There are animals and, of course the fairies, but they're more a nuisance than anything."

"I haven't seen any animals in this part of the forest. Is it because of the Imminent Darkness?" Again everything seems to grind to a halt: the chatter, the clinking of knives and forks against plates, everything stops. After a beat it all resumes again. "Why do they keep doing that?"

"Because you speak of things that make them uncomfortable,"

Qildor explains.

"And what about you?" Sloan asks. "It doesn't make you uncomfortable?"

Qildor shrugs. "It does, but avoiding the issue doesn't make it go away. Sometimes we need to confront that which makes us uncomfortable." It's those words that make me realize who the true warrior is, and it isn't Hennie and her pretend play at going after the Imminent Darkness. If there's a battle, I've already decided I want Qildor on my side.

Hennie leans in across the table, almost spilling her glass of golden liquid across my empty dinner plate. "Did they tell you who they are, Qildor?"

"This is Ka and her friend the water creature, Sloan." This seems to be a game they've played before because Qildor answers with a measured patience.

"That's their names, but who are they truly?" Hennie grins and stands back up. Someone calls her name and she teeters away.

"Is she ever not annoying?" I ask.

Qildor laughs, and it's the first moment the serious façade seems to melt ever-so-slightly. "No. She's always like that. It's just Hennie."

"You seem to have a lot of patience with her."

"She's like a small child. You must have patience with small children."

"Wait. How old are you exactly?" I ask realizing that it's quite possible to him, Hennie really is just a child.

"I'm nine-hundred and forty-two years old."

This time I'm glad I'm not eating anymore because I surely would have choked on that response. "And Hennie?"

"Like I said, but a child. A mere three-hundred and twenty years old."

"Everyone looks good for their age," Sloan quips taking a swig out of his glass.

Qildor turns to me. "You never did answer the question. Who are you truly?"

"I'm Ka."

Sloan levels me with a stare. "You know what he means. He's going to find out sooner or later. Would you rather tell him or let Hennie have the satisfaction?"

I let out a sigh. "I'm the daughter of Anuja and Absalom."

Qildor grins. "Ah, the Impossible Girl of Legend. I'd been wondering whether or not you were real. They said you were, but I had my doubts."

Now, it's my turn to be witty. "Yeah, likewise."

Qildor laughs again and it has the same melodious quality of my mother's laughter. "And what brings you to the Land of Wood, Impossible Girl and her companion?"

I lower my voice, not wanting to cause another awkward silence. "The Imminent Darkness. And the Wood stone. I need to retrieve the Wood stone and destroy it. Then I will have three of my Elements returned to me: Fire, Earth, and Wood."

"Is that all?" he presses.

"And the forest. I want to help the forest. It's apparent it's dying. The Imminent Darkness is destroying it. I want to help stop it. Before…before it's too late." I don't want to say out loud, before it destroys you too, but from the seriousness of my stare, Qildor appears to get the message.

"Then, Impossible Girl, you have found your most loyal of servants. It would be my honor to accompany you and your friend on your quest for the Wood stone, and in the process destroy the Imminent Darkness and save my home from its energy of death and destruction."

"No," I correct. "It would be mine—" I glance at Sloan and he nods ever-so-slightly. "I mean *our* honor to have you by our side."

Suddenly, an upbeat tune of fiddles, guitars, and tambourines fills the air of the dining hall. Nymphs and elves jump up pushing the tables off to the sides, creating a large open space in the center of the room. They begin dancing, dipping, and bowing. Looping arm and arm, swinging around. Singing and laughter fills the space.

"Ah," Qildor smiles, the heaviness of our conversation dissipating as quickly as it had appeared. "Now the real fun begins."

CHAPTER 8

It feels as if we dance for hours. I can't even feel my legs. There's just arms entangled and bodies pressed together. Spinning, swirling, and pirouetting across the dirt floor of the dining hall. I feel light as air and almost elated by the mesmerizing music that permeates the room. I've never experienced anything like this. Nothing on Xon 9 even comes close. It's as though the rest of the world: the stones, the Elemental Abyss, the Imminent Darkness…are all gone. My head almost feels empty as if the thoughts just flitter in and out, never staying long enough to take root.

I've lost sight of Sloan and my legs seem to have a mind of their own. I end up locking arms with Qildor who smiles his pointed-teeth smile, his blonde hair, which is much too long, fans out over his oversized eyes. "I told you it would be fun!" He spins me around and the room becomes a dizzying blur. He catches me by the waist and dips me so low my head nearly touches the ground before bringing me back up and spinning me in the opposite direction, off to someone else. This time I lock arms with Hennie.

"This is my favorite song!" she grins. We fall into a sort of hopping, waltzing dance. Everyone is bumping into one another, but no one seems to care.

"Do you guys do this often?"

"Every day." She puts distance between us so we are no longer locking arms but holding hands with our arms outstretched. She pulls me in so our arms are bent, then pushes me back out again. Each time I catch little pieces of what she says.

"…surprised…drank…wine…most humans…good." She spins me around and before I can process what she was trying to say, I'm locking arms with an elf I haven't yet met. This one has shoulder length brown hair that's more lustrous and shiny than mine could ever be. He has sapphire blue eyes and a scabbard around his waist. The jewel-encrusted hilt of the sword peeks out of the top.

Wait. Did she say wine? I don't remember drinking any…the sparkling golden liquid! If I had a free hand I'd smack myself in the forehead. Why didn't I realize it? No wonder everyone is so dang happy and dancing the night away. I only had alcohol once and it was in the Black Bazaar. And it was by mistake. Suddenly, I feel the urgent need to find Sloan.

I unravel my arm from the long-haired elf who frowns, but is immediately entangled with a blonde-haired nymph. I catch a glimpse of Idaia's long red hair. She's dancing with someone who has shaggy brown hair and appears to be Sloan's height and build. I head in that direction, bodies press against me and the music now seems intrusive in my ears. I reach out a hand to put it on Idaia's slender shoulder and just as I do, I get a glimpse of the person she's talking to and it's not Sloan. It's just another elf. I tap her on the shoulder anyways.

"Have you seen Sloan?" I ask

She shakes her head *no*. Where could he be?

I wander away from the throng of people and away from the sound of the music. I open the door from whence we came earlier and a rush of cool air greets me. It closes with a soft thud behind me. Almost instantaneously, I feel like my head is clear and that I can think again. Was it the wine? Or was it the music? Maybe it was both. I shake my head as if I could shake the remnants of the magical trance right out of my head like droplets of water.

Still no Sloan. I start to make my way up the tunnel and as I do the air gets cooler. I shiver. I left my jacket in the dining hall, but I still have my messenger bag. My messenger bag is something I'm not willing to part so easily with. It's my tether to both home and to my mother. The Imminent Darkness had broken into our house and almost killed my mother, leaving her to die. Luckily, I found her before it was too late, but very few places feel safe for me anymore. Sloan's house and Mrs. Chatfield's is about it. Even Bina's house— and Bina herself—have been attacked by the Imminent Darkness. Anything I have that I value I keep in my messenger bag which is always by my side. Or up here. *Tap, tap.* But with the Imminent Darkness, even our memories aren't always safe. I almost experienced that firsthand.

I pull out a flashlight and shine it around, studying the tunnel more closely. Have you ever noticed how on your way somewhere new you're so excited (or scared) that everything is a blur? You think that you're noticing all that there is to notice, but then on your way back home you realize there were a lot of things you missed. Like the small, iron door you walked by earlier, completely oblivious.

I stop and crouch down shining my light on the door. It has no markings and appears to be sealed. The door confuses me because this tree, this entire place around me, is Nahele. It's his very being. What then could be locked away behind such a nondescript door? More importantly, why?

Curiosity gets the better of me. Sloan couldn't have wandered far. To the door's right is a small electronic keypad. For magical creatures, they sure must like their modern day touches. Or maybe whoever put the door here was from my world. I put my hand over the keypad and visualize the Fire in my veins rising to the surface. Just a few sparks and it should short-circuit. If it short-circuits I should be able to pull the door open. It only takes a few seconds before the electronic keypad begins to spark and then emits a series of short beeps and then one long final beep that eventually fades to silence.

There's no door handle to pull it open, so I gently push on it. It doesn't give and I realize that if it's made of iron, it may need a little extra effort. I lean my shoulder into it. It moves slowly inward. I push it open until there's a space small enough for me to squeeze through.

Once I'm on the other side I push it back closed. The ceiling is low and I need to crouch. I sweep the flashlight around the space.

I'm in a small room. In the middle of the room is a table. On the table sits a box. I sink to my knees and make my way across the dirt floor and over to the table. Even kneeling the table is about chest height. I shine the flashlight onto the box. The box is made of iron and has rivets. There's a keyhole in the front of the box. I'm more confused—and more curious—than when I first noticed the door. A tiny door leads to a tiny room with a tiny box?

A door and box made of iron. What did Hennie say about iron? The doors to the dining hall were made of wood, but they had iron handles. *Keeps the fairies out.* Fairies. I pretty much know nothing about fairies, but Hennie spoke of them like they were foul creatures. I chuckle to myself. I've met a lot of human beings recently who I would consider foul creatures. Diadona and Tristen among them.

The box must be important to be protected, but what is it that the nymphs and elves would consider to be so important? Gold? Jewels? The Wood stone? Or maybe none of the above. I place my hand over the top of the box. It's warm, not cool to the touch like you'd expect. I close my eyes. There's a slight pulsating. Like a beating heart. Before we destroyed the Earth stone, Sloan said whenever we were getting closer to my mother's location, the stone would beat like a heart. A heart. Nahele is very old, a tree grown from a seed planted by Constancia. He has lived centuries, with nymphs and elves dancing in his bowels. Could it be that this box contains Nahele's own heart, his life-force? And if so, was it too placed here by Constancia?

There's a soft thud behind me. Crap. I bite my lip, too fearful to turn around. My own heart pounds loudly in my chest. I could turn off the flashlight, but it's too late, I'm sure. I am regular-sized again and practically take up one-third of the space in this tiny room. Even kneeling my head practically touches the ceiling. There's no hiding a giantess in a world that's miniature. I should have known that I could be followed, or that I would be followed. A stranger in a strange land, Impossible Girl or not. It doesn't mean that everyone is fighting on the same side as me.

A deep voice causes my heart to seize in my chest.

"You shouldn't go exploring on your own. You never know what you might find. It's quite possible that you end up finding something that you wished you never had."

I close my eyes and take a deep breath, whirling around and shining the flashlight on the owner of the voice. The beam catches the glint of his pointed teeth, curled into a snarl.

Qildor.

. . .

"I was looking for Sloan." The half-truth rolls off my tongue easily.

"In here?"

He's got me. Of course, Sloan wouldn't be in here. The door was sealed. As usual, my curiosity got the better of me. Story of my life.

"Well, no. What can I say? I'm easily distracted." He closes the distance between us in what seems like two steps. Even though I have to kneel, he's somehow eye-to-eye with me. "How do you guys do that?"

"I don't even think about it much anymore. It's almost like we just think it, and it happens. Our bodies adjust to meet our needs. If we want to hide, we become very small. If we want to be full-sized, it just happens."

"I wish I had that ability," I turn back toward the box on the table. "This ground is killing my knees."

"You shouldn't have wandered where you shouldn't be."

I ignore him. "Why was the door sealed? Why was this little room built for this little box?"

"Who said the room was built for the box? Perhaps it is the other way around."

He's got me there. "You mean the box was built for this room?"

"You don't give up easily, do you?"

"Of course not. If I did, I would have given up back when I was initiated into Fire."

He chuckles, a deep, melodious sound. "Your title is apt; you *are* impossible."

I reach out and touch the box gently, feeling the pulse beneath my fingertips. "So I've been told on more than one occasion."

"You feel it?" He reaches out a pale hand and places two fingers on the box, like he's taking a pulse. He closes his eyes.

"I do." I pause. He'd said I may find something I wished I hadn't. Well, that's already happened like a thousand times since I found out I was the Impossible Girl. "What is it?"

He doesn't answer right away. His chest rises and falls with the beating that I feel in my fingertips. Soon I find that my own heartbeat begins to match that of the box. *Ba-boom, ba-boom, ba-boom.* When he opens his eyes, they're softer.

"It's a heartbeat."

"I gathered that much."

He smiles. "It's the life-force."

"Of Nahele?"

"And of every nymph and elf."

I pull my fingers away, rubbing them absent-mindedly. "Wait, you mean to tell me that inside this box is the life-force of everyone who was in that dining hall? Of Hennie, Idaia, and you?"

He nods. "That's why it is hidden and locked away."

"Behind an iron door and inside an iron box."

"Fairies can be quite the tricksters."

"That's horrible."

"They lack foresight. They often do without thinking of the consequences of their actions."

He takes my hand. His hand is cool and dry compared to my warm, clammy one. He places my hand back on the box. He doesn't take his hand away. "Close your eyes."

I obey and close my eyes. The rhythmic beat pulsates in my fingertips. I feel him take my other hand. I feel the roughness of the fabric of his shirt beneath my palm. The same rhythmic beat pulsates beneath my hand. Beat for beat. When Qildor's heartbeat quickens, so too does the beat from the box. My eyes fling open. He lets go of both my hands. I awkwardly leave my hand over his heart a moment too long. I blush as I pull away. His eyes look deep into mine. He's searching, but for what?

"You said that I may find something that I wished I hadn't. What is it?"

"You're not telling me something."

"There's nothing to tell."

"Your eyes beg to differ. Sloan, who is he to you?" It's a weird question, unless Qildor's in the market for a half-mortal girlfriend.

"Elves aren't my type. Sorry."

"He's your boyfriend then." I nod. He tilts his head as if listening to a faraway sound. "But he's more than that."

"He's my protector." I shift uncomfortably. "Listen, I don't understand what any of that has to do with this box."

"But it does. The heart is not just what gives life. It has a funny way of showing us the things we need to know, if only we listen."

"You can quit waxing poetic on me."

He reaches beneath his shirt collar and pulls out a leather cord with a tiny key on it. He holds it up and makes a face, as if to say have it your way. I feel my eyes grow wide as he takes the key and in one swift motion, unlocks the box with a single click. He lifts the lid and sets it on the small table beside the box. "Look," he demands.

I take a deep breath. I'm not one for blood and gore, but in true form, my curiosity has the best of me. I peer inside the box. I was expecting a bulging red heart, but instead the box is lined with a beautiful, sapphire blue velvet and in the bottom of the box is a single teardrop-shaped seed. I feel so stupid. Of course. Nahele grew from a seed planted by Constancia, why then would his life-force not be that same seed? The same seed that gave birth to all the nymphs and elves who call him home.

"Pick it up," Qildor instructs.

I shake my head. "But I couldn't."

"But you must." He places his hand on my shoulder. "Ka, it is no coincidence that you have come here and found this room. That means that Nahele *wanted* you to find this room."

"How do you know?"

"Because I am the Keeper of the Genesis."

"Is that what this seed is called? A Genesis?"

He nods. "Genesis means the root, the beginning. So much life has been given from such a tiny seed." His hand drops from my shoulder. He reaches into the box and gently takes the tiny seed out, as if he is handling the most precious gemstone, and in a way I suppose he is. He takes his other hand and unfurls my fingers so that my palm is facing up, fingers scooped up like a small dish. Carefully, he places the seed in my palm, gently curling my fingers back over it. "Now close your eyes and just feel it."

I do as he says. I close my eyes and feel the gentle pulsing in my hand, the soft *ba-boom* of the beating of every elf and nymph's heartbeat. The rhythm is soft and steady. I soon find myself not only feeling it, but hearing it. A gentle throbbing in my ears. Then it moves to behind my eyelids where it is accompanied by swirls of colors: greens, browns, and reds like the fallen leaves in the forest. I'm beginning to feel disoriented, but I can still feel Qildor's hand resting over my own.

The swirling colors begin to shift and take form, soon an image starts to materialize before me. I've seen weird things before. Sloan has visited me in my dreams to deliver messages and I've traveled in my own Mindscape. I've even almost had my MindCleansed, still recalling the burn as the memory was extracted from my brain. But somehow this is different. It's kind of like watching a dream, except there's a dense fog that makes it difficult for anything to materialize clearly.

I can make out Sloan's lean, muscular form. His shaggy brown hair and deep sea-colored eyes. But it's difficult to make out any other distinct characteristics. I only know it's him because I'd recognize him anywhere. He's standing in the forest, among the blackened tree trunks of the part of the forest that has been permeated by the Imminent Darkness. He appears to be looking for something. His mouth moves, but I can't hear his words. It looks like he's calling my name. I want to call out that I'm right here, but I can't.

He begins to walk about as if he's confused. Even though I can't quite see his face, I can see the fear and frustration in the tenseness of his muscles and in the way he's searching around the forest. He falls to his knees and I try to rush forward to help him, forgetting that I can't. This is simply something for me to observe. It isn't happening now. Or is it?

Suddenly, he's on the ground writhing in pain, his body contorting in ways in which nobody should be able to bend. I cry out and hear the echo of my voice in the small room. I feel the hot sting of tears running down my cheeks as I watch Sloan fighting against an invisible opponent. He swings his fists at nothing, kicks the air. The vein in his neck, just beneath his scales bulges as he lets out a bloodcurdling scream. And then the scream is stifled, as if strangled by an unseen force. His head flops back to the leaf-strewn ground and his body goes limp. My chest feels like it's on fire; my stomach is made of lead. I find myself pleading, please just let him move, please don't let him be still. He wouldn't stop fighting. Whatever it is, he would never stop fighting. He's smart and strong. He took an Everlasting Vow. A breeze ruffles his hair, but otherwise he lay unmoving among the dead trees and leaves.

This must be what Qildor meant when he said I would find things that I wish I hadn't because right now I wish that I wasn't seeing this. Anything but this. Not Sloan. Not ever. Why is this what I need to see? And a second later I find out why.

Sloan's lifeless body slowly begins to move. First an arm and then a leg. He sits up then slowly gets on all fours before pushing himself back up to standing. The movements are jerky. Regardless, I feel my heart open with joy and relief. He's alive. He lifts his chin and this time, as if truly seeing, he stares right at me.

With yellow eyes.

CHAPTER 9

My own eyes fling open. My hand is pulled back and I'm poised to launch the stupid seed across the room. Only Qildor's icy fingers grip my wrist, stopping me. I let out a shuddering breath. I can feel the well of tears threatening to overflow my already tear-stained cheeks.

"I told you, you may learn things you wished you hadn't." He carefully lowers my hand, peeling my fingers away from my palm where my nails have dug out little half-moons. He gingerly plucks the seed out of my palm and places it gently back in its velvet-lined box.

"When?"

He closes the box slowly and uses the key to lock it before placing the leather cord back around his neck.

"I don't know."

"Is it now?"

He shakes his head. "I don't think so."

I grab the rough fabric of his tunic into my fist. "Why?"

He shakes his head. He tries to unravel himself from my grasp, but even though I am kneeling and he is standing, I have more leverage. He sighs. "I don't know that either. I told you the life-force shows you what you need to know, if only you become still and listen."

Something my mother said to me tugs at the fringes of my mind. *Be careful of who you trust because the Imminent Darkness can cause them to say or do things they wouldn't normally do. You have Sloan, but even Sloan can be affected by the Imminent Darkness.* I let my hand drop from Qildor's shirt, instead reaching it into my pocket where I pull out the Bloodstone.

"Heliotrope." Qildor says. "Protection."

"My mother said…" But I shake my head. "If it hasn't happened yet, then it can be changed, can't it?"

Qildor ignores my question and strides across the room. I scurry after him. He pulls the door open and ushers me out before closing it behind him. The burnt smell from overheating the keypad still lingers in the air. It feels good to stand up to my full height again. I find that Qildor is taller than me now. He opens a pouch on his waistband, hidden beneath his shirt. He pulls out a pinch of whatever is hidden inside and tosses it into the air. It glitters in the beam of the flashlight and he mutters something beneath his breath. Like a mirage, the door seems to fade away as if it was never there at all.

"I don't understand."

"The door only appears when one needs it. You found it. You received the message. It is no longer needed."

Once the door has fully disappeared, he continues down the tunnel leading back up to the forest. I have to walk double-time to keep up with him. The flashlight beam bounces uselessly across the ground.

"You never answered me."

He doesn't stop and turn.

I press on. "If it hasn't happened yet, then it can be changed."

"The Imminent Darkness is powerful."

Another memory rises from the recesses of my mind back to the surface. Something else my mother told me: *You know the Imminent Darkness is growing stronger. But as you grow stronger, it grows just a bit weaker, which infuriates it, so it will continue to recruit...to feed...in order to grow stronger.*

"So am I."

At this he stops, causing me to practically run into him. He whirls around, his boots digging into the dirt floor. His eyes are angry and accusing, but I don't know what it is that I've done wrong. I just want to find Sloan. I just want to find Sloan, get the Wood stone, and return home. I didn't ask for the stupid life-force's message. I didn't ask for Qildor to intervene.

"Yes, but the Imminent Darkness is ancient. Old as time itself. Older even. And you, you are nothing but a foolish, half-immortal girl. If I were not there to stop you, you would have destroyed the life-force of countless nymphs and elves in one reckless moment.

Why? Because you saw something that you didn't want to see. You are weak and you are selfish."

The words sting as if he's slapped me. But he isn't finished.

"As you grow stronger, the Imminent Darkness weakens, in order to keep itself stronger it will need to feed. And who do you think it will feed on? My friends. My family. My entire world. You know nothing of loss."

My body moves before I can react. The flashlight drops to the floor and I hurl myself at Qildor, knocking him to the floor so that I'm sitting on top of him, my fist poised to smash in his stupid, elf face.

"You. Don't. Know. Me." I growl through clenched teeth. "I didn't ask for this. I didn't ask for the weight of the Universe to rest on my shoulders." He tries to move beneath me, but I squeeze my knees tighter around either side of his ribcage until he winces. "I watched an innocent woman get evaporated trying to help me. *Poof!* Gone like smoke. I watched my best friend turned into a soldier programmed to kill me. Now I have to watch him bear the scar of me saving myself. I watched my father's heart break when my mother disappeared. But you know what else I've watched? I've watched countless people risk their lives to help me and to help each other. All the while you live in your safe, little tree, hiding from the big, bad Imminent Darkness. And you call me selfish, Qildor?" I slam my fist into the ground beside his face, causing him to flinch and my knuckles to scrape and bleed. I climb off him, resisting the urge to give him a swift kick in the ribs. I grab the flashlight from the ground and storm up the tunnel without turning to look back.

. . .

When I reach the top, the hollow widens and opens, leaving just enough space for me to pass through. The sky is dark. Night. The ground is covered in a blanket of white. We don't get precipitation on Xon 9, but I learned about this in Earth Science. Snow. I crouch down and dip my fingers into the cold softness. I rub it between my fingers feeling it crumble and liquefy from the heat of my body, cooling my bleeding knuckles.

Fat, white flakes fall from the sky, landing in my hair and on my eyelashes, where they cling momentarily, then melt away as if they were never there at all. They melt into the skin of my cheeks. I look around. No sign of Sloan. Nahele is a giant tree. By far the largest of the forest. I make my way over the bulging roots that break out of the ground as if they are trying to free themselves. I get halfway around the base of the tree when I find him.

No lifeless body. No yellow eyes.

He's sitting on top of the roots of the tree, his back against the trunk, head tilted up to the sky, watching the snow fall down. There's a small smile on his face. Even though it is night, the snow seems to have a sort of illuminating effect on the world, giving it light where there should be dark.

"I couldn't find you." I climb over the roots so that I'm sitting in between his legs, my back pressed against his chest and stomach, a leg wrapped protectively around me from either side. He pulls his hands out of the pockets of his sweatshirt and wraps his arms around me, resting his chin on my shoulder.

"I was too warm and it was too loud."

"You should have told me."

"You were having fun. Besides, I thought that I'd be back before you even noticed I was gone."

"But you weren't."

"I know. I'm sorry. But this...I've never seen this before. Not in person anyways. It's as if the sky is letting the ground below know that it's going to be okay. Like it's saying, *Rest my friend. Sleep. And when you wake up everything will be better.*"

"Do you think that's true? Do you think that everything will be better?"

He's quiet a moment then says, "Yes. I think so."

The silence settles in the space between us, and suddenly I want to tell Sloan all about Qildor and the seed. Unburden my heart with what I've seen, in the hopes that he'll reassure me that it never could happen. That the Imminent Darkness will never fill his body and those evil yellow eyes will never peer out at me where calm green ones should be. I want him to tell me that we'll find the Wood stone and go home. And I want him to tell me that no one else will get hurt or die. I want him to tell me that everything is going to be okay, including me and including us. More importantly, I want him to tell me that I am not weak and I am not selfish, because I fear that the words only bother me so much because I feel that they hold some element of truth to them.

Instead, I say nothing. Just feeling his solidness pressing into me and watching the real magic of the snow falling quietly to the forest below, hiding the blackened, dead leaves beneath its blanket of pure white. I say nothing because Qildor never answered me. If what I saw is in the future and hasn't happened yet, then can't it be changed? The future isn't a set point in time. We can change it. I say nothing because Sloan wouldn't lie to me. And I'm not sure that I can handle the truth.

. . .

There's the sound of boots crunching on snow.

"I thought you might be cold." It's Qildor. He's wearing a heavy cape along with a gray bycoket. The bycocket appears to be felt and has a white feather pinned to it. He has a quiver slung across his shoulders, like Hennie, and a long bow. He holds out my jacket and two wool capes.

"Nice hat." I mumble getting up and taking my jacket along with one of the capes. Sloan takes the other. I suppose I'm relieved that Qildor isn't mad at me. But I'm not sure that I can say the same just yet.

"Thanks. I thought it was quite sporting."

"Is the feather from Constancia?" I ask buttoning the cape across my chest. It even has a hood. I lift the hood to protect my damp hair from the falling snow.

"For good luck." He pauses, peering at me carefully. "I owe you an apology, Ka. I think I was wrong about you. Forgive me for my words earlier." He bows slightly. Sloan raises an eyebrow but I give a slight shake of my head. Not now. Maybe not ever. If you don't speak of the unspeakable, the unspeakable can never happen, right?

I'm not about to apologize for my earlier behavior. So instead I say, "Thank you."

"And for the capes," Sloan says. He looks a bit ridiculous, what with the juxtaposition of his jeans, sweatshirt, and beat-up boots along with the fancy, wool cape. At least it's warm.

"It's no problem. Most nights now, it snows. But it usually melts by daybreak. Although, each day and night seems a little colder than the last."

"I noticed that," I say. "When I came out of the dining hall I could feel a cold breeze drifting down the tunnel. Does the weather change here?" The weather is always balmy with a slight, warm breeze on Xon 9.

Qildor frowns. "Not usually. It seems…" he lowers his voice. "It seems that the deeper into the forest the Imminent Darkness infiltrates, the colder it gets."

"I assume you didn't come find me just to apologize?"

"Ka, I'm insulted." He feigns a hurt expression. Then smiles. "But you are right. I have come to again offer my services to you. The Imminent Darkness grows stronger and I'm not sure how much longer Nahele can withstand it. He's doing his best." We look up at the still-green foliage in Nahele's branches. "But he is old. And he is tired. After you left, I realized that in order to defeat the Imminent Darkness, I need you. But you also need me."

"Oh, really? How do you figure that?" Sloan gives me a gentle nudge in the ribs. But like I said I don't forgive all that easily.

Qildor's eyes sparkle in the luminescence of the snow. "You are in an unfamiliar land. A land filled with nymphs, elves, fairies and, more importantly, magic. You need to find the Wood stone. This is my home. I can help you."

Unfortunately, he's right. Things could go much quicker if Qildor can help us find the Stone. The stone could be anywhere: on top of a mountain, deep inside a frozen lake, or buried beneath a grove of trees.

"Okay then, we accept your help, Qildor."

He grins. "I thought you might say that."

CHAPTER 10

Qildor pulls out a gemstone-encrusted dagger. Sapphires, emeralds, and amethysts are embedded in the handle. Its blade is tucked into a worn-leather sheath attached to a belt. He hands it to Sloan.

"You may need this."

Sloan takes it and fits it around his waist so that the sheath is on his left. "Thanks."

"Do you really think that's all necessary?" I nod to the dagger then to the quiver.

Qildor nods. "You don't? The Imminent Darkness can take on any form it sees fit." He glances at Sloan then back at me. "Including one of us. Or any other creature that still resides in the forest. That includes beasts as small as a rabbit or as large as a bear. Do you want to be caught empty-handed in such an encounter?"

Sloan nods in agreement. "Never bring a knife to gunfight."

I look at him. "What the heck does that mean?"

He shrugs sheepishly. "I'm not sure actually, but Bina used to always say it. I think it boils down to always be prepared."

Qildor glances up at the sky. "It's getting late. We should be going."

I follow his gaze upward to the sky, still black with thick gray clouds, bellies lit from within. "How can you tell if it's late? Regardless of whether it's day or night, you can never see the sun or moon for the clouds and trees."

"All the creatures of the forest—animal or elf—is in tune with one another. It's part of this Land's interconnectedness." He starts across the freshly fallen snow, heading back in the general direction of the path.

The snow-filled clouds emit a soft light that casts eerie shadows across the frozen ground. The crunching of our boots is the only sound in the otherwise silent forest. The festivities of the dining hall now feel far away, the warmth and delight like a feathery memory. I'm a bit angry at myself for allowing the distraction. Then again, if I hadn't been distracted I wouldn't have met Qildor. Even though, I saw things that I didn't want to, it's not necessarily his fault. Constancia sent me on this path. And my mother had warned me that I should be cautious. As we walk, I absent-mindedly reach for the Bloodstone in my pants pocket. Only my pocket is empty.

I must have dropped it when I was fighting with Qildor. We've been walking a while already so there's no going back now. I can only hope that I don't need it. I twist my turquoise ring around my left index finger nervously. Really, I don't need a silly gemstone to protect me, even if it was a gift from my mother. This ring has all I need. It contains fragments of my enemy, was created by a friend, and was blessed with the power to take me to my parents whenever I need them. Still, I feel a tinge of sadness at my own impulsiveness.

I never used to be that way. I was always boring. Ordinary. Blended in with the crowd. A rule-follower. And then suddenly, it was as if everything I knew about myself had been torn to pieces and thrown into the wind, only to float back to the earth below for me to reassemble it all. Never in a million years would I have stood up to Qildor like that or let my anger bubble over. I could say that it's the Fire inside me, except I think that would be a lie. Because even though I retrieved the Fire stone and restored that piece of my personality, I think it was always in me lying dormant. Waiting.

And that's what scares me. Those parts of my personality that are lying dormant, waiting to be awakened, what if I don't like them? What if I become someone so unrecognizable that I don't even like myself? One time Li had said something strange. He thought I hadn't heard him. It was after another one of our spats: me blaming myself for the scars he now has to bear, he accusing me of treating him like he's broken. He'd stormed off, but not before mumbling something about liking me just the way I am, as in the old Ka. Because that's how I've come to look at myself. There's the old Ka, the one who couldn't make a decision to save her life, and when she did make them they were often the wrong ones, and the new Ka, the one who isn't afraid to speak her mind and go after the things that she wants, the one who will take a stand even if she's standing alone. I've changed so much in such a short amount of time. How do I know where it is that Ka ends and the Elements begin? Worse, what if who I am becoming is someone that I don't like?

"There." Qildor's voice slices through my thoughts like the dagger sheathed at Sloan's waist.

"What's where?" He's staring straight ahead. The forest seems to open onto an empty area. I don't see anything except an expanse of open space. It's so vast that I can't even see the other side.

"There. That's the lake."

"I don't see a lake," I reply.

"That's because it's frozen. It's covered with snow," Sloan says.

"Where does it end?" I ask looking to both my left and my right as we keep walking. It seems to go on forever in either direction which means going around it isn't an option.

"The forest continues on the other side."

"There's another side?"

"Every lake has another side."

"So how do we get there?"

Sloan walks carefully to the shoreline. He bends down and swipes some of the snow away, revealing a glass-like surface. "Maybe we could walk across."

"No, remember what I said. The temperature warms too much during the day. The ice hasn't accumulated, and isn't very thick. It could give way and if you didn't drown, surely, you'd freeze to death," Qildor says.

"Gee, there's a happy thought," I mumble.

Qildor ignores me and continues. "There's an old wooden bridge not too far from here. We just need to walk down the shoreline a ways. It's in need of repair, but it's less dangerous than risking the instability of the lake ice."

"Sounds as good a plan as any," Sloan says rising to his feet. "What is it exactly that's on the other side of this lake, besides more forest?"

"There's an enchanted fairy grove. And I suspect that the Wood stone is kept there."

"I thought you said that fairies are tricksters," I say.

"They are."

"Then why would the Wood stone be kept in a fairy grove?" I ask. Qildor looks at me like I've confirmed his suspicions that I am quite clueless when it comes to magical creatures.

"Why for exactly that very reason."

. . .

Qildor and I have very different definitions of what constitutes a bridge, and I can tell from the expression on Sloan's face that he feels the same way.

"You're kidding, right?" I ask. The bridge before me appears to be made of branches. The branches are bent into U-shapes with the base of the U forming the walkway and the sides of the U forming a short wall on either side of the base. Branches are also attached along the top of either side like a railing to prevent you from tumbling into the lake. Despite its appearances, it arcs gracefully from one side of the frozen lake to the other.

"Surely not."

"But it's just a bunch of sticks!"

Sloan steps forward and places a boot onto the walkway, testing it out. He steps completely onto it with both feet and jumps up and down a couple of times. "Seems sturdy enough."

"We couldn't use iron. The amount of iron would have been detrimental to the fey's ability to cross the lake."

"Can't they just, you know, fly or whatever?"

Qildor rolls his eyes. "That is such a human thing to say."

"Should I be insulted by that?"

"Fairies don't fly!" Sloan calls out from the bridge.

"And how do you know that?"

"Folklore. The notion that fairies are tiny people with wings is an erroneous notion," Qildor explains. "Like myself and the nymphs, fairies can take on any size that the situation dictates. Furthermore, some do have wings, but most do not. And the ones who do have wings, can only travel short distances, not across an entire lake."

"Sheesh! I never even knew nymphs and elves were real, let alone fairies," I say trying to cover up my apparent ignorance.

"Oh, we are very real indeed. We bleed just as our human counterparts bleed. Now, shall we be going? Dawn will be here before we know it."

"Do you turn to stone or something at sunlight's first break?" I scoff stepping onto the bridge behind Sloan.

"Of course not. But even the Imminent Darkness needs to rest. It seems to be more active during the daytime. Now, let's get on with it."

. . .

Walking across the bridge creates an odd sensation deep in the pit of my stomach. When I went to the Land of Earth and retrieved the Earth stone, there was a pyramid and it had a glass floor. I realized that despite my knowing that there was something solid beneath me, I couldn't walk across it unless I closed my eyes. The sensation now is the same. If I look down at my feet, it seems impossible to be walking across a bridge entirely comprised of sticks. And yet, it feels solid beneath me. Don't get me wrong, it wouldn't be my first choice in building materials, but it seems to fit the environment.

As we walk across, the lake is silent. Frozen. No fish, no birds. No loud sounds, just the soft hush as the snow falls, dotting the shoulders of Sloan's cape as he walks in front of me. Qildor is behind me. Out here, without the forest blocking the view, I can see the entire sky, filled with tiny pinpricks of light: stars. Because of the never-setting sun on Xon 9, we don't see much in the way of stars. But I wish that we did. To think that there are billions of stars out there and that they're billions of years old—maybe even trillions— really puts things into perspective. Are there stars out there that are older than the Imminent Darkness? Older than Raj and Katayun?

I stare up at the sky, not paying much attention to where my feet are landing. And that's why when I take my next step, my boot hits nothing but air and I fall straight through the bridge's bottom, breaking through the thin layer of ice and splashing into the freezing waters of the lake below. I scream Sloan's name, but it's swallowed up by a rush of cold water into my mouth as I sink. I'm drifting away from the hole that I fell through and there's nothing but solid ice above me. I recall Qildor's words in a panic: *It could give way and if you didn't drown, surely, you'd freeze to death.* I pound my fists on the ice above me. But it's no use because with nothing solid beneath me, I can't get enough leverage to break through.

The cold is piercing and seeps through my skin and muscles, and deep into my bones. I could conjure up some Fire, but what then? I could try and melt the ice, but it would take minutes. The coldness stings my lungs. I've never been good with water, which is maybe another reason I went against the box's recommendation at Pronouncement. Sloan once told me that water has the ability to sustain life, but to also take it away. In that way, it's not that different from Fire. But right now I feel more of the taking away part.

I drowned once before, in the Elemental Abyss. It was how I had to break the waterfall's enchantment. I remember the burn in my lungs and the dark, dancing spots in front of my eyes. Except then, Sloan had reassured me that I would awake in the rowboat with Doran. That I wouldn't truly die. But that's not what is happening now. This time, I will not wake up safe and sound.

Around me is nothing but darkness. As above, so below. My body feels heavy and my muscles ache from the effort of trying to tread water. But what's the point when you can't take a breath? When there's no oxygen making its way to your brain to tell your body to continue to fight. My eyelids slide closed and I can feel the weightlessness as I begin to sink away from the frozen ceiling above me.

It's not how I thought it would end. I've survived worse. I've survived an army of fire, the fangs of a wolf, even the living dead. One of my own, as of yet unclaimed, Elements is my own death. I press my thumb to the ring on my index finger. I could wish myself home, wish myself to safety and to the comfort of my parents' love. What then would happen to the stones? I wouldn't be able to return to the Land of Wood and the portal would be sealed shut forever. Would the Imminent Darkness devour everything in its path? But if I die…can a half-immortal die? *Yes*, a voice whispers from deep inside me. It may take me a bit longer, but it is the Universal cycle of life. Everything must die eventually. Even me.

Strong arms surround my chest and I'm being pulled upwards. I'm moving quickly, I can feel the water flowing around my body. Voices from far away. "Here, I've got her." Another set of arms, not as strong as the first. A blast of air. A hard surface beneath me. I turn onto my side and throw up lake water. I thought the burning would stop, but now it only seems worse. I open my eyes, but everything is blurry. I can make out Sloan's shivering form in front of me. He's shirtless and his hair is wet and matted to his forehead. He quickly pulls his shirt back over his head and before I know it he's pulling the layers of my clothes off and tossing them aside, ignoring my garbled protests. I'm shivering and he's only making it worse. My brain is in slow-motion, trying to put together the pieces of what's happening. He takes the cloak he was wearing earlier and wraps it around me.

"She needs more." Not a request. A demand.

Another cloak materializes and Sloan wraps me inside it, bundling me like a small child. My teeth are chattering uncontrollably and freezing droplets of water push out of my hairline and run down my cheeks. Sloan scoops me up in his arms and I press my head against his chest, listening for the reassuring beat of his heart next to my ear.

"We need to hurry, Qildor."

There's a shuffling sound and then the sound of someone running. Sloan doesn't run, but he begins walking quickly, following Qildor across the bridge.

"I wasn't planning on going for a swim tonight," he says softly, trying to make light of the situation, but I can see his eyes and his eyes always tell me the truth. That he is afraid.

"Neither was I," I say, but my voice comes out harsh and ragged-sounding, raw from the water.

"There was a loose branch in the bridge. Qildor thinks it was typical fairy trickery." His words come out in a rush, trying to talk to fill his head, so that he doesn't have room to think, or room to worry. "How I missed it and you didn't is beyond me. But Ka, we need to restore your body temperature. If we don't…"

"Half-immortal," I say forcing the words out.

But he only confirms what I already knew. "Half-immortal doesn't mean invincible."

"We're almost there!" Qildor calls out from somewhere ahead of us. "But we'll need to gain entrance to the grove before we can get her inside."

"What does that mean?" Sloan calls back.

"Don't worry! I'll take care of it!" Comes the reply.

"Kata, this is very important." Sloan's voice is a hushed whisper and I can't help but wonder if he's using that tone to soothe me or to soothe himself. "You need to fill your body with Fire. It will give us some time, before we can get you completely dry and warm. Do you think you can do that for me?"

My eyelids feel heavy again as if I am drifting off to sleep, like I'm slipping in and out of consciousness. One minute Sloan's words make sense, the next they're a jumbled mess inside of my head and it takes all my effort to put them in order again. Fire. I nod.

"That's my girl." And even though I can't see his face anymore, I can hear his smile.

Anger. Passion. Life. Death. That is what makes up Fire.

I can feel the heat percolating just beneath the surface, waiting. All it takes is a spark to ignite an inferno.

Suddenly, it hits me. The concern in Sloan's voice. He already knows what I have yet to realize. The shivering and the confusion. Each breath an exhausting, painful, Herculean effort.

I am dying.

Chapter 11

I'm so cold. I'm not used to the cold. Xon 9 always has the perfect, constant temperature. My teeth are chattering, my chin moving up and down of its own accord. I can feel the coldness deep in my bones and they ache. My hair is still damp and matted to my head. I'm alone here. It's dark. But in the distance I can see the smallest of flames. Where there's fire, I know that there's heat.

The fire seems so far away, nothing but a faint glow in the distance. I know it's there but I can't quite grasp it. It's inside me, but I'm lost. I can't find my way. Maybe if I just focus on the faint spark, just maybe I can get it to flare. The small flame twirls, but I need it to dance, to pirouette across my field of vision. I rub my hands up and down my bare arms, but it's no use. My fingers are like icicles that steal away whatever body heat I have left. I need to get to that fire. I take a step forward, but it's as if my legs are made of lead. All I need is a little at a time.

As I drag my feet I concentrate on the small flame imagining it getting bigger and bigger. I know this isn't right, that this isn't how it ends. Bina would have seen it or Sloan would have somehow known. I am just in a sort of between space and need to get from one side to the other. I struggle to keep my eyes open as I fall to my knees. It's better to crawl than to stand still and do nothing.

This place makes me feel sad and alone, but what is it that makes me feel love and warmth? Sloan. Home. My family and my friends. Despite the cold and dark, I imagine my body filled with a soft, glowing light that radiates through every cell. I picture Mrs. Chatfield's house. I can see Doran and Zora sitting on the worn sofa drinking hot chocolate. My father sits beside them, smiling and laughing. In the armchair across from him sits Sloan, animatedly telling a story. This is the last place that I felt safe. My ring is still on my finger and I turn it thrice, thinking of the safety of my family and friends. I open my eyes. The flame seems to grow brighter in the distance, beckoning me to come closer.

I continue to crawl towards the flame. Despite our personal hardships and heartbreaks, we can still come together. We can still smile and laugh. We can still love. The flame seems to ignite in a giant burst of blinding light. Before me now is a roaring bonfire, flames almost licking what I imagine is the ceiling of this invisible space. And the warmth! It feels so good on my cheeks, the slight burning prickle of heat.

You can take it all away.

But in the end, the things that truly matter are still there.

If not physically, then at least as a wisp of memory in the recesses of our minds.

I smile into the feeling.

. . .

"She's waking up!" Sloan's voice is both relieved and urgent. I can feel his hand in mine and I know that I'm laying down on something soft and fluffy. There's a warm blanket pulled all the way up to my chin.

My eyes flutter open and his green eyes come into focus first, followed by the curve of his lips and then the glisten of his silvery scales. His brow is furrowed with worry. I try to squeeze his hand to reassure him that I am okay, but I can barely grasp his fingers with my own.

"Here," a gruff voice says. "Have her drink this."

Someone hands Sloan a small teacup and he takes it, holding it up to my lips. "Drink it," he instructs. I obey, allowing him to tilt the cup so that the warm liquid touches my lips. I open my mouth and drink. The liquid is sweet and thick.

The unfamiliar voice returns. "Agave nectar. It will boost her immune system." I finish sipping the syrupy liquid and turn toward the voice.

A very old woman stands in the corner of the room. She has small spectacles over large pale blue eyes. Her hair is a faded blonde, swept into a messy bun on top of her head. She's plump, but in a soft, inviting way. She's wearing an apron over a flowery printed dress. I am laying in a small bed with Sloan sitting beside me on a small wooden chair. It would appear I am inside some kind of infirmary, only it's cozier than that, as if it's part of someone's house. There are pictures on the wall and shelves lined with glass jars and bottles, not unlike Bina's own kitchen of concoctions. A fire crackles in a brick fireplace against the far wall.

The woman waddles over. She's quite short, only as tall as Sloan and he's seated. She takes out a wooden cylinder with a hole at one end and a hollowed out cone shape at the other. She places something inside the funnel end and presses it to my chest, placing her ear over the opening. Waiting, she listens, then satisfied she removes the plug and follows the same procedure, listening. Satisfied, she pulls away, dropping the wooden cylinder into a pocket of her apron.

"Everything sounds good. Strong heartbeat. Her lungs sound a little watery. But in a few days' time she should be fine."

Sloan turns to her. "Thank you, Althea."

"It's no problem. I save those who need saving. Whoever loosened that part of the bridge, their consequences should be severe. These fairies nowadays have no concept of the dangers their trickery may cause. If it wasn't one of the nymphs or elves, it could have been one of our own. Not to mention a human girl!" Althea shakes her head. "It isn't often that we have guests and they wonder why!" She bustles over to one of the shelves and the sound of clinking glasses drifts over to me. She returns and places another teacup on the little table beside the bed. "It's good to see you are doing well, Dear. Quite the fright you gave us all. I think you nearly scared your beau here half-to-death. Thank goodness for his and Qildor's quick thinking! Speaking of which, I am going to leave you two alone a moment and go see if I can find Qildor. I'm sure he'll be relieved to know that you're awake."

Her face is kind. "Thank you," I say but it comes out all muddled sounding.

"Hush, Child," she smiles placing a wrinkled hand over my own. "Anyone with half a mind and half a heart would have done the same. Healers help those who need helping." She pats my hand and then flurries out the door to go find Qildor.

The room doesn't have electricity, instead there are little glass jars and other containers everywhere with little blinking lights inside them. There are so many that it gives enough light to feel like a bedside lamp is turned on. Sloan sits back in the little wooden chair and rubs a hand over his tired face.

"Althea's a pretty good Healer. She even healed my collarbone. Carrying you that distance hadn't done me any favors, but now it's good as new." He moves the collar of his shirt to show me there's no evidence of injury, but my mind is on other things.

"You saved me," I whisper.

He stares at me hard. "Of course I did."

"You could have died, frozen to death, you're a Water, but even you could have drowned…but…you still honored your vow."

He leans forward and I see the smallest flicker of anger in his eyes. "You think I saved you because of a vow?" He slouches back again, allowing his head to flop back so that he's looking up at the ceiling. "Ka, I didn't jump in and save you because of the stupid Everlasting Vow. I didn't even think about it. There was no debate or reasoning. Almost as soon as you hit the water, I jumped in after you. There was no choice. I wasn't honoring a vow. I was honoring my love for you."

I can feel the burn of tears behind my eyes. I know that Sloan loves me, but to hear him say it now feels so different, foreign almost. Not because we don't tell one another, but because suddenly the words have a certain depth to them that they lacked before.

He brings his gaze back toward mine, taking my hand again and pulling it toward him. He carefully scoots the chair nearer to the bed so that his elbows can rest on its edge.

"And not only my love, Kata, but my fear of losing you. I told you earlier, that your lack of fear is what frightens me the most. The fact that you walk so willing into death's open arms. And for a second there, when I held you in my arms as I followed Qildor into the enchanted grove, your eyelids slid closed and your lips were tinged with blue. Your breathing became so soft, so shallow that I thought surely, you had succumbed to death's embrace. I knew long ago that it wasn't the vow that drew me to you or that has kept me by your side. It's just you, Kata, in all your self-centered, annoyingly reckless glory. Love made me jump off that bridge to save you. Nothing less."

His words sink in and the same warm feeling from when I was alone in the darkness seems to fill my body, starting in my chest and radiating outward toward my fingers and toes. Sloan smiling and laughing in the comfort of Mrs. Chatfield's living room. I reach out and take his cheeks in either hand and pull his face toward mine, feeling the softness of his lips upon my own. Warm and alive. I pull away slowly and look deep into his eyes. This love—and the fear it holds— is not one-sided. It never was. It never will be.

"And your love is what brought me back."

CHAPTER 12

There's the sound of someone clearing his throat at the door. Qildor. His hat and cape are removed and he looks fairly at ease despite being in a fairy abode.

"Sorry to, uh, interrupt your little thing there, but Althea told me you were awake and alert, so I had to come and see for myself."

Sloan lets go of my hand and I carefully push myself to a seated position. It's the first time that I notice I'm wearing a long, white cotton nightgown and a pale pink cardigan with flowers printed on it. My feet are beneath the blanket but I can feel the itchy wool of the socks that cover them. I pull the blanket up and over my chest a bit self-consciously.

"Yes, I'm feeling a lot better, thanks."

Qildor steps into the room and stands awkwardly beside Sloan who is still seated in the small wooden chair.

"That's a relief. I thought for sure—" He coughs. "What I mean to say is I reported the incident to the Fairy King and he was most displeased."

"The fairies have a king? Don't they just obey Nahele and Constancia like the nymphs and elves?" I ask.

Qildor leans onto one of the large wooden bedposts. "Yes and no. Everyone in the Land of Wood must follow the rules of Constancia because she is our goddess. But Nahele's jurisdiction is the nymphs and elves. Constancia tends to focus her efforts on the other plants and animals. The Fairy King rules the Grove and the fairies that live here."

"Some of the fairies don't live here?" Sloan asks.

"Most of them do, but not all. Some like to be solitary. They still respect the Fairy King, but will obey the laws set forth by Constancia."

"What will happen to whoever messed with the bridge?" I ask.

Qildor runs a hand through his hair. "Most likely they will be sent away."

"Sent away?"

"Solitary fairies are a peculiar thing. Some fairies are just drawn to being alone and have a fierce independent streak that doesn't lend to living in a colony with their brethren. But others are forced away for disgracing the others. Fairies may be tricksters, but almost causing someone's death is considered crossing the line."

"Accidents happen," I say even though I'm not sure I believe the words myself.

"That was not an accident," Qildor replies.

"So what happens now?" I ask changing the subject. "I'm alive. We're here. What happens next?"

"Well, it's very late into the night. So first, I think you should rest a bit longer. Then we can meet with the Fairy King first thing in the morning."

"You said you think the Wood stone is kept here."

Qildor nods. "I do."

"So, what, are you just planning on asking the Fairy King to give it up? Neither of the other two stones were that easy to retrieve."

Qildor gives me a dim smile. "Certainly not. The Fairy King will most likely offer up the information willingly; however, as I've said before, the fairies are tricksters. Simply knowing the stone's location does not mean that it will be easy to retrieve. In fact, quite the contrary."

. . .

I'm dreaming that I'm home. I'm alone and I'm wandering down the sidewalk that I know leads to the Black Bazaar. It seems like forever since I've been here. I see the familiar wooden signpost and head down the cobblestone stairs. As usual in these situations, my feet seem to have a mind of their own.

I walk past Bina's banged up trailer, still not repaired from when the Imminent Darkness's henchman kidnapped her. They wanted to cleanse her mind, which I know firsthand is excruciatingly painful, only it backfired on them. It's not so easy to MindCleanse someone with the Sight. She barely got out alive and when Sloan and I left for the Elemental Abyss she was still recuperating at Michaela's.

People move about me, but I don't hear any sounds. I walk past the tattoo shop where I first met Zora. No hum of the tattoo needle. I continue past one of the bars. No clink of glasses or rough, drunken laughter. *Okay, this is a bit weird.* If I'm not hearing anything, what is it that I'm supposed to be seeing?

My feet lead me on, past the other vendors and toward the outskirts of the Black Bazaar and the rest of the Underground. That's when I realize where I am headed and begin to fight back. I try to dig my heels into the ground, grab onto one side of an awning, but the efforts are futile. Only recently have I began to understand that my dreams aren't simply the nighttime whispers of my imagination. Bina, Sloan, and my mother all have this gift, why then should I be any different? If no one is here to deliver the message perhaps I am simply supposed to bear witness, like the time the Imminent Darkness almost devoured my mother whole. Its messages can be disturbing to say the least.

The small, shabby vendor comes into view. It has a dilapidated awning over a concrete patio. I don't want to see this. I don't want to know. No more. I pinch my cheeks, trying to wake myself up, but my feet plod on. I close my eyes, but somehow I can still see. My efforts are useless. The first thing I notice are the overturned chairs. Was it that long ago that Doran and I sat here as he shaped the wire for the very ring I am wearing? I use my thumb to rub against the cool metal, to comfort myself from what I don't want to see.

The next thing I notice is the overturned shelves, the shelves that displayed the various pieces of jewelry and other odds and ends. Smashed to tiny pieces across the concrete. My feet continue to the open door, crunching over the remnants. The living room sofa is ripped to shreds and the armchair is overturned. Every cabinet in the kitchen has been emptied of its contents, shattered glass is scattered across the kitchen floor. I find myself heading down the short hallway. There are three small bedrooms. The first belongs to Mrs. Chatfield. The small closet is open and there are clothes scattered about. The bed is unmade. The second belongs to Zora and it is in much the same condition. Maybe they escaped. Somehow they got away. Why else would there be clothes strewn about? Unless they had to pack in a hurry.

The last bedroom belongs to Doran. The door is closed and I reach my hand for the knob. I find that I am holding my breath. When I first met Doran, I didn't care much for him. Actually, I quite disliked him. I thought he was a punk. I smile recalling the smug smirk he'd always wear when we were first initiated into Fire. And how quickly things changed when I discovered him at the mercy of Tristen and her cruelty. I was on my way to the transportation portals, but one glimpse at his brokenness and I knew I couldn't just walk away. And you know what he did? He had the nerve to act like he didn't need my help. Even at his most vulnerable, he wouldn't let anyone else in. But I helped him anyway because that's exactly when someone needs you the most.

Little did I know my compassion would lead to a companion. He traveled to the Land of Fire with me and I'm pretty sure I wouldn't have survived the trip without his bravery and ingenuity. Later, I learned that Doran's father was an Unbalanced Water and that his mother was the keeper of a safe house from the Imminent Darkness. He wasn't a punk; he was merely trying to protect himself. Like we all do.

This house brought me home. The warmth and love that I felt here called me back to the living in my time of need. Now it's in shambles, a shell of its former heart. One more room. I now realize this entire dream trip was for this sole purpose: me entering into this room. What will I find behind door number three?

I take another deep breath and turn the knob. It comes out in a whoosh of relief. It's a mess alright, but no Doran laying helpless and as far as I can tell no bloodstains on the carpet. I step into the room. Dresser drawers are half-pulled out, their contents spilling onto the floor. There's a knocked over picture frame, its glass broken into pieces. I follow the pieces of shattered glass to near the bed. There's a facedown photograph on the floor. I pick it up and turn it over.

It's Doran and he's smiling like I've never seen before. Sure, I've seen him smile and tell jokes, but this smile is different. He's grinning ear to ear and it reaches his eyes because they are full of sparkle. Beside him is a man. The man has black hair like Doran and almost the same skin tone, a soft, mocha color. His nose is wide and flat, a perfect match for Doran's. The man has silvery scales running down the right side of his face, but he too appears happy and wears a wide, toothy smile. Doran's father. I saw the images, when we traveled through the Elemental Abyss together, just like with Sloan, little glimpses of memories that don't belong to me. I remember the anger, but worse, the hatred. How can this be the same man as the one in those memories?

I lower myself to the edge of the bed. Is this what I was brought here to see? I feel it beneath me, hiding beneath the covers. I place the photo carefully down beside me and reach my hand underneath the bedspread. I feel something cold and metal in my hand. I pull it out. It's a slender, silver tube. A message tube. And it's blinking green. Looks like someone left me a message.

. . .

I hesitate before pressing the button. But as usual, my fingers are moving of their own accord. I press the button. Doran's deep voice comes over the tiny speaker in a hushed whisper. "I don't know how you'll find this. I just know that you will because, well, because you're you. It's coming. It's all over the Underground. When you come back home don't expect it to be the same. In fact, don't even come here. Don't trust anyone." There's a long pause, as if he's listening to someone telling him what to say. Zora? Mrs. Chatfield? Or something more sinister? No, not Doran. He'd rather risk his own life than be a traitor, unlike some people. "If you need to find us the wind will take you there. Now don't waste any more time. Get out before it finds you. Because it will." The last couple sentences come out in an urgent rush. The message tube beeps: transmission over. Then it deletes. Messages can only be listened to once. Good idea, in case your messages land in the wrong hands.

I get off the bed, shoving the tube into my pocket next to where the Bloodstone should be, but isn't. Wait. Doran said to get out before it finds me because it will. My heart quickens in my chest and the hair on the back of my neck prickles. I make my way toward the bedroom door, but it's too late. A thick, gray smoke is curling through the doorway. It's too fast. It permeates the room, swirling around me, encompassing me in its suffocating sulfur-y smell. I hold my breath and hear the faint whispers of laughter. It's found me.

. . .

"Ka! Ka, wake up!" Sloan's voice brings me back to the present, back to reality.

"What time is it?" I mumble.

"Morning," Sloan replies. The window is open and the curtains pushed aside. Pale sunlight enters through the window.

"I thought that the Imminent Darkness had penetrated this side of the forest?" I stretch and run a hand through my chin-length brown hair, pulling out the nest of tangled strands.

"Apparently, it hasn't reached the Fairy Grove." He leans over and peers out the window. I stumble to my feet and shuffle over to stand beside him at the window. The grass is lush and green, kissed with dew from the morning. There are trees with bright green leaves and cascades of vined flowers in every brilliant color. Sloan smiles. "Beautiful, isn't it?"

We don't have beauty like this at home. Xon 9 doesn't have cornucopias of colors. Because of the red landscape and the never-setting sun, the shades of light vary from a deep red to a pale pink when the twin moons rise. There's no precipitation, so the vegetation has taken on a grayish-green tinge, whether it be shrubs, trees, or grass. Of course, there are manmade lights in a pale green to cancel the overwhelming redness, providing a "truer" sense of things, around buildings and homes. But what I see outside right now, Xon 9 pales in comparison.

"I've never seen anything like this. It's as if everything sparkles."

A soft, female voice comes from behind me. "That's because it does."

Althea.

We turn from the window. "How?"

"Fairy dust, of course. It's an enchantment, keeps away that darkness thing, at least so far it has. We have to reapply it regularly, but the flowers have really taken a liking to it." She holds up a pile of clothing. "I've taken the liberty of washing your things."

I pull the flowered cardigan tighter around my waist. "Thank you."

"Oh, and Basal told me to let you know that breakfast is ready."

"Basal?" Sloan asks.

"The Fairy King," Althea smiles, sets the clean clothing on the bed, then disappears back out the doorway.

"Well, you better get dressed. It isn't every day that you get to have breakfast with the Fairy King," Sloan says. "I'll wait for you just outside the door."

I slip out of the cardigan and pull the dowdy nightgown up and over my head. I pull my own t-shirt down over my head. I slip into my jeans. Michaela's coat that she lent me is there too. I was wearing it, along with the cape, when I fell into the lake. But the Grove looks so beautiful today that I don't think I'll be needing it. I look around for my messenger bag which is lying next to the nightstand. My boots are beside it. I roll up the jacket and shove it into the messenger bag, double-checking to make sure that the jars, map, book, flashlight and other things are all still there, which they are. I bend over to pick up my boots and feel a stab in my right hipbone.

I reach into my pocket and my breath catches in my throat. I pull out a long, slender metal tube. But it can't be. There's no green light flashing. No message. With shaking hands I stick the message tube back into my pants pocket, fling my messenger bag over my shoulder, and head out the door.

It's time to meet the Fairy King.

CHAPTER 13

If I thought the nymph and elf dining hall was fancy, they don't have anything on the Fairy King. There's a long wooden table that reminds me of the one my father, mother, and I sat at when we were all reunited in the Land of Earth. It has a bright purple, velvet table runner with golden tassels running its lengths. Above the table is a driftwood chandelier alit with candles. In the center of the table is a row of various colored flowers: blue, purple, pink, yellow, orange, red, white…you name it and it's there. On either side of the table are high-backed wooden chairs, but at the end is a much taller, more ornate chair and in it sits a very plump, very old man with a ring of flowers around his head. Qildor sits to his left.

The first thing I want to exclaim is: "You're the Fairy King!?" But I bite my tongue because I know it would be rude and not only would my mother be ashamed of me if she knew, but so would I.

"Ah, the Impossible Girl of Legend and the Protector of the Everlasting Vow! Please, please come sit and feast. You must be quite hungry after your ordeal."

"Thank you, Your Highness." Sloan pulls out a chair for me across from Qildor and then seats himself in the one beside me. The table in front of us is covered with food: fruit swollen with ripeness, little dishes of agave nectar in varying shades, and soft-boiled eggs along with golden goblets filled with golden liquids. The magical creatures seem to really like their golden beverages. I push the glass aside, not wanting a repeat of the other night. If I am going to find the Wood stone, then I need a clear head.

The Fairy King has a tuft of white hair beneath his flowered crown. His eyebrows are bushy and white too, hovering over his light blue eyes like hungry caterpillars. The folded lines of time wrinkle his face, but his cheeks remain a rosy pink. His belly rests on the table just in front of his plate. In addition to the crown he's wearing a long, purple velvet mantle that appears to match the table runner.

"You're looking much better than upon your arrival. I'm glad that Althea could be of service to you."

"Yes, she is a wonderful Healer," I say taking a bite of an apple, so tart that my eyes almost water.

"That she is. I do apologize for the, uh, incident. Please know that dire consequences were issued to the perpetrator."

"I hope not too dire," I say remembering what Qildor said about solitary fairies.

"I assure you, trickery is one thing, but endangering the life of another is never acceptable. It puts a tarnish on the Fairy reputation and we have a no tolerance policy on such behavior."

Qildor interjects, "The King is quite fair and just in his consequences."

Basal beams like a school child just given a golden star. "Thank you, Qildor."

"You two know each other?" Sloan asks.

"Everyone knows of Qildor. He's a fine warrior. The best!" says Basal.

I raise an eyebrow and a blush creeps across Qildor's pale skin. "Surely, Your Highness, perhaps the second best."

"Oh, nonsense!" Basal pounds his fist playfully on the table. "Qildor here's simply being modest. Nahele is an old and dear friend to me, he wouldn't send just any old elf to offer us protection."

"Is it often that you need protecting?" I ask pouring a bit of a light-colored agave nectar into a teacup.

"Only since that atrocity has shown up."

"He means the Imminent Darkness."

"Must we name it? The things which we name to which we also give power." Basal frowns and I can see when he said Nahele was an old friend he meant quite literally. The Fairy King could easily be millenia old.

"Ah, but to the things which we fear to name, and refuse to call forth, do they stealeth our power from us for if we cannot name our enemy, how then can we defeat it?" Qildor replies.

I pause with the teacup at my lips, waiting for the Fairy King's reaction. I've learned that royalty can sometimes be fickle. Will Basal turn in a moment's notice to lash out in anger at Qildor's turn-of-phrase? Instead he lets out a jovial laugh. "As usual, you are right, my warrior friend!" I let out a relieved sigh. "Brave and sharp, Qildor is. I'm honored to have his services." The Fairy King pats Qildor roughly on the back, but I can tell that Qildor appreciates the praise. "Now, let us finish our breakfast because we have business to attend. I hear someone's looking for the Wood stone and I just may know how you can find it."

. . .

We're sitting in an office where the walls are lined with mahogany bookshelves. It smells of leather, dust, and parchment. There are four overstuffed armchairs and a fireplace with a fire already going when we arrived. The large picture window is flanked by gauzy white curtains and reveals a stunning view of homes built into and around the trees. The view is a bit higher up, so we're looking down on what appears to be the entire Fairy Grove. The sun shines down and, as before, everything appears to sparkle.

Basal sits with his back to the fire. Qildor and Sloan are on either side. I've taken the seat across from him. There's a small table with a tray of water glasses. I wish those had been at breakfast; my mouth is still sticky with the sweetness of the agave syrup. The King takes a glass of water and leans back comfortably into the chair which seems to fold up around him.

"So, you are the Girl of Legend. I've heard much about you."

I smile awkwardly, embarrassed at being so well-known, when I've only just began to know myself. "That's me."

"The girl who consists of all possibilities and yet none, half-immortal, seeker of the five stones. Your reputation precedes you, but if I am being honest, which unfortunately is a fault of mine, you don't look like much of anything. Just an ordinary girl." The words sting, but I cannot deny their truth.

"Looks can be deceiving," I say. "And, Your Highness, if I am being honest as well, your words don't strike me as being very honorable, as the words of a king should be. I have the fierceness of Fire and the stubbornness of Earth in my veins." Qildor gives me a beseeching look. Apparently, he thinks my honesty will get me nowhere, but if that's true then neither will the king's. As I see this, it's a mutually exclusive deal. I want the stone and the Fairy King doesn't want the Imminent Darkness infringing on his Grove.

"I must say she appears to be a worthy opponent of the Imminent Darkness, Your Highness. She is spirited, quick and intelligent. Her strength is deceiving," Qildor says.

"Show me," Basal orders. Qildor shoots me another look letting me know that if I know what's good for me, I'll set to impressing the King. King or goddess, they're all the same. They're like small children; always needing their egos fed and needing to be entertained. But I am not someone's amusement.

"No." I say sternly. I lean back in the chair and cross my legs like I don't have a care in the world. "I will not show you. This is a business deal. As I see it I need you, but you also need me. I need the

Wood stone in order to restore back to me what's already rightfully mine, and defeat the Imminent Darkness. And, if we're still being honest, you're shaking in your floral undies about the Imminent Darkness getting hold of your Fairy Grove. There's only so many enchantments that you can cast before the Imminent Darkness can find a way in. It's pure energy; it can take any form it pleases, including yours. Would your enchantments know the difference between the real king and a doppelganger?" I lean forward placing my elbows on my knees. "It's already penetrated the enchantments of the Elemental Abyss which were cast by Raj and Katayun. Do you really think your fairy enchantments stand a chance? You need me as much as I need you."

The King's blue eyes grow wide as saucers in his face and he goes slightly pale. "How do you…How did it…?"

I shrug. "I was told from a reliable source and have seen it with my own eyes. If the ID gets hold of your precious Grove, all those beautiful flowers, the happy, sparkling homes, even the shining of the sun would all wither away and turn to rot. And I don't think you want that, now do you?"

Basal shakes his head. He leans forward and sets his glass back onto the tray. I can see the slight shake of his hand. "Qildor's words are true. You are both quick and intelligent. I apologize if I've insulted you. Forgive me."

"Thank you, but it's not about being intelligent, it's about getting the job done. I didn't ask for this task, but it's what I was assigned to do. And, quite frankly, it's personal. Something of mine was taken away and I'd very much like to have it back." I let out a long sigh because isn't that the truth? We don't always ask for the situations that happen upon us, but sometimes it's simply what we have to do to move on to the next thing.

"The Wood stone is made of amber. About eighteen years ago, Constancia came to me and asked me to place it in a place of protection. I thought long and hard about where to keep an item so precious."

"It's somewhere in the Grove, isn't it?" Sloan asks.

"The Grove is quite large, several kilometers wide," Qildor explains.

"About a kilometer north of here, there's a fairy mine. Can you guess what the mine contains?"

"Amber," I say.

"Yes."

"So the stone is located inside the mine?" Sloan asks.

"Yes, but unfortunately it will not be as simple as you're thinking to retrieve it."

"Listen, Your Highness, I've been into the base of a volcano that erupted with me inside of it and I've been inside a gemstone-laden pyramid where I was chased by the living dead. I think I can handle it."

Basal smiles. "I do admire your bravery, Impossible Girl. However, it's not the location itself that you will find problematic, it is the process of retrieving the actual stone. As you now know, fairies do enjoy a good practical joke or two, even though, admittedly, some take it dangerously far."

"The mine is booby-trapped?" Qildor asks.

The King nods. "It is. But you see, we had to ensure that the stone would not be easy to retrieve. You, of anyone Qildor, know how the fairies, elves, and nymphs can get carried away on the elixir. It had to be set up so that the stone couldn't be snatched away as a bit of fun, because oh my dears, if the stone had ever been misplaced or lost…I'd dare not think of the repercussions."

"So how do we get past all the traps?" I ask. Still, in my head, I am thinking nothing can be much worse than raining fire and the smell of rotting flesh.

"I wrote a poem."

"A poem?" I ask. How will a poem get us past fairy practical jokes? Because from what I've experienced we do not have the same idea of either fun or funny.

The Fairy King hoists himself out of the chair and waddles over to the mantle, an intricately carved frame of wood. The top is lined with trinkets: little glass bottles, dried flowers, porcelain animal figurines, and a small, metal dish. He picks up the dish.

"Your Majesty, that dish is made of iron, is it not?" Qildor asks.

The King removes the dish's lid. "Indeed it is."

"I thought iron was dangerous to fairies?" I ask.

He smiles. "It is. But I am very old. The oldest of all the fairies. The iron doesn't burn me as it used to. Now, it's more of a nuisance than anything." He pulls a tiny scroll of parchment out of the dish. "As I said, when I hid the stone I did not want it to be easily retrieved. But Constancia had warned me that one day an Impossible Girl, the half-mortal daughter of Anuja and Absalom, would come seeking it and that when she did I must help her to find it. Like I said, I am very old, so I wrote it down, lest I forget."

"So it's not so much a poem as it is a set of directions?" I ask.

Basal nods. "Yes, this paper tells of the stone's location. It also describes the traps and how to get around them."

I think of the Elemental Abyss. "I'm about used to traps by now."

But the King shakes his head. "But these are fairy traps and fairies do not always play fair." He hands me the scrolled parchment. "I'm afraid I don't remember much besides what's written here." He places the dish back onto the mantel and turns toward the window. "It's still early. You should go. It will take some time to get to the mines. I will have Cook pack you a meal."

"Thank you," I say slipping the parchment into my pants pocket.

"You may not be thanking me once you see what lies ahead." A funny expression comes across the King's face and Qildor frowns. I've met some pretty cryptic people lately, but the Fairy King seems to take it to a whole new level. He's both inviting and abrupt; kind but selfish; helpful yet fearful. He snaps back to the present and we follow him to the door of the study. He opens the door and we step into the hallway. "I wish you well, Impossible Girl, but when you find what it is that you seek, please don't judge me too harshly for I was simply doing what was asked of me."

CHAPTER 14

Several kilometers turns out to be a lot farther than you think. I'm just thankful it's north of the Grove so that I didn't have to walk back over that bridge just yet. Or ever. Even though the day looked sunny and warm through the windows of the Fairy King's house, it's quite cold outside. I've unfurled Michaela's jacket and slipped it back on. The frosty earth crunches beneath our boots as we walk along a flower lined path.

Qildor leads the way. He explained that the amber mines are closed, no longer open for mining. The Fairy King was afraid all the amber would be used up because fairies, in general, tend to get a little carried away. Not only would they create jewelry with the amber, but they'd also extract the sap from it. Those gold elixirs everyone seems so found of? Sap extracted from amber at extremely high heat. Essentially, it's gem juice. No wonder they all look so young and radiant all the time.

Anyways, the mines have been abandoned for some number of years. In the distance, just north of the Grove as Basal had told us, is a small range of purple colored mountains. Inside those mountains are the fairy mines. Qildor also mentioned that fairies don't have the best work ethic in the world, constantly fooling around, so it wasn't exactly in the best interest of time nor safety to have them working in the mines. I asked why not just hire the elves or nymphs to do it instead? But Qildor had shook his head and explained that the fairies are also quite territorial and don't play well with others. If the King is any representation of the fairy population, I could see that. There's an odd paradoxical nature about them, like they want to have all these gemstones and fancy elixirs, but don't want to do the work to have them.

Qildor stops walking and I almost slam into his quiver. "That path there." He points. "It used to have a sign, but I guess they don't want any uninvited guests creating mischief."

"From the sounds of things, I think they do enough of that on their own," Sloan says.

The path is a bit overgrown with tall blades of brown, purple, and green grass on either side. It winds along leading up to the base of the mountains. There's snow at the mountain peaks and a crystalline stream runs alongside the path. We walk in silence a bit longer, the only sound the bubbling of the stream, until we reach the base of the mountain. Set into the mountainside is a set of large wooden doors, with intricately carved images of flowers and dancing fairies. A large iron padlock hangs on a thick chain which is woven through the wooden handles of both doors.

"For a long time this was considered a sacred site. Because the amber was used as a nectar type drink, the fairies thought they were essentially drinking the nectar of the gods," Qildor says.

"Weren't they though? If Raj and Katayun created each of these lands, then they're the ones who put the amber here. Those crazy elixirs you all drink really are the nectar of the gods," I say.

"Basal gave me the key." Qildor pulls another necklace over his head and there's a very large, very old looking key tied to a leather cord.

"What's with you and keys?" I ask.

He shrugs as he steps up to the doors. "I'm trustworthy." He sticks the key into the padlock and, with some effort, it unlocks. Sloan helps him to unravel the rusted chains. Above the entrance to the mines, there are some carved out words, but not in a language that I recognize.

"What does that say?" I ask, pointing above their heads.

Qildor places the chains to the side of the door, near some shrubs with large, red flowers. He takes a step back and reads it, his mouth moving silently with the words. "It's a warning."

"I don't recognize the language," Sloan says.

"It's an ancient fairy language, back when the woodland creatures and the fairies spoke different languages."

"So what does it say?" I ask again. I appreciate Qildor's intellect, but it takes forever for him to get to the point.

"It's not a direct translation, but basically it says: He who enters with great wealth shall leave empty-handed."

"That doesn't sound like much of a warning to me."

"But it is to the fairies. They tend to be unable to look at the bigger picture. Basal can somewhat because he's developed the skill over centuries, but younger fairies only see the here and now. It's saying that if you enter into the amber mines you will lose all that you value. It's a warning to not let the discoveries inside the mines become an obsession at the cost of everything that's important to you."

"Do you think that's true?" I ask.

He considers this before speaking. "What's the most beautiful thing you've ever seen?"

"The most beautiful? Well, the gemstone pyramid in the Land of Earth was pretty magnificent, not to mention the waterfall in the Elemental Abyss…but honestly…" I turn to look at Sloan. "The first time I went to the Water Building and saw the underground pool, with the tiny window filtering in the red light, causing the pool of water to take on a purple shade. Just that single bit of light, dust particles dancing in its beam. I think that's the most beautiful thing I've ever seen." As I look at Sloan, I feel transported back to that moment. Seeing it for the first time, this place where Sloan first learned how to be a Water, and in that moment feeling like we were the only two people on Xon 9 that existed. It was like entering into another world. He smiles at me and I see in his eyes that it's a fond memory for him too.

"Then my answer is no, I do not think it's true for you. Because even though you describe the beauty of the place, I can see from the expression on your face that it is who you were with, not the place itself that gave it value to you. Fairies don't have that kind of rationale. They are fickle and they like pretty, shiny, sparkling things. It would be easy to become obsessed with both the beauty and the riches inside these mines." He puts a hand on one of the wooden handles. "Have you read what the poem says?"

I feel in my pants pocket for the tiny scroll of parchment from the iron dish on Basal's mantle. "I haven't. I was waiting until we got here because I figured it wouldn't make any sense anyway until we arrived." I hand it over to Qildor and he opens it carefully. "Is it written in that ancient fairy language too?"

Qildor shakes his head. "No, thank goodness. It doesn't translate exactly and a lot of the words have double meanings. It would have confused us more than anything. Here, take a look."

Enter into the gemstone of the gods

And know that Wood stone is nigh

It will not be easy to find

But search low and search high

Beware the facets of the stones

Something deadly hides inside

And just when you think you are near

Know that the mines have lied

Kill the beast that lurks below

But don't waste time to weep

If you get out in one piece

The stone will be yours to keep.

"That is one extremely depressing poem," Sloan says when Qildor's finished reading it.

"What do you think the beast could be? Typically, I have a no kill policy, unless absolutely necessary. Trap inside a stone and destroy into a million pieces? Guilty as charged, but I'm not sure I'm prepared to kill anything."

"I think that we cannot draw any conclusions until once we are inside. It may not be meant to be taken literally. What I do know is that the Fairy King took every precaution that he felt was necessary in order to protect the stone. Considering the Wood stone is made of amber, it's going to be a bit like looking for a needle in a haystack in a mine that is full of amber stones." He turns to Sloan. "You still have the dagger I gave you?"

Sloan pats his waistband where the belted sheath is still secure. "Yep."

"And I have my quiver and bow. What about you, Ka? We need to be prepared for any circumstance we could encounter."

"I have the ability to generate fire out of my fingertips and vines that shoot out of my wrists."

"Are you joking?" He gives me a dubious look.

I turn my hands over to show him the tiny green openings on the inside of my wrists. "Nope, not kidding."

"Peculiar. What gift do you think the Wood stone would bestow upon you?"

"No idea. I just know that I need it and from what I've seen, we're beginning to run out of time."

Qildor nods grimly. He rolls the parchment back up and hands it to me. I stick it back inside my pants pocket. Again, Qildor reaches for the wooden door handle. Sloan grabs the other one and together they slowly pull both doors open, revealing a space large enough for us to pass through. The doors groan under their own massive weight. I pass through first. The first thing I notice is the smell: must, dirt, and the faint hint of something sweet. It's an odd combination. I feel Sloan and Qildor come up behind me on either side. We're greeted by total blackness. I reach inside my messenger bag and pull out the two flashlights, handing one to Sloan. We flick them on at the same time and what's before us is enough to take my breath away.

We're standing in a cavern. The floor is compacted dirt, but every other surface is covered in orangery-red amber stones. Jagged pieces protrude from the ceiling and walls, smooth pieces cover the spaces in between. In the beams of the flashlights it sparkles and glistens. I reach out a hand and drag my fingers along the wall to my right. The gems are cool to the touch, but the energy emitting from the gems is warm and inviting. There's a subtle hum in the air.

"I think I understand the warning now," I say.

"The amber comes from the pine trees that cover the mountains above us. This particular mountain range is called the Bijou, which means jewel. The pine trees form a resin that seeped into the ground below. When the resin fossilizes it forms these amber gemstones."

"That must take a lot of pine trees," Sloan says.

"In some areas, the forest is so dense it is said one cannot see past one arrow's length in either direction. The resin is what is extracted from the gemstones, partially because of its healing properties. The gems are said to clear away negative energies and provide a clear mind."

"Kind of like Heliotrope."

"I almost forgot," Qildor reaches into the pocket of his cape and pulls out a small stone. "You dropped this before. I meant to give it back to you."

I take the Bloodstone from him and slip it into my pocket where it's snug against the scroll of parchment. "Thanks for that. My mom gave it to me before she left."

"Well, if it does keep away negative energy you may need it. This mine goes further down. We've only just scratched the surface and I'm not sure what we'll find once we're in the belly of the cavern."

Qildor begins to walk and Sloan and I follow, flanking either side. "How are we supposed to find an amber stone in an amber mine? I mean how will we know which is the actual Wood stone?" Sloan asks.

"Oh, I'll know. And it's not usually just sitting there. It's usually, what's the word I'm looking for? *Presented* in some way. I don't know how to explain it, but it's like I'm linked to each stone and in a way I suppose that I am." We continue to head down the path at a gentle downward slope. "I'm more concerned about the 'beware the facets of the stones, something deadly hides inside,'" I say reciting the lines from the poem.

Qildor comes to a stop. He sticks out either arm, blocking us from continuing. And now I see why. The path dead ends into a cliff. I shine the flashlight down and either side of the crevice is covered with amber gems, but my flashlight beam doesn't reach the black bottom of whatever lies below.

"'Kill the beast that lurks below,'" Sloan recites.

"I don't like this," Qildor says. On the other side of the crevice is about a half-meter of space and then an amber-covered wall.

"Looks like we only have one choice. Down," I say.

"Yes, but how do we get down there?"

"There must be some way." Sloan shines the beam of his flashlight over the surrounding area. "Over there." He scurries over to an outcropping of amber gemstones protruding from a low corner of the wall. There's a coil of rope laying there, perhaps something left behind from the mining days. He brings it over. "We'll have to climb down."

"We don't know how deep it is."

"Well, the beam of the flashlight is about five meters, if I had to guess. It looks like we have at least that if not more in rope length." Sloan takes my flashlight too and shines both down into the crevice again. "I think I can see the bottom." He takes an end of the rope and knots it around an amber stone that's tucked between the wall and the floor at an outward angle. He knots it again, then several more times going down the length of rope, once he reaches the end he walks back over to the crevice and tosses it into the darkness. We hear a faint *thunk* as the rope hits the ground. "That's encouraging." He gives the rope a satisfying tug. "I'll go down first then Ka, then Qildor."

We nod in agreement. "I'll shine my flashlight down and then when I come down you can shine yours up to light the way."

Sloan takes the rope into his hands and nears the edge of the cliff. He puts one foot down and against the side of the crevice. Then the other foot, carefully backing his way over the side. I shine the flashlight off to the side so I don't blind him as he slowly lowers his way down, first his right foot then his left. He grips the rope tightly using it to guide himself downward. Soon, he's past the beam of my flashlight, but it's only moments before I hear him call back. "Okay! It pretty much looks the same down here as it does up there. The path only goes one way and there's amber everywhere. It's a bit colder though and smells kind of funky." He shines the flashlight back upward.

"That's probably you," I say. "When's the last time you showered?"

I hand my flashlight to Qildor and grab the rope in the same fashion as Sloan. Qildor helps me lower myself over the cliff-face.

"Just take your time!" Sloan calls up.

I lower my left foot first, pressing it against the solidness of the amber wall. It's strange because my first impression would be that the amber would crumble beneath the pressure, but I guess if it were that easy, it wouldn't have had to been mined. It would have just snapped off in your hand. I lower my right foot, then my left again. I close my eyes, going methodically and feeling the solidness beneath my feet and in front of me. Right, left, right, left.

"You're almost there!" says Sloan. "Just a little bit more!"

Right, left, right, left.

I feel my right foot slip and my eyes fling open. The beam of the flashlight illuminates the amber wall in front of me. Staring back at me is a face. I scream and lose my footing, before I know it the rope is sliding through my hands and I'm tumbling down to the bottom of the mountain. Luckily, Sloan breaks my fall. He lands backward and I land on top of him, knocking the wind right out of both of us.

"What's going on down there?" Qildor sweeps the beam of the flashlight back and forth frantically. "Are you okay?"

I groan as I roll off Sloan. "Fine!" He calls back up.

"What happened? Is it safe for me to come down?"

"I don't know. I mean, yes. I just thought I saw…never mind, Qildor. Yes, it's safe to come down."

"Are you sure?"

"Yes, here." Sloan picks up the flashlight and shines it upward to illuminate Qildor's way the best he can, even though the beam doesn't quite reach the top. We hear the thud of Qildor's boots as he lowers himself down the mountainside.

I check to make sure none of the glass jars broke inside my

messenger bag. Somehow they didn't. That fall could have been even more gruesome if the glass had broken, especially if Sloan hadn't been there to cushion my landing. Looking back up the cliff side, I realize I didn't actually fall all that far. Only about half a meter. It was more awkward than anything. I rotate my right wrist. It had gotten squished beneath me and there's a dull ache, but I think it will be fine.

Sloan doesn't move the beam, but he glances over at me as he shines it up the mountainside. "What was that exactly?"

"You're going to think I'm crazy," I say.

"I already think you're crazy."

"Gee, thanks." I roll my eyes even though he's turned his gaze back toward Qildor's descent.

"I don't know. I just thought that I'd seen something."

"You screamed like you saw something horrifying."

"I did?" I don't remember screaming. Just opening my eyes and seeing the contorted face trapped behind a façade of amber, then falling.

"What is it that you thought you saw?"

"Well, I had my eyes closed. I just wanted to concentrate on the descent down. But then my foot slipped and I opened my eyes. And when I did I saw a face looking back at me."

Sloan shrugs. "Maybe it was your own reflection. The amber is smooth in some parts."

"It definitely wasn't my face."

Qildor is now in view of the flashlight beam. He continues to lower himself gracefully down the mountainside. It's almost as if his feet barely touch the side as he glides to the base, his feet finally touching the ground. He takes the flashlight and tosses it to me. Like Sloan said, there's only one direction to go. The smell is strange, like a combination of cooked meat and sweat, but with a hint of something fruity. The temperature is about twenty degrees cooler. The whisper hum of energy from above is no longer present, instead replaced with a deeper, monotonous sound, almost as if the ground beneath us is groaning. The amber in the walls down here is darker in color, more red and brown, less orangey-yellow.

"Is everything okay? You had me worried up there that something had happened," Qildor asks.

"Everything's fine. I just missed a foothold and fell the last half meter or so. But Sloan was there to break my fall."

"Yeah, my back thanks you for that by the way."

"You're the one who took an Everlasting Vow to protect me.

It comes with the territory." I shine my light and the path curves to the right just in front of us. "I don't like the way it feels down here."

"Me neither," Sloan and Qildor say at the same time.

"Then let's get this over with." I let out an involuntary shiver. I know what I saw. There was definitely a face behind that amber stone. I'm not sure what I'm more afraid of: what lies behind the facets of the stone, or the beast that lies below.

. . .

We follow the path downward to the right. I sweep the beam of the flashlight in front of us. As we walk the cavern seems to narrow into a singular tunnel. One way in—one way out? The effect of the shrinking tunnel is that the flashlight beam seems to bounce off the smooth surfaces of stone, giving the illusion that they're emitting a soft orangey-red glow.

"Wait," Qildor says holding up a hand. "Do you hear that?"

We stop walking and listen. I can still hear the low reverberation, as if the ground itself is breathing, but nothing else.

"There it is again."

I look at Sloan and he shakes his head. Then we hear it: a soft rustling sound, like the sound of someone walking by. It's faint, but not undeniable.

"What could it be?" Sloan asks, sweeping his own flashlight beam up and down the walls of the tunnel. "We're alone in here right?"

Qildor carefully removes his bow from behind him and pulls an iron-tipped arrow from his quiver. "As far as I know, we're the only living people in here."

"Besides whatever the beast below is," I point out.

"Like I said: people."

"You're not a people. You're an elf." He gives me a smoldering look, brown eyes ablaze. "Fine, people," I correct.

"Let's continue down the tunnel. Carefully," he says. Sloan and I obey, turn, and continue the descent toward what I hope will be the Wood stone. Qildor's footsteps are barely audible behind us. Wait. I whirl around and shine my flashlight. But no one is there, only a faint wisp of amber-colored smoke that slowly evaporates. Qildor is gone.

CHAPTER 15

"QILDOR! QILDOR!" I cry out frantically. "Seriously, this isn't funny. I thought the fairies were the tricksters, not the elves."

Sloan sweeps his flashlight beam up one side of the tunnel. "He was just here. Where could he have gone that fast?"

I sweep my flashlight up the other side of the tunnel. The hair on the back of my neck prickles and I know that what I am about to find isn't going to be good, in fact, it is probably going to be all kinds of bad. The flashlight beam catches a glint of metal. I close my eyes willing what I am about to see to not be there.

"Sloan...Sloan, I think I found Qildor," I whisper because I'm afraid to provoke whatever it is that put Qildor there.

"Whe—?" Sloan's words stop abruptly as if swallowed up by the air itself. "But how is that—that's not even possible."

I was right about the face behind the amber on the cliff side because now looking back at me behind a facet of amber is Qildor. His small pink mouth caught in an *o* of surprise, brown eyes wide with shock. His right hand still holds the metal-tipped arrow, but his bow has fallen to the ground just outside of the amber gemstone. I reach down carefully and pick it up, holding it tightly in my left hand as if it's some kind of inseparable link between us, if I let go I may really lose him, lost forever in some amber mine to an unknown assailant.

"I don't know how it's possible," I say as calmly as I can. "But it happened, okay? So, now we just need to figure out how to free him."

"Ka, we don't know what put him there. What if it takes one of us and does that to us?"

"Well, if we're constantly with each other and never turn our backs, never take our eyes off the other one, it can't happen, right?"

"You don't know that for sure."

"I don't. But that's what happened, isn't it? We turned our backs. We were walking ahead of him and we turned around and he was gone. So whatever it is that did this is quick."

Sloan knocks on the amber stone in front of Qildor's face. Qildor has no reaction. "How do we get him out of here?"

"I don't know." I focus the flashlight beam on the stone, feeling around with my free hand for any cracks or breaks, but it's perfectly smooth. "*Beware the facets of the stone, something deadly hides inside.*"

"I'd say that's a gross understatement. So something lives inside the amber stones and somehow comes out and snatches people?"

"He said he heard a sound, then we heard it too, the rustling as if someone was walking."

"But there wasn't anyone there."

"The wind."

"There wasn't any wind. We're in the middle of a tunnel almost five meters below the surface."

"Okay, maybe not the wind literally, but maybe something like the wind. Think of the Imminent Darkness. It can take on the appearance of almost anything, maybe something trapped inside the stones takes on the appearance of a sort of vapor. It gets released and traps its victims, then disappears."

"Alright, if I play along with this theory then why does it do it? Why trap people in the stone?" Sloan asks. I unshoulder my messenger bag looking to see if there's anything to help us get Qildor out from the stone.

"Maybe it's lonely?"

"Or hungry."

"That's morbid."

Sloan shines the flashlight further down the tunnel. "Look." I stand up, following the beam of light. Even without going further down the tunnel I can see the shadows within the stones. More people. Trapped for how long? "That breathing, you've felt it too right?" I nod. I have. The breathing of the tunnel itself. "The beast. Ka, what if the breathing that we feel is actually the beast and these people are its food source?"

"*Kill the beast that lurks below.*" It's too gruesome to even think about. "We have to rescue him. We have to get him out of there. If I had to guess, I'd guess that whatever the beast is, that it's protecting the Wood stone. And if we're going to get it we need Qildor's help."

"What do you suggest?"

I kneel back down in the dirt pulling items from the bag. The map, the mason jars of herbs and plants, the tiny burlap sack that Bina gave me. The sack. I pull out the remaining three items: the speckled feather, a pack of matches from The Old Tavern and the Sea, and a small, clear crystal.

"Qildor said that the golden elixir they all drink is extracted from the amber stones."

"Yeah, so?"

"Well, what if we could extract Qildor from the stone he's trapped inside?"

"I don't quite follow."

"Maybe if we apply heat, the stone will soften and when it softens, maybe we can somehow pull him out of it."

"I thought you said those items were supposed to be used to destroy the stones once they were recovered?"

"They are. But I'm running out of ideas." I pick up the pack of matches.

"There's not enough heat from only one match."

"We only need one."

Sloan bites his lip and nods slowly, finally understanding my plan. He voices my only reservation. "What if Qildor's not alive in there? What if it's like a catacomb?"

164

I shrug and strike the match along the strip on the matches' pack. It illuminates into a beautiful flame. Something real and tangible in my hand. "There's only one way to find out."

. . .

I hold the match as close to the surface of the stone as I can and close my eyes, concentrating as hard as I can on the fire that's inside me. *Come,* I call to it, *come and give me the strength that I seek.* Fire is eager. Almost instantly, I can feel the rush of warmth beneath my skin, making its way to the surface. As I call to it, it comes, and I feel it trickle out of my fingertips holding that single match, and it grabs hold of the wooden base, igniting it. Only it doesn't burn me. It would never hurt me because it's part of who I am, blood of my blood. The flame grows hot and as the flame burns brighter I gently blow it toward the stone that Qildor lies trapped behind.

Sloan stays off to the side, never taking his eyes off me, nor the rest of the tunnel. I take a deep breath and blow again, directing the heat toward the amber surface. I see a slight tremor, like a ripple. "It's working." *Come, flesh of my flesh, blood of my blood. Come.* Softer and softer as if it's melting, but it's still solid, not melting, turning permeable. "Sloan, it's happening." I take my free hand and push my fingertips gently against the stone, it gives beneath them and my fingers push through the molten orange stone. *More. Give me more.* I push my hand all the way through the softened amber and my fingers find Qildor's wrist. I can feel his pulse beneath my fingers as I pull him toward me. Sloan is ready for the catch, as with a swift yank Qildor tumbles out of the stone's facet. As soon as does, the match snuffs out, falling to the dirt floor. The amber surface glistens back at us as if nothing had ever happened, sure and solid.

Sloan is holding Qildor in his arms and even though I felt the pulse, there is no rise and fall of his chest. His eyes are closed and his body appears limp and lifeless. Somehow the stone entrapment had been keeping him alive. But now that I've pulled him from it…oh, what have I done? I was supposed to be saving him, not killing him! "Do something!" Sloan says lying him carefully onto the dirt floor.

I drop to my knees and fold my hands over his chest and give a solid pump. Two solid pumps. People. People have hearts. Qildor is a people. If I wasn't so frightened, I'd smile at the thought. I need to feel that beat beneath my palms. Pump. Pump. Pumping again and again. Until, the deepest breath of air I've ever heard is taken. Qildor's eyes fly open, darting around confused before finding my face.

"Thank. You." There's a long pause before he asks, "Why did you save me?"

"That's a dumb question," I reply. He takes a slow and steady breath, pushing himself up to a seated position. He closes his eyes and shakes his head.

"Clearly, you don't need my help. What you just did, your bravery and inventiveness, not to speak of your intellect. You don't need my services."

"Qildor, you're ridiculous," I say looking at him like he's lost his mind. "Don't you have any friends? That's what friends do, real ones anyways. Besides your people, remember? Sometimes people need

166

saving." I get up from my knees, tossing the matches back into the burlap sack and into my messenger bag before dropping the strap over my head. Qildor's bow was dropped on top of my bag and I pick it up and toss it to him. He catches it with his left hand. Back from the dead without missing a beat. "You're going to need that. We figured out some things about the beast below, and I have a feeling he isn't going to be happy we messed with mealtime."

. . .

We don't talk about what happened. Some things are just better left unspoken. What I do notice is that all three of us are now on edge. The Fairy King has a wicked sense of humor, if you could call it that. As we walk I try to avert my eyes from the periodic faces trapped behind the facets of amber like living catacombs. Amber-colored smoke that can capture human beings and other creatures, then entrap them in solid stone? It's more than my brain can handle at the moment. I knew the Imminent Darkness could take on any form because essentially it is only made up of energy, an ancient dark energy, but I hadn't thought about other things having that same ability. How can a stone go from a solid to a liquid to a vapor? I didn't pay super close attention in Science class, but what just happened seems to defy the logics of matter.

The tunnel curves again, this time to the left and the stench is almost unbearable. It fills my nostrils and suffocates me. No longer is it the smell of sweat and rot, but of death. The breathing of the earth is palpable here. It is no longer as if we are breathing, but that the beast seems to be breathing us. I have a feeling what I'm about to see is going to stay with me for a long time. *Basal was only doing what he was told,* I tell myself, *protecting the Wood stone.* He probably never thought in a billion years that I'd actually show up to claim it.

Qildor's about to round the corner, but I reach out a hand to stop him. This is my stone and my battle. I want to be the first to see what beast we will face. But I'm not prepared for what greets me as I round the corner. Bones. Everywhere. Fairy? Elf? Animal? Does it matter? Every. Where. There are piles and piles of bones stacked on top of one another. Some of the bones appear to have rotting flesh still dangling from them, like a tantalizing morsel overlooked. I feel my stomach clench and then heave and I don't even care, I throw up right then and there. Retching over and over.

I am not brave.

Yes, you are.

I can't do this.

You can.

I don't want to.

You must.

Once, I've thrown up anything that could be remaining in my stomach from the morning's breakfast, I wipe the spit from my mouth with the sleeve of my jacket. Sloan gives me a sympathetic look. Qildor brings a finger to his lips to silence the already silent. His bow and arrow are at the ready and for the first time I notice that Sloan holds the jewel-encrusted dagger in his fist. The abandoned dinner bones rattle with each inhale and exhale of the beast.

Kill the beast, but do not weep. Why would I weep for something that has caused such destruction? The tunnel of bones opens onto a small cavern. Qildor is in the lead. He stops, lowering his bow ever-so-slightly.

"Ka. Stay where you are," he orders.

But that's not how I roll. I peer over his shoulder and what I see confuses me. Instead of a monstrous beast, there's only a boy. So thin you can see his bones jutting out beneath his skin. He's wearing tattered rags, his hair is a matted mess, smudges of dirt on his arms and legs. There's an iron cuff around his ankle and he wears a heavy chain that leads to an iron stake in the ground. Bones are scattered around his barefeet. I feel my heart sink. A dawn of realization hits me. This is my weakness. Helping those who need helping. Everly. Doran. Li. My mother.

"Ka," Sloan whispers.

The girl in the cell beneath Council Hall. The girl who looked at me with glowing yellow eyes.

"It's not real," I say but the words are barely audible. "It's not real," I say again, louder this time.

Qildor is as still as a statue. "You can't be serious. It is as real as you or I."

"It's not. It-it somehow knows my weakness. I need to help those who need helping. I can't turn my back on those who need me. That's why it's the little boy. It knows I'll help him." Tears are welling up in my eyes. Even though my brain knows it's not real, that it's some sort of trap, my heart begs otherwise.

"Little boy?" Qildor asks. He's still as a statue, but darts his eyes back toward me. "What little boy?"

"The little boy right there! In front of you! The half-starved one with the chain around his ankle!"

"Ka," Sloan says calmly, in the voice I recognize as the one he uses when he's unsure of how I'll react to what he's about to say. "There is no little boy."

"Yes! There is! He's right there…" If my weakness is to help the helpless, and this truly isn't real, then what is it that Sloan and Qildor see? The little boy looks up then, big blue eyes imploring. He makes a feral sound and my heart tightens in my chest. "Quick, Sloan, what do you see?"

"I-I see…I see my father," Sloan whispers. Finn Braden. Sloan sees his dad, the dad who is now blind and locked away in a prison for crimes he didn't commit. The father he won't visit because it's too painful. It makes sense that Sloan's weakness is his father.

"Qildor? Qildor, what is it that you see?"

"I, uh, I see a beast as tall as four men and as wide as twenty. It has orange-brown fur that is filthy and matted with blood. Its teeth are long and curved, like a saber tooth. Its paws are as big and round as my head. Do you not hear it roaring?"

"I hear a child screaming out in hunger," I say at the same time that Sloan says, "I hear my father begging for his life." We look at each other.

"Qildor," I say. "I don't understand." The boy leaps forward, but is caught and snapped back by the chain. He still tries to reach out a hand toward us. Qildor ducks, crouching low and aiming his bow.

"We must kill it."

"It's just a boy," I say even though I know that it isn't true, that it's some sort of elaborately concocted illusion. But my heart battles with my head. *Help the helpless. Save those who need saving.*

"Where's the stone?" Qildor asks. The stone! In my distraction I completely forgot about the stone. I look around, but every wall is the same: facets of amber shining back at me. And then I see it, right next to the little boy. There's a large mat of straw and on top of the straw is a small, perfectly round amber stone the size of an egg.

"There! On the straw mat! Near the boy!" At my words the boy growls at me, baring his teeth. He stands up and raises his arms, as if trying to make himself as large as possible.

"Please," I find myself saying. "If you let me have the stone, I promise I'll set you free and we will take you to the Fairy King. You can have all the food you'd ever want and never go hungry." The boy tilts his head.

"Stop talking to it like that," Qildor orders. "The poem said we have to kill the beast in order to retrieve the stone." Qildor pulls back his arrow and aims it at the boy's chest.

"Qildor."

"Ka, it's not what you think. Fairy magic is very strong, especially that of the King. It's a trick. An illusion. The beast is real. Look at the bones, Ka. Think of all those people. I could have been one of those people if you hadn't saved me." He never takes his eyes away from the target.

I look around at the piles of bones. How many? Did a young

boy eat all these people? Of course not. The boy I see is poor and starving. If he had fed on all these innocent people then how could he be starving? It can't be. But it feels so real. There's a monstrous roar and when I turn around I see it. A large furry beast, with fangs. It is still chained to the floor and I feel a pang of sadness, but not at the cost of all the lives it has taken. Then again what choice did it have?

"I see it!" I say. The beast lunges forward and I hear the snap of the chain. Qildor pulls back his arrow and just as he's about to release it, Sloan rushes into him tackling him to the ground and the arrow misfires, bounding off one of the amber stones and hitting the floor. "Sloan!"

I rush over, but Qildor's already knocked him off, grabbing for his bow that scattered to the floor and immediately pulling another arrow. The warrior. Sloan gets up, ready to grab at Qildor a second time, but I knock him to the ground, pinning his arms to his sides.

"It isn't him, Sloan. Finn is at home. On Xon 9. It isn't him. Look." I grab his head and move it around so that he can see the piles of bones. "Innocent people. Fed to the beast below. All these bones. Death. Destruction. Your father would not do this. I know your father being tortured and put in prison hurts you. It hurts me. But it isn't your fault." I force his head to the side so that he's looking at the beast. The beast is stalking straight toward us. Its chain broken. Preparing to pounce on its prey. Dinner time. Qildor pulls back the arrow. Sloan strains against me. "This isn't your fault. This is not your father," I say again as the arrow soars through the air and pierces the beast directly in its heart. There's an excruciating howl and black, tar-like blood rushes out of the chest of the beast. Sloan's head drops in my hands and I feel the tears that wet his cheeks, his body shakes with silent sobs.

The enormous beast crashes to the ground and lays still, orange eyes wide open in surprise. Qildor's a good shot. He runs to the straw mat and picks up the Wood stone. As soon as he does, there's a thicket of amber-colored smoke that seemingly appears out of nowhere. It rushes around the dead body of its beast, surrounding it, enveloping it. The smoke is so thick that we can't see anything else. And after a moment it clears. Qildor stands with the Wood stone held triumphantly over his head and before him lies nothing but a massive pile of bones where the beast once laid.

Sloan shakes his head from side to side, as if he could shake out the memory. "I-I'm sorry. I didn't protect you. I completely freaked out."

I help him to his feet then put my arms around him in a hug. "It's okay. I know how important your dad is to you. If I thought that were my dad, I would have reacted the same way."

Qildor comes over and tosses me the stone. I catch it with both hands. It's heavy and solid. Smooth and cold to the touch. "The Fairy King knows that the heart is stronger than the mind." He slaps Sloan amicably on the shoulder. "Come on you two, let's get out of here."

"Wait. Qildor. I don't understand. How come you could see the actual beast and we couldn't? Is it because the fairy magic doesn't work on you?" I ask, slipping the stone into my messenger bag.

"No, it worked on me," he replies slipping his bow back over his head.

"But you saw the beast for what it was."

"Yes, but it knew my weakness."

"Which is…"

"You saw the helpless because your weakness is helping those in need. Sloan saw his father because his weakness is most likely the one person he couldn't protect." He glances at Sloan and I see a different level of respect in his eyes. He turns back to me. "As for me, I saw the beast because that's what my weakness is."

"A huge furry, saber toothed beast is your weakness?"

He smiles his pointy toothed smile. "No, my weakness is being the hero."

CHAPTER 16

I stop Qildor once we're back in the tunnel. "If you're weakness is being the hero, then be a hero right now. Help me to free the people trapped inside the amber."

"How?"

"I have an idea." I explain to Sloan and Qildor my idea. We'll burn the piles of bones using my Fire, hopefully causing the remaining amber to soften and melt, freeing the people trapped inside the facets.

"We could just report it to the Fairy King," Sloan says.

"Are you crazy? He's the one who entrapped them all here! That beast was his creation."

"It was only doing what it needed to survive."

"Well, now that it's dead, we can't just leave these innocent people trapped in a living catacomb. Unless you have a better idea?"

Qildor shakes his head.

Sloan shrugs. "Then let's do this."

He and Qildor move piles of bones in the vicinity of each victim trapped inside the amber facets. Some are elves or nymphs, a few are fairies. None are human, but I don't suppose many humans travel to the Land of Wood. After they form each pile, I strike a match and begin to use my Fire to ignite the bones. My hope is that my Fire burns at a high enough temperature to burn through the bones and generate enough heat to melt the amber. To go up to each individual trapped, there must be thirty or forty imprisoned here, would drain my energy possibly for the rest of our trip. But to light several fires, that gives me hope that I can help these people.

The flames trickle but not enough to catch. "We need something else! Something fibrous!" I shrug out of the cape and begin to pull as hard as I can, tearing it along any available seams. If I'm lucky, they're not one-hundred percent wool, but some kind of blend. I throw a couple strips onto the pile of bones and it hungrily ignites. I move on to the next pile, working methodically. When I run out of fabric from my own cape, I take Sloan's and continue to do the same. Soon, we have seven piles burning. We're dripping with sweat and before our very eyes I can see the fruits of our labors taking shape. The amber begins to form pools of oil as its temperature increases. How long have these people been locked up here? Years? Decades? Centuries? Hard to tell in Fairy Time. I run back down to the first burning pile, its flame burning bright. The heat is smoldering and I see a beautiful brown-haired nymph with wide green eyes behind the amber facet.

As the stone softens I see her long, nailed index finger move ever so slightly. I push my hand through the syrupy resin and clasp my fingers around her wrist. She comes out easily, falling into my arms. Unlike Qildor who wasn't breathing when he emerged, she takes a huge gulp of air. She looks at me in wonderment, but doesn't speak, instead she wraps her arms around me in a fragile hug.

"Help us free the rest?" I ask. She nods eagerly. The nymph, Qildor, Sloan, and I work from the back of the tunnel to the front, pulling people from the softened resin. Some fall to the ground and stop breathing. Sloan or I perform chest compressions until they take in a satisfying gulp of air. Only one never takes a breath. A small fairy about the size of a squirrel with pink wings and a delicate face. But we don't leave her behind, one of the fairies insists on carrying her back to the surface for a proper fairy burial in the Grove.

"It's only appropriate," she explains. Once everyone is free, we leave the fires burning and head to the cliff side. This mine is full of death and dark magic. I could care less if the entire place burns to the ground, precious elixirs or not. There's a reason this mine was closed and if it were up to me no person, fairy or otherwise, would ever return.

As we head for the rope that's still dangling, an elf stops us. "There's another way out of the mine."

"How do you know?" Qildor asks him.

"Because it's the way I came in."

"We didn't see any other tunnels between here and there. It's been a long time, friend, it could have caved in and no longer be there."

But the elf insists. His clothes are torn and even more old timey than Qildor's if that's possible, with laced up boots and a button down shirt with a vest. We finagle the thirty or so other people and return down the tunnel, doubling back the way we just came. Just past the first pile of bones, which is still burning strong, I see it—another tunnel behind a large outcropping of amber gemstones. We make our way to the entrance, the elf leads the way and I usher the others in after him. Qildor falls in behind them. Just as Sloan and I are about to bring up the rear, I hear the rustling of the wind, as if someone's behind us, only I know that no one's there. I turn around and there's a plume of amber-colored smoke rushing right toward us.

"Run!" I yell, grabbing Sloan's hand. We dash down the tunnel and I call up ahead. "It's coming! Whatever it was, it's coming after us!" I had mistakenly thought that by killing the beast we would kill the thing that had trapped the people, but I was wrong. No green vines, dagger, or arrow is going to kill something that's not even really there. The vapor is fast, it coalesces through the air, tendrils reaching out toward us.

"We're almost to the end!" An unfamiliar voices calls out.

"Hurry!" Sloan yells back.

I see the light of day ahead of us. Nymphs, elves, and fairies pouring out of the tunnel's mouth and back into the world outside. For how long were they lost? Are their loved ones even there anymore? I'm running so hard my lungs burn and I feel like my chest could rip open with the effort. My breath comes fast and hard. The sound of my boots hitting the dirt with each step is like a tremor. Walls of orange rush by me in a blur. I feel the hair on the back of my neck prickle and I fear that I'm too late.

Cold, airy fingers grasp at the back of my neck. Sloan runs through the opening and out into the light. "Ka!" he yells my name but it seems far away. The fingers grasp tighter, pulling me back. I see the words "NO!" form in his mouth. He reaches out to me as amber colored-smoke hugs me tight. A jewel-encrusted dagger slices through the smoke, causing it to recoil, and a familiar hand grabs me, yanking me back to reality. Sloan practically throws me onto the ground as he and Qildor slam shut an iron door in the base of the mountain. I push myself up into a seated position and rub my elbow.

"Thanks," I say, not wanting to admit how frightened I truly was.

"I almost lost you twice," Sloan says referring both to the incident when we tried to destroy the Fire stone and the accident with the bridge earlier. "I'll be hard-pressed to have it happen again." He extends a hand, helping me to my feet. "Sorry about your elbow."

I shrug. "Right now it's the least of my worries."

Some of the others have scattered, either eager to get home or too frightened to return, I can't be sure. We bid good-bye to the nymphs and elves, for now, and join the few fairies who are heading back to the Grove. We have one last visit to pay to the Fairy King.

CHAPTER 17

It's only been the rise and set of one sun when we return. The moon is high in the midnight black sky. The Fairy King lives in an elaborate house shaped like a cluster of giant mushrooms attached to one another. Its top is made of moss and the sides are made of faded wood. All of the houses pretty much look the same to me, but the other fairies have smaller, single mushroom homes. When we knock on the door—eleven of us in all, the brown-haired fairy with the small fairy who didn't survive tucked like a baby in her arms, and six others—Althea opens it and her eyes grow wide in her rotund face.

"Oh, my," she whispers. She immediately takes the still bundle from the fairy girl's arms and bustles into the house. "Come in, my children. I will fetch the King."

She's gone for a while and we stand awkwardly waiting in a small entryway with a table and nothing else. Althea returns. She is still carrying the small bundle. "The King will receive you in the chamber."

We follow her to the chamber, which is a small room with a narrow carpet of moss rolled out leading to an elaborate driftwood throne on which Basal is already perched. His crown of flowers sits jauntily on his head. He was awoken from his slumber and his face is creased with both the wrinkles of sleep and time. He's wearing a fluffy, white robe, the collar of his blue and white pinstriped pajamas peek out the top.

"Come forward, my warriors and my missing." Qildor glances at me and gives a slight shrug. We step forward. Althea stands off to the side, clutching the bundle to her chest. She too is wearing a purple robe over a long sleep dress. Her bun tilts sloppily to the side.

"Qildor, Sloan, and Ka, I am relieved to see that you were successful in your mission. However," he glances at Althea and she gives a little nod. I wonder what Althea is to the King, besides his Healer. Is she also his wife? Companion? Or maybe confidante? Even though Basal can come across as paradoxical: friendly and crass at the same time, Althea is like a calm lake despite a raging storm. "I was not anticipating you returning with your group more than doubled in size."

"The more the merrier," I say sarcastically.

Qildor jumps in. "If I may, Your Highness? The fairy mine is a dangerous place. Not only should it be closed for good, but it should be destroyed if possible. Deep in its belly not only lay the beast, but a magic much older and darker than your own."

Basal hides his surprise well, if you don't notice the twitch of his right eye. "That's not possible. My magic is the oldest in the Grove."

"We've seen it, Your Majesty," says a small, male fairy stepping forward. "It traps people into the amber and saves them to feed to the beast."

"But that won't be a problem anymore," I say. "We killed the beast. And we freed the people that were trapped in the facets of stone."

"How brave of you," Basal smiles, but it doesn't reach his eyes. Something is going on here, but I haven't figured out what just yet. "Althea, will you tend to the burial of the young one in your arms and show the rest of our guests to their rooms? They may stay here the night."

Althea nods. "Yes, of course." She leads the other fairies away, bustling out of sight. A door thuds closed behind them, echoing in the empty chamber.

Basal sighs and rubs his forehead. "You've made a grave mistake, Ka."

"How so?"

"In freeing those fairies."

"They were left to die there, to feed the monster. There were piles of bones everywhere. It was horrifying."

"How did you free them?"

"With my Fire. I realized the amber could be softened, even melted, when Qildor told me how the resin was used for those elixirs you all drink all the time. That weird mist had trapped Qildor. I had to save him."

"It trapped Qildor?"

"Yes, Your Highness. But Ka saved me. I don't know how I got inside and I couldn't see or hear, but I knew I was still alive."

"And he almost died when we got him out, but he didn't. I saved him."

"Yes, perhaps. But you should not have saved the others."

I'm confused. I don't understand what he's getting at and then I realize what it is that he means. "Wait. Your poem." I pull it out of my pocket and unfurl it. I reread the lines about what hides behind the facets. "You knew." My tone is accusing.

Sloan looks at me as if I'm crazy, but now it's all starting to make sense. Basal's odd reaction to our return and his odder reaction to the saved fairies. "You put that mist thing in the mines."

"It wasn't meant to entrap someone like Qildor."

"Why would you do that? Why would you do that to innocent people?" I cry ripping the stupid poem into a million tiny pieces and throwing it to the ground, feeling the anger boiling up inside me and singeing the edges.

"Because they were not innocent people."

"Explain," I demand. Beside me Qildor has grown very quiet. Qildor, who's so smart, even he didn't figure it out.

"They were guilty of various crimes and sentenced to death by the Fairy Court. What I did for them was a favor."

"A favor! Being trapped inside a stone and left to be devoured by some beast of your own creation? I don't think that's a favor, I think that's a cruel, wicked way to die."

"Some fairies who commit wrongdoings, are given the option of becoming Solitary, but others are not so fortunate. Order needs to be kept. The rules need to be followed." Basal's voice is calm and even. "Tell me, Ka, what was your weakness?"

"What?" The question catches me off-guard.

"The beast I created to protect the stone was an illusion conjured to show you your greatest weakness. Everyone has one."

"It—it was a little boy, dirty and half-starved."

"And what did you do?"

I glance at Qildor. "I begged Qildor not to kill him. I wanted to save him."

"And that is your weakness. Some of the people you try to save are those who should not be saved."

"Everyone deserves to be saved."

"I think you will find that to be untrue." Basal stands. "Now, if the three of you will excuse me, I have several Solitary Contracts to draft before the sun rises for the fairies you have released. It will be considered a Reprieve of the most unlikely circumstances you have generated. I think you know how to find yourselves out." He bows slightly then strides away out the door that Althea exited through earlier.

"I didn't know," I say to Qildor.

"There's no way you could have known. You saw an injustice and you acted," Qildor says. "And I think that you are right, no one deserves a fate such as the one those others would have faced."

"If the fairies had been sentenced to death, what about the nymphs and elves?" I ask.

Qildor shrugs. "Some may have been in the wrong place at the right time, but if a nymph or elf comes into the Grove and commits a crime, they could be sentenced by the Fairy Court."

"What about the others? Some of the ones we saved didn't return with us. What have I set loose? What have I done?" The greater consequence of what I've done makes me feel sick to my stomach. "Maybe I am no better than Basal."

"No," Sloan says. "No, that's not true, Ka. You did what you thought was right. You set those people free and saved them from a cruel and gruesome fate. You are much braver than Basal could ever be. You gave those people a second chance. I don't think the opportunity will be lost on them."

"Indeed," agrees Qildor, grabbing me by the arm and guiding me toward the door. "The Fairy King, and perhaps even you, may think that your desire to help those who are vulnerable is a weakness, but I think that it is a strength."

I stop walking and turn to him. "You do?"

"I do. Look at Basal. He is intelligent, but calculating. He appears hospitable on the surface, but deep down he is manipulative. He has lost touch with what it means to be a…"

"A people?" I smile thinking of our earlier conversation. People, not creatures.

"Yes, he's lost touch with what it means to be a people. People are dangerous: we can be cruel and selfish, but we also can be compassionate and selfless. Sometimes, Ka, people need saved. So your desire to save others is not a weakness, it is your greatest asset."

…

When we finally reach Nahele, there are no celebrations to be had. Qildor welcomes us to spend the night. Nahele is a maze of tunnels and rooms within his roots system. Qildor says they go on for miles and miles, housing all of the elves and nymphs who wish to live among the rest of the community. Sloan and I sleep on the floor beside Qildor's elaborate wood-posted bed. We don't wake until morning.

After a quick breakfast with none of the fanfare of our first night with the elves and nymphs, Qildor leads us out and back to the forest above. It's still quite cold, but it isn't snowing even though there's still some snow on the ground. It crunches beneath our boots as we walk toward the forest path.

"It has been my honor to walk beside you, Ka, and you too, Sloan." He gives a slight bow, but I surprise him by throwing my arms around him in a big hug. He looks confused for a second before putting his arms around me. I give him a big squeeze.

"Thank you, Qildor. For everything." I pull away and his pale skin is flush with embarrassment. "I have to be honest. At first I wasn't sure about you, but you turned out to be a worthy ally."

He smiles. "I must say the same about you. But I am glad I was able to get to know you better on this journey." He turns and shakes Sloan's hand. "You as well. I am honored to call you my friend."

Sloan reaches for his sheath and begins to take it off in order to return it, but Qildor puts up a hand to stop him. "No, you keep it." He looks around at the darkened forest. Even though it is day time, the Darkness is here. No doubt about it. "You never know when you may need it."

"Thank you," Sloan says. "I'm glad we have you on our side, Qildor. The Fairy King was right about one thing. You're a fine warrior." He turns to me. "So, ready to finally head home?"

"Yeah. We have a portal to find and a stone we need to figure out how to destroy."

"Here, I brought these for you too. In case you need it." Qildor pulls out two wool scarves and hands one to each of us. "You know, since the capes got destroyed."

"Thanks." It feels bittersweet to say good-bye to Qildor. I feel like I'm always leaving wonderful people behind. Some of my fellow Fire initiates come to mind. And Doran, who was left home with some broken ribs from our last adventure. Only. The dream.

"Good luck. Maybe someday our paths will cross again," Qildor waves us off.

"I hope so," I say but my words are whisked away by the breeze and I'm not sure he even hears me.

. . .

The scarves prove useful. It's cold and dark. The wind has picked up significantly and the air is biting at our cheeks and noses. If it's even possible, the forest seems even darker yet. As we walk in silence, we are both looking for the portal. Sloan's never seen one before, but they seem to kind of appear around wherever you fall through, so this one will most likely be in the light, beautiful part of the forest near where we first met Constancia.

But what does finding the portal even mean at this point? The Imminent Darkness is infiltrating all of the Lands, not just Xon 9. And Doran's message has risen back to the surface from the recesses of my mind. *Don't come back. It's here. It's all over the Underground.* If I don't go back then where do I go? *The wind will take you where you need to go to find us.* I have Zephyrus seeds in my bag which my mother's map told me are good for summoning the wind. I still haven't told Sloan about the dream. There's too much for him to lose in the Underground.

There's a rustling in the trees to our left and we pause on the path, unmoving. I take a deep breath and feel the Heliotrope pressed against my hip bone. I remember my mother's words that the Imminent Darkness can take on any form. Even Sloan. *But it won't,* I think. *Because he would never let it. His weakness is the one he couldn't protect. He would never fail a second time.* When no crazy wolves with yellow eyes or any of the living dead come jumping out at us, we continue down the path.

Soon in the distance I can see blue sky and sunlight. I know then that the portal cannot be far away. There's a noticeable difference in the atmosphere as we near the fork in the forest. The temperature gradually warms and I can hear the faint chirping of birds and the soft chittering of other smaller creatures. The grass is greener and the forest floor is once again littered with different, vibrantly colored flowers. As we emerge from the darkened side of the forest, it's as if a burden we didn't even know we were carrying has been lifted. I somehow feel lighter and freer. We step into the sunlight and I feel the gentle caress of its rays on my cheeks, warming the frozen parts. I unwrap the red wool scarf from Qildor and tuck it into my messenger bag.

"So, what are we looking for again?" Sloan asks handing me his navy blue scarf so that I can put it in my bag too.

"A big black hole. I don't know. It kind of looks like a spinning, swirling mass of time and space."

"Okay. And how does it get us home exactly?"

"It's hard to explain. It just, like, pulls us up and in. Sort of like the portals in the Abyss, but in reverse."

We walk for a little bit, letting the sun warm our backs and shoulders. Enjoying the brightness after being in the dark for so long. I wish home was like this. I wish that the sky was blue and the grass was a true green, and that animals could scramble about. We stop beside a pool of clear blue water. We each take a long, satisfying drink. To live in a world with surface water—or even the snow! Even though it's been so long since our ancestors left Old Earth, I can still feel a longing for our true home deep inside my bones. Home. I have to tell Sloan.

"The other night I had a dream."

Sloan looks up from the pond, a palm full of water poised just beneath his chin. He empties his palm and comes to sit beside me. "That phrase has never started out good."

"It isn't good. I was at Mrs. Chatfield's and it was a wreck.

190

Furniture overturned, cabinets empty. Like someone was looking for something."

He nods slowly. "The Imminent Darkness. As you already know, its members are not above terrorizing the people it suspects of speaking out against it."

"That's not all. I was walking through the house and when I got to Doran's room, I found a message tube." I pause, feeling it pressed against my hipbone beside the Bloodstone. I pull it out. "I listened to it in the dream, but then when I woke up, it was still in my pocket."

"How is that possible?"

"You tell me."

"You're not a Seer or half-Seer. Normal people don't have the ability to dream walk."

"My mother did it once. She visited me, like you do."

"Then maybe it's part of an older magic. Like immortality." He frowns as he considers the possibilities. He takes the tube from me and twirls it between his fingers like a small baton. "What did it say?"

"That's what I didn't want to tell you. It was Doran. He said that if I needed to find him that the wind would take me there. He said that the ID had infiltrated the entire Underground and that I shouldn't go back there."

At first he doesn't say anything and I know he's thinking of Bina and Michaela. The Black Bazaar is only a small part of the Underground. The Underground is vast to accommodate the amount of Unbalanced Metals. It also includes our military compound and our sole prison. He stops twirling the message tube.

"Did he say for how long?"

I shake my head. "But time isn't the same here as there. Usually, it seems like several days that we've been gone but when we get back it will only be a day or two."

"That's all it needs. Something must have shifted."

"But I haven't gained any new power. I've found the stone, but have yet to destroy it. The balance is still the same as when we left."

"Maybe it's fearful." He looks up and hands the tube back to me. I drop it into my messenger bag. "Maybe it's recruiting."

"That didn't work out so well for the army of Fire and Tristen."

"Yes, but there are some that are still loyal to it. And the Leadership Council. We still don't know whose side they're on. Even though I don't agree with your assumptions, it doesn't mean they aren't right. They just have yet to be proven."

I think back to the statue in front of Council Hall and how it resembles the codger from the story of *The Five Goddesses*. I swear for a moment that it looked back at me with yellow eyes. For me, that's all the proof that I need.

"We need to find that portal." Sloan stands and pulls me to my feet.

"It could be anywhere."

"Well, we need to find it. And fast. Because I'm not sure what we'll find once we return to the Elemental Abyss."

"You think the Imminent Darkness is there?"

"I think the Imminent Darkness is everywhere. Brooks said they saw it. And from what you're telling me it sounds like things are only

going to get more dangerous the closer we get to home. Come on."
He takes my hand and pulls me away from the serene pond of water
and back toward the sunlit path. "We have a portal to find."

CHAPTER 18

"There!" I call out. Hovering just above a bush with bright pink flowers is a space of swirling black nothingness. Sloan tugs me toward it. It's just above our heads. Together we roll a log across the path and over to the flowering bush. Sloan climbs up then reaches out a hand to help me.

I find that I'm a bit sad to leave. Despite everything—the near drowning and facing my weakness—I enjoyed being in this world. I enjoyed dancing with the nymphs and elves, drunk on the amber elixir. My curiosity was piqued by the Genesis Seed as well as by Qildor himself. I hate making new friends and then having to leave them much too soon. Our adventures with Qildor won't soon be forgotten in my mind. But this Land, split between the peace and beauty on one side and the Imminent Darkness's fear and death on the other. It needs to be saved and I'm no good to the friends that I'm leaving behind if I don't return home. I let out an audible sigh.

"Are you ready?" Sloan asks, but his eyes are really asking me if I'm okay.

"Yeah. It's just...I like it here. In the other Lands, besides my mother, I didn't meet any other people. There's an entire world here and once the portal closes, I'll never be able to come back. We'll never be able to see Hennie, Nahele or Qildor ever again." My eyes start to brim with tears.

"Hey, now." Sloan lets go of my hand and wipes the tears away with his fingers. "I'm sure we can find a way back if we really wanted to. Constancia or your mother, they'd find a way, wouldn't they?"

I nod. "Probably. It's just...I feel like I'm always leaving someone behind. If not you, then my mother and father, or Doran, or Finn. Rhian. Even Ahna and Li. Now Qildor. As soon as I make a friend, our paths always seem to diverge."

"Well, that's part of life isn't it? It's the natural ebb and flow of things. Sometimes people get left behind, but it doesn't mean that they can't eventually catch up." He's right and perhaps he's thinking of Finn. Maybe Sloan's finally catching up. He looks above us at the swirling vortex. "Ready?"

"Yeah, just one more thing." I wave out to the happily blooming forest. "Good-bye! Good-bye, Constancia! Good-bye, Nahele!" I turn back to Sloan. "Okay, now I'm ready."

He smiles at me, grabs my hand and reaches for the portal above our heads.

. . .

It sucks us up in a *whoosh!* Back into that space where time seems to happen all at once and not at all. No seeing, no hearing. Just being. The memories come back in a rush. Finn's blind eyes staring back at us. Sloan peering at me from behind his desk at school. Li, Ahna, myself, and Sloan huddled together as Sloan reads from *The Five Goddesses.* Then I see water everywhere. Ice is above me. I see myself floating downward my brown hair splayed in a halo around my head as I sink. The playback of memories is almost too fast to keep up. As we hurtle through time and space, the nothingness, they seem to come faster and faster, blurring together until they're intertwined and I can't separate my memories from Sloan's memories. Just as my head feels like it might implode, I see the brilliant blue-white light pulsating at the end of the tunnel-like space we're traveling in. The portal. The pressure becomes greater as we get closer and then with an ungraceful burst, we're pushed out through the other end of the portal and tumbling back into the Elemental Abyss. The door to the Land of Wood slams closed behind us, forever forbidding us entrance to go back.

I push myself up to standing. I've yet to have a graceful landing going into or out of the portals. Three doors are now darkened: The Lands of Fire, Earth, and Wood. Water and Metal still remain illuminated. I pull the Ignis Flos out of my bag and step over to the chasm of Fire. I pluck a few petals out of the jar, shoving it carefully back into my bag. I sprinkle the petals into the fiery pit and say out loud. "Brethren of Fire, we summon you for safe passage across this chasm. Please take these petals of the Ignis Flos as a sign of my respect and loyalty."

A plume of gray smoke shoots out of the chasm. It contorts into a grotesque face with little fiery eyes. It peers down at me. But it doesn't reconfigure into the bridge right away like it normally does. It blinks at me and I look back at Sloan. "What's going on?"

He shrugs. "I'm not sure. It—it seems like it's waiting for something."

A small orange flame rises out of the chasm and floats up near the beast's face. It floats right to where I'd imagine its heart would be, if it were a person and not a column of smoke, next to the petals of Ignis Flos. Once the flame is settled it flickers and a very old, rough sounding voice emerges from the smoke. The beast is speaking.

"Passage is dangerous, Impossible Girl."

"You know who I am?"

There's a long pause as if it's trying to figure out how to use language once again. "Of course. I've granted you safe passage before." Another long pause. Fiery eyes blinking at me patiently. So many times I was afraid of this smoky beast, but right now it seems more friend than foe. "It has been here."

"The Imminent Darkness?" Sloan asks.

"Yesssss." The smoke breaks apart briefly, then reintegrates, as if it's struggling to stay in this form. "It comes and goes. It takes many forms. It can slip around the cracks to the portal doors. It can be human, smoke, or creature. But, Impossible Girl, what you may find on the other side of this chasm. You may not want to see."

His words ring of Doran's message about the ID taking over the Underground. Not just the people who represent the ID, but the Imminent Darkness itself. But it was also in the Land of Earth and in the Land of Wood. And it's here in the Elemental Abyss and at home in the colony. How then can I defeat something that is everywhere at the same time? I am only one girl. I may be all possibilities, but I can't be in more than one place at a time. *All possibilities, yet none.* There's something I think I'm missing, but I can't quite figure it out yet. I need to destroy the stone. I need to get home and find Doran, make sure Ahna and Li are okay. Make sure Bina and Finn are still alive.

"I may not want to see it, but I have to return home. There are people we need to help and people we need to save. Please." My heart feels heavy. With each retrieval of the stones I thought things would get easier, but it's only proving to be more difficult each time.

"Very well. I am sorry for whatever may lie before you. Great measures were taken to protect you and great measures are being taken to destroy you." The flame flickers gently. "I grant you passage, Sister of Fire, and, despite the challenges that lay ahead, may the spark of Fire burn brightly in your heart." The little heart flame turns to an ember and then sinks back slowly into the chasm, like a speck of fairy dust.

The fiery red eyes blink at us, then the column of smoke twists and contorts until it forms a bridge between the battlements that leads to the other side. I take Sloan's hand. "Thank you!" I call out and dash across the bridge, still fearful of the illusion of solidity beneath my feet. As soon as Sloan's feet land safely on the other side, the smoke bursts up in one last great show, and then dives back into the chasm below, disappearing from view.

We run up the tunnel leading to the enchanted lake with a new sense of urgency. We weren't gone that long, but when you can be everywhere at the same time, I suppose time isn't something that you grapple with. Just as we're about to round the corner, Sloan stops and puts a hand on my shoulder.

"Promise me."

"Promise you what?" I ask, panting slightly from the sprint up the tunnel.

"Promise me that no matter what you see that you won't stop. That you won't run away or that you won't turn your back on those who need you because you're too afraid."

"I told you earlier. I'm not afraid."

But this time the words don't feel true like they did before. I am afraid. I'm terrified. I'm afraid to keep losing people I care about, whether it's leaving them behind or actually losing them, like Everly. I'm afraid that I'm not enough, that I'm just a girl who happens to be half-immortal, but in the span of time and space I am small and finite compared to the Imminent Darkness. How can I ever defeat something that is as vast and infinite as the Universe itself? I'm afraid that I won't be able to save those who need me. I'm afraid that I will fail. My eyes must betray my words because Sloan nods as if I've confirmed everything he's already suspected.

"Promise me," he urges. He looks up the tunnel, his brows furrowed nervously. He turns back to me. "Promise me you won't give up. On me. On Xon 9. On what's good and right." This is much, much bigger than just me. Who am I kidding? It's never been just about me, no matter what I thought it was.

"I promise." I look him right in the eye. "No matter what I see or hear or what anyone does. I won't give up. I won't give up on you. Or on our colony. I refuse to stop fighting for what I know is good and right." I promise to honor the sacrifices of those who've come before me. Finn. Bina. Everly. Li. Sloan. My mom and dad. I promise to not give up on the Universe, because even though there is loss, there is still life. I promise because I really am afraid. Afraid of what lies ahead. And even more afraid of what could lie inside.

"Okay." He takes my hand and we round the corner to the enchanted lake.

I wish we hadn't.

CHAPTER 19

The rowboat is there, but it's not the only thing that's waiting for us on the bank. There are maybe twenty of the sea creatures from the enchanted lake, lying motionless. My hand finds its way to my mouth to stifle an involuntary cry. Sloan knew. Maybe he'd seen it. Maybe he hadn't. But he'd known something was very wrong. That's why he wanted me to promise. He wanted me to promise because he knew I'd see something horrifying and that I'd want to turn back. But I can't. I promised. And I can't let the deaths of these innocent creatures be in vain.

We walk among the bodies. There is no blood, for that I am thankful. The creatures are both male and female. Knotted seaweed-like hair pressed to their scaly foreheads. Some of their mouths rest open, revealing their jagged teeth. I never had seen the full body of any of the creatures. These half-man, half-water creatures. From the bellybutton down, they have a thick tail covered in silvery-blue scales that then trickles up and over the right side of their body and then covers most of their face.

"Is it true?" I ask bending down to slide a female's eyes closed. "That they're Unbalanced Waters?"

Sloan's tone is terse. "Yes and no. They're called Aqua Bestiam. They are Unbalanced Waters, but they can also reproduce on their own."

"But there are no children here." For that too I am grateful. I'm not sure I could handle that. "It's all adults."

"The adults are used as protectors. They're protectors of the Elemental Abyss. They were put here by Raj, but they stayed willingly."

We continue walking and it's only a matter of time before we find Brooks. I remember some of the last things he'd told me before we traveled to the Land of Wood. He'd said that the Imminent Darkness had been here and that not everyone was loyal to the Impossible Girl. He'd also warned me that as I grow stronger the ID grows angrier and won't stop until it destroys me. Or everyone I care about. I kneel down beside his lifeless form. His eyes are already closed. He looks peaceful, like he's sleeping which makes me feel a little bit better. I can tell myself any lie if it's convincing enough. I take his webbed hand in mine. His nails are long and tinged green in the nailbed. His skin is a pale shade of blue.

Sloan comes and kneels beside me. He gently moves Brooks' head revealing his gills which have gone still in his neck. He looks over his chest and stomach, then investigates the tail. He's examining him. Looking for evidence.

He shakes his head. "I don't see anything."

"Something's different," I say absent-mindedly rubbing my thumb back and forth over the scaled-skin on the back of Brooks' hand.

Sloan's brow furrows as he thinks. He stands up and looks around. "The enchantment."

"What about it?" I lay Brooks' hand carefully across his stomach and get up to stand.

"There isn't one."

I pause, listening. There's no rush of the waterfall. Everything has gone still. Sloan walks closer to the water's edge. The once cerulean lake has gone dark, almost stagnant in appearance. The water is black and murky. Sloan reaches a hand out and I rush over to slap it away.

"Are you crazy? You're a Water! These are your kin. What if whatever happened to them happens to you if you touch it?" I ask. "One's enough. I can't handle another."

He pulls back his hand. "I can't be sure what happened, but if the waterfall recirculated fresh water, then maybe the lake filled with some kind of bacteria."

"A deadly bacteria." I finish walking among the bodies, making sure that each creature's eyes are closed so that it appears as though they are sleeping. "What do we do?" I finally ask.

Sloan shrugs, but it's not meant to be apathetic. "They're magical creatures. I have a feeling that when we return—"

"If we return."

"You made a promise."

"The Elemental Abyss has been compromised. We need to find another way."

Sloan walks over to the row boat and helps me inside. Then he unwraps the rope from the small wooden stake. He tosses it into the bottom of the boat and climbs inside. He pulls the oar and begins to guide us across the lake. After he's got a good pace going he continues what he was saying before I interrupted him. "They're magical creatures. Yes, they're Unbalanced Waters, but they've been given magical protection by Raj and Katayun. I have a suspicion that it's kind of like the old Biblical saying: ash to ash, dust to dust. They'll return to their original source."

I stare back at the shrinking shoreline. "We still can't come back here."

"You're right," he replies. We're already halfway across the lake. Sloan is wasting no time in getting us to the other side. I can't say it makes me feel any better. I know he wants to get home to make sure Bina is okay, but I'm not sure I want to see whatever's become of the Underground. Although I do want to know if Ahna and Li are safe. I know Doran's safe, at least at the time he created the message he was.

Sloan interrupts my thoughts. "How do you think we destroy the Wood stone?" he asks.

I shrug. "I don't know. I only have the matches, the crystal, and the feather left in the sack from Bina. I'm not sure how either of those could help."

Sloan continues paddling, moving the oar up, down, and around to the right side of the boat, guiding us carefully toward the opposite shoreline, the one that will take us to the cavern's entrance. "Maybe it will be the matches. If the stone has the same chemical make up as the rest of the amber in the cavern maybe it will melt too."

"I don't know. That seems too easy, don't you think?"

We reach the bank and Sloan pulls the oar back into the boat, but as he does several drops of water land on his arm. There's a hissing sound and he takes a sharp intake of breath, dropping the oar to the boat's bottom. I grab his arm and there are two tiny holes burned into his sweatshirt. I push up his sleeve and there are two red marks. Burn marks. Sloan turns, peering back at the far shoreline where the Aqua Bestiam still lay.

"It wasn't the bacteria that killed them," he says.

"What then?" I ask.

"They were trying to escape it. They died because they can't breathe air but for a few moments. Whatever's in the water, they knew they had to get away from it."

"So either way they were going to die. It was just a matter of being burned to death or suffocating," I say bitterly.

Sloan looks down at the marks on his arm then back up at me. His eyes are clouded with worry. "We have to go."

He helps me out then ties the rowboat to the stake, although I'm not sure it matters to us anymore. I don't think we'll be using it again. The Imminent Darkness is every bad thing that I don't want to think about it. At first, I thought it was just a trickster, manipulating people to bend to its will. But it's so much more than that now. It's death. It's poison. It's evil. Wherever it goes, it leaves a trail of pain behind in its wake. Sloan knew that I'd be afraid of the things I would see. And I am afraid. But I'm also angry. I'm angry that people I love keep getting hurt. I'm angry that people have to die because the Imminent Darkness knows no bounds. And I'm angry that as I jump through each of the hoops set up to protect me, the Imminent Darkness causes more chaos and destruction. Like it's trying to do as much damage as it can before I can defeat it. Because what then? If it destroys everything that I love or care about, everything that's important to me, I may defeat it but what will I have left once everything is said and done?

We run up the tunnel that leads to the cavern opening in the mountainside. The twin moons are high in the sky and the lights of Xon 9 twinkle back at us. Only there are much fewer lights than usual. Instead of hundreds of tiny lights winking in the distance, there are probably fewer than a hundred. Doran's right. Something has happened. Something bad.

I reach into my bag and pull out the jar of Zephyrus seeds. I twist the lid off and sprinkle a small handful of seeds into Sloan's open palm. I put the lid back on and place the jar back inside my messenger bag, nestled against the Wood stone.

"Ready?" he asks.

I shake my head. "No. I'm not."

He takes my hand with his free hand then opens his palm

containing the seeds. Gently, he blows the seeds out of his palm and into the open air above the cliff side. "Wind," he summons. "Take us home."

. . .

The wind arrives. It wraps around us like a baby in swaddling and carries us in its warm arms. Even though it defies all logic, I feel safe here. The wind rushes around us so quickly that I can't see the ground or the sky, just Sloan holding my hand next to me. It's similar to floating in the space of the Elemental Abyss, except I can actually feel and see my body. We float through the air and the sensation is much like I'd imagine flying to be: free.

The wind sets us down just outside the northernmost colony limits. Close to home. Or what used to be home. I whisper my thanks as the gale turns back into a gentle breeze. The Underground is east of where we've landed. We're just outside the perimeter. Doran's message had said that the Imminent Darkness had infiltrated the Underground, but had it reached to other parts of the colony? I know Sloan's first instinct is to check on his mother. I'm priority one, but only because of his Everlasting Vow. If she hadn't had him take it, I'm sure I'd be running a close second to Bina. But if Doran's right and the Imminent Darkness is in the Underground, we may need help. That's why I think we should find Ahna and Li first.

"You're right," Sloan says, agreeing with my thoughts before I've even expressed them. "If the Imminent Darkness is in the Underground we might need their help in order to find Bina."

"And Doran."

"The message said they left, didn't it?" I nod. It did. "Bina may have gone with them. But we can't assume that. We're going to have to go to Michaela's to be sure."

Michaela's. The last time we'd visited her, just before leaving for the Land of Wood, she'd been acting strange. Usually, in our limited interactions, she'd been friendly. Not exactly warm, but I figured that's just not part of her DNA. Sloan had explained to me how he was very close to both Finn and Bina, but Michaela was always a bit different. She was always Balanced and very driven in her military career. Sure, he was close to his sister and she was there to help Bina recuperate when she was almost MindCleansed, but during our last visit she made it quite clear to me that the safety of her family and her career came first, and that my being who I am put that safety in jeopardy. I can't say I blame her. If I didn't know my government was somehow infiltrated by a dark, evil force—or if I refused to believe it—then I'd be a bit more cautious too. And I do have the uncanny knack for attracting trouble.

We head toward the Solloman's house, located right next door to my parents' house, which now remains vacant since I stay with Sloan and both my mom and dad are, hopefully, safe in the Land of Earth. It's a short walk from where we landed. The colony isn't really all that large and we've inhabited only a small part of the planet. Our numbers haven't grown much since the original 3,000 colonists. With no surface water and limited food sources (what we do have is grown and farmed from specimens brought from Old Earth and their subsequent offspring) I can see why population control would be of the utmost importance, especially since it was a major issue on Old Earth before the sun died: how exactly does one feed fifteen billion people? The oddest part about our colony is how little we've progressed. Sure, we have some advanced technologies: like cloaking devices and teleportation portals, not to mention the elaborate technology of the Mindscape, but most of the so-called technology I've encountered has been more magic than anything.

The twin moons cast a pinkish glow as they flank the sun of Xon 9. Our sun never sets and during the day the landscape takes on almost a blood-red appearance, but at night the moons rise and the landscape softens. I'm sure it's past curfew, but I'm not sure that it really matters anymore. I pull the hood up on my jacket. I don't know how long we've been gone. Maybe two or three days' time at most if I had to guess. But the last time I was home I freed numerous prisoners of the Imminent Darkness who were being kept beneath Council Hall, so I don't think I'm exactly on the military's good Samaritan list since the Imminent Darkness has probably infiltrated their ranks.

Everything is very still. Few lights are on inside the stone and wood houses that we walk past. Most of the houses on Xon 9 are made of stone, but some are made of a combination of wood and stone. The wood on Xon 9 is very strong, yet flexible, kind of like the Wood Elementals themselves, like my father. There's no outside light on when we reach the Solloman's. My house appears empty to its right, but I try not to look. Too many bad memories near the end of our time there, that I'd rather not remember.

Sloan leans in and whispers, "It doesn't look like anybody's home."

I shrug. "But where else would they be?" I knock quickly two times, wait a beat then knock a third time. Sloan gives me a quizzical look. I shrug. "It's how we knocked as kids." I've lived next to Ahna and Li my entire life and we've been best friends all that time too.

We wait a long time, long enough that if it were normal circumstances we would have walked away. But we don't. There's a rustle behind the door and then it pulls open just a sliver, caught on a small chain that never used to be there. An almond-shaped brown eye peers back at me.

"Ka?" Ahna whispers.

I nod. "It's me." Then I hold up Sloan's hand which is still in mine. "Us."

"No one else is there? No one followed you?"

I turn around and look. We hadn't noticed anyone. "No. In fact we haven't seen anyone at all."

"Come in. Hurry." She closes the door to undo the chain and pulls the door open, practically yanking us inside before shutting the door and re-doing what seems like countless chains, bolts, and locks.

The last time I was here my father had been kidnapped and Ahna and I had discovered how to destroy the Earth stone, well at least how to remove the protective outer casing to reveal the true stone inside, the stone that was later shattered into a million tiny pieces trapping Tristen inside. The lights are off except for a couple of kerosene lamps, one to the left sitting atop the kitchen table and another to the right in the living room area.

"Where is everyone?" I ask pulling my hood down.

"Li's asleep. You know how he is since what happened." I do. Drunk. Ever since the army of Fire nearly killed him—ever since I nearly killed him—he's been weird, spending too much time in the Black Bazaar. "My parents are asleep too. Most nights I can't sleep."

She leads us into the living room. She's wearing regular clothes—not pajamas—and her hair is in a long braid down her back. The kerosene lamp sits on a table in the middle of the room. She pushes the sole armchair closer to the table and then motions for me to sit beside her on the couch. Sloan sits in the armchair.

"I was worried," she says. "You've never been gone this long before."

"How long?" I ask, lifting my messenger bag strap up and over my head and setting it on the couch next to me.

"Five days."

"Five days?" I ask. Ahna puts a finger to her lips, reminding me to be quiet. "How is that possible? Time in the Elemental Abyss is supposed to pass faster. Three days there would only be a day here."

She shrugs. "I don't know how to explain it. I just know that it is."

"That explains how the Imminent Darkness had enough time to take over the Underground. Maybe it somehow manipulated the time vortex, buying itself more time with me gone."

"You know about the Underground?" Ahna asks.

I nod and pull the empty message tube from my bag. "Doran

left me a message. He said to stay away."

"And you're going to stay away, right?" she asks raising an eyebrow. I can hear Sloan chuckle under his breath.

"Of course not. I have to see what's happened. What I'm up against. And we have to make sure Bina is okay."

"I'm sure she's fine." Ahna only met Bina once, but usually that's all it takes. "But I can see how making sure would put your mind at ease. So, what's your plan?"

"Plan? Do I ever have a plan?" I ask. I reach into my bag and pull out the Wood stone, even in the dim flame of the kerosene lamp the amber glistens. I hand it to Ahna. "The Wood stone."

She takes it turning it over in her hands. She's an Earth Elemental. Even since I've been gone the curlicue of green vines and tiny leaves has continued to blossom around her right ear and up the side of her face. "It's exquisite."

"That was more work than any of the others. Each one somehow seems to get harder and harder to retrieve."

"Have you figured out how to destroy it?"

"No clue. I was hoping you'd have some ideas. All I have left is the pack of matches, a feather, and a crystal."

"I'll try and think about it." She hands the stone back to me. I cup it in the palm of my hand. It fits perfectly.

"What's with all the lights out?" Sloan finally asks. I'd been wondering the same thing, but when you haven't seen someone in a while and a lot has happened, it's hard to focus on the minute details.

Ahna pulls her braid over her shoulder and fiddles with the hair at the bottom. Ahna is brave, smart, and kind. It's not like her to be anxious or scared. That's always been my role in the friendship. "New rules."

"New rules?" Sloan and I exchange a confused glance. There haven't been new rules on Xon 9 since the implementation of curfew and that was more to save the youngest of the population from exposure to the drunkards coming and going from the Black Bazaar. And even that was put to a vote by the Council of Leaders.

"Curfew was tightened. Now it is at moon rise. Anyone out past that time is taken in for questioning as to their whereabouts and intentions." She lowers her voice even though it's already a whisper. "And then no one comes back."

"No one comes back?"

"Yes. They're taken in for questioning and then don't come back. After the first few people went missing, well, people catch on pretty quickly these days."

"Where do they go? The prison beneath the Council Hall has already been exposed, so I can't imagine they'd be taken there. The Imminent Darkness' MindCleanse was destroyed." I had seen to that by quite unintentionally catching the entire place on fire. Okay, maybe not so quite unintentionally.

"Mom and Dad have speculated that they're taken to the military prison. But no one knows for sure. Ka, the Metals aren't part of the Imminent Darkness, are they?" There's a fear in Ahna's voice that makes me uncomfortable because I'm not used to it. I'm not used to her relying on my courage, instead of the other way around.

"No," I say emphatically. "There's no way. If I've learned anything since Pronouncement and all that's happened, it's that if one Element is grossly misunderstood it's Metal. Bina, Doran, Zora, Mrs. Chatfield, Finn, even Michaela—there's just no way."

"Then why else would it go there? Why else would the Imminent Darkness decide to hide there in plain sight, if not to convert the willing?" This is not like Ahna at all. Never would Ahna make such assumptions. She'd conduct research and analyze the situation from its various angles before drawing her conclusion. It strikes me that fear makes people behave in uncharacteristic ways. For me, as Sloan has shown me, it's made me angrier and more determined than ever to right others' wrongs. But for Ahna, my sweet friend, it's made her prejudiced against her better judgment. Fear: the power to inspire or the power to conspire.

"Because of just the opposite. Ahna, we've been friends a long time—our entire lives—and you have to trust me—believe me— when I tell you that the Metals are the least dangerous of all the Elementals. If I was worried about any, it would be the Council of Wood. The Metals, they're strong, tactical soldiers. The Unbalanced ones in the Black Bazaar may be scheming, but what choice have the rest of us given them? They've been ostracized, but instead of curling up in a ball and admitting defeat, they've banded together and formed a community. A community of people who stick together. If that's not the thing that would scare the pants off the Imminent Darkness then I don't know what is."

The glimmer of fear in Ahna's wide eyes retreats and she nods.

"You're right. I-I don't know what's come over me."

"It's what the Imminent Darkness does: it creates fear, then chaos, and finally destruction. I've seen it. I've seen the pain that it can cause." I reach out a hand and place it over hers.

She smiles at me and it's not fearful, but genuine. "You've changed so much. If I hadn't known you almost my whole life, I don't think I'd recognize you now."

"I'd know her." A sleepy male voice drifts over from the stairs. Li pads into the living room, his black hair sticking every which way. He slaps Sloan on the shoulder in a friendly enough way before plopping down on the couch on the other side of Ahna. "What's up, Princess?" he asks. I feel a pang of loss as I'm reminded of Brooks. Maybe that's why I found Brooks so endearing on our few meetings; he reminded me of Li.

"Oh, you know, saving the world one stone at a time"

"So you got the third stone? Can I see it?" I pick the stone up off the top of my messenger bag and hand it across Ahna to Li's open hand. "Crazy. It looks like it would weigh a ton, but it's light as a feather."

"What did you say?" I ask.

"I said it's light as a feather."

I reach inside the messenger bag and pull out the sack from Bina. I undo the drawstring and pull out the white and brown speckled feather.

"There are no birds on Xon 9. At least not wild ones," Ahna says, reverting quickly back to her logical fact-loving self.

"Right. But there are in other Lands. In the Land of Earth and Wood, both had birds."

"Or it could be from Old Earth. The Gift runs in our family. It could have been something that was passed down," Sloan says.

"I wonder then if the feather is what will destroy the Wood stone?"

Li hands the stone back to me. "I don't see how a feather is going to destroy a stone."

"That's part of the fun of it," I say sarcastically because destroying the other two stones was anything but fun. "In all seriousness, it always comes together in the most unlikely of ways, so it's just a matter of time before it plays out in all its epic glory." I drop the stone into the burlap sack along with the feather and draw the string closed.

"Speaking of fun, what's the plan for tonight?" Li asks.

"Li, they probably haven't even slept in who knows how long," Ahna points out. And she's right. But at the same time, there's no time. The Imminent Darkness is growing stronger and people I love could be in danger.

"Li's right. We need to find Bina and Michaela, and make sure they're okay. Then we need to find Doran."

"What else did his message say?"

"It said not to go to the Underground and that the wind would take us to him when we needed to find him."

"That's not cryptic or anything," Li says. "So, that means you're going to the Underground then?"

I smile. "Of course."

Whereas Ahna is usually the logical twin with a plan, Li is the adventurous, impulsive twin. Don't get me wrong he has his soft spots too, but I've seen Li take my certain death in his hands and break a collective consciousness to warn me. Even though we've been on the outs since I destroyed his ability to be a Fire Elemental, his loyalty runs deep. And the outs are more my own guilt than his, although he's been dealing with it in his own way. Except, I get the feeling that isn't so much about the loss of his Element as his loss for something else.

Li and I were never an actual thing, he usually teased and bothered me more than anything. But he was my first kiss and I think there was always something extra there that neither one of us cared to acknowledge. When he declared Fire at Pronouncement, my heart followed what was familiar. But then Sloan came into the picture in a whole new light, once our Universal History teacher, and now my Everlasting Protector. How can anyone compete with the allure of an Everlasting Vow? Not that he should, but as Sloan's helped me on my quest to retrieve the stones, I've learned a lot about who I am and who I am not. And I think that Li might be in love with who I was, and not who I am. Only, he hasn't figured it out yet and although I interpret his longing for the return of his destroyed Fire, I think, too, it's a longing for when I was more familiar to him. The black tattoo of fiery filigree lines the right side of his face giving him an eerie, almost menacing glow in the dim cast of the kerosene lamp. What do you have to lose when everything you've ever wanted is already lost to you?

"So, when do we leave?" he asks.

"Ideally, I'd say now," Sloan replies.

"Except the curfew." Ahna goes over to the window on the far wall and moves the heavy burgundy colored curtain to the side. "Moonset is near. It will be safer. You can rest a little while and we'll leave before our parents wake up. If they knew, they'd only worry more."

I nod. "Sloan and I will sleep down here. It will be good to even sleep on this couch after the other places we've slept the last few days."

Ahna gets up. "Li and I will gather some supplies. We'll need a cloaking cuff, at least for you, and some other things."

Li stands and salutes his sister. "Right on it. You two champs get some shut eye. Ahna and I will take care of the rest."

They disappear back up the stairs.

"You can have the couch," Sloan offers.

"Are you sure?" I ask.

"After the last few days, this armchair is like sleeping on a mattress made of clouds." He leans back in the chair and lets out a soft sigh. "Sweet dreams," he whispers.

"See you in the morning," I whisper back, resting my head on my messenger bag for a pillow. It smells like the bitterness of smoke and a reassuring earthiness from the Land of Wood: pine, dirt, and even a hint of the freshness of snow. In a few short moments Sloan's breathing slows and softens. He's asleep. But I can't sleep. The events of the last few days replay in my mind over and over again, interspersed with my fears of what lies ahead. I'm afraid of what I'll see if I close my eyes this time. Instead I just lay there, counting the pockets in the stone ceiling and listening to Sloan's gentle breath as I wait for the twin moons to set and morning to come.

CHAPTER 20

The Underground isn't far from where I grew up. It's where I spent the majority of my life thinking that the Unbalanced Metals were forced to live there—shunned from the rest of the colony—but I now know it was a choice not a consequence. The Underground pretty much runs from the Black Bazaar to the military base where Michaela lives. The Black Bazaar is part of the Underground, it's known as a place of forbidden luxuries. Basically, anything that you shouldn't find, you will find. Feeling down and need some cheering up? Try an Elation patch. Need to drink away your worries? No problem, sidle up to the bar. The Black Bazaar is full of fortune tellers, tattoo vendors, bars and mood-altering patches. Needless to say, Li's always hung out there, maybe a little too often lately. But this morning he seems mellow, nevertheless alert.

He hands me a sleek silver cuff, the likes of which I've seen before. The cloaking cuff. I slip it over my wrist and press the button on the underside of the bracelet. The cloaking cuff hides your physical body as well as anything on your person. I can see you, but you can't see me. It's quite convenient for sneaking out of the University Complex or for hiding from the Imminent Darkness's minions. For a long time I thought the Imminent Darkness was the people who were appearing around the colony, shrouded in ruby-colored hooded cloaks, even Sloan had infiltrated their ranks in order to learn more about them. But the ranks are so secretive that other members don't even know what occurs in each one. Now I know what the Imminent Darkness truly is—it's not a person, even though it can take human form, nor is it a beast. It's ancient and it's pure dark energy. It can manipulate people, fills their minds and hearts with darkness—like Tristen. Yet, the ranks must have a leader— surely, there's a figurehead at the very top. I haven't figured out who, but I don't think it's a coincidence that there was a prison camp for dissenters of the ID hidden in plain sight beneath our Council Hall. I'm still trying to put the puzzle pieces together, only I'm hoping that I don't figure it out after it's too late.

Sloan comes up behind me and places a hand on the small of my back. "Are you ready?" he asks softly.

I know better than to be surprised that even though I am hidden from view, Sloan can still see me. No matter where I am, he can somehow sense me and I know, too, that no matter where I am he can always find me, even if it is only in my dreams. Li once said something similar to me, that he could always see me. I didn't think much of it then. Our friendship has been through a lot, especially recently. When he said it to me, I thought he just meant that he could always feel my presence, like Sloan does, but now I'm not so sure. I thought Li—and Ahna—knew me better than anyone, but only now do I feel like I'm learning who I truly am. If I didn't even know who I was, how could someone else?

I nod. I am ready. I am ready to see what Doran warned me to avoid. It's one thing to see the devastation in the Lands of the Elemental Abyss, but it's an entire other thing to see the destruction here on my home planet. Sloan straps the sheath with the dagger around his waist. Li notices.

"That must have cost a pretty piece. Where'd you get that? The Black Bazaar?" he asks.

Sloan shakes his head. "It was a gift from a friend."

"Fancy friend."

"More like really old friend." And I know that Sloan is referring to Qildor's age and not the length of time that they've known each other, because in Qildor's life our time together was probably the blink of an eye.

"Do we have everything we need?" Ahna asks.

"Cloaking cuff, hologram transmitter, audio scrambler…oh, here, I almost forgot." Li pulls out two thin, silver wristbands and slaps one onto my wrist. He puts the other one on himself. "In case we get separated. These are from one of my dudes. They're two-way communicators."

"Why would we need these?" I ask, inspecting the bracelet

which has tiny holes for listening and speaking. Along with the cloaking cuff, it looks like I went on a jewelry binge in the Black Bazaar.

Li looks at me like I am completely clueless. Maybe I am. "In case we get separated."

"Which might happen. Michaela lives in the apartments at the military compound. They have security and three of us marching in could arouse suspicion," Sloan says.

"Good point," Ahna agrees.

We head to the front door. We step out onto the front stoop. The moons have set and the red sun is high in the sky. No one is outside yet. Too early. It's quiet and almost peaceful. Everything seems so still. Once, in Earth Science, we were learning about the weather patterns that began to grow out of control on Old Earth, right before the sun died. Our Science teacher—Teacher 15—had explained to us how there would be wind and rain storms, called hurricanes. And smack dab in the middle of this raging storm, there would be what's called the eye of the storm—a place of total calmness, before the rest of the storm raged on. That's how I feel right now. I feel as if I'm stepping out into the eye of the storm, an eerie sense of calm permeates the landscape. The only problem is that a hurricane could be predicted. Its course could be tracked. Old Earth Scientists had gotten the patterns down so precisely, that they could predict the exact route a hurricane would follow including wind and current adjustments. They could warn people ahead of time so that they could get out of harm's way. I could warn people. I could tell them that something more evil than they have ever known is coming, and that it will fill their hearts with darkness, death, and destruction. Only no one would believe me. The storm is coming, but I have no way to get people out of harm's way and nowhere to take them where I know that they'll be safe. It's coming and I have no idea how to stop it.

We walk past my old house. I pause. It is dark and vacant. No one is home. There is none of my father's stories. None of my mother's talks in the middle of the night. It will never be my home again. The Imminent Darkness changed that, my home is now an empty shell of what it once was. It may have taken that from me, but I refuse to let it take everything.

"So should we go the long way around?" Ahna asks.

"No. Let's go the direct route. I want to see what's happened. What it's doing."

"It's not doing anything," Li says. "It's creating."

"Creating what?" I ask

"Fear."

. . .

Li's right about that. Every housing complex we pass seems dark and vacant. I know that people are here. They mistakenly think that if they pretend they're not here the Imminent Darkness won't be able to find them. But they're wrong. We pass the University Complex with its scrolled iron archway bearing the words *divide et conquer*. I used to think that meant if we divide ourselves—into our respective Elemental affiliations—that it meant we could conquer anything together, that somehow that division would also create unity. There's an oxymoron if ever I've heard one. I know better now. I know that it's somehow linked to the Imminent Darkness.

Long ago the Imminent Darkness tricked the five sisters—who later became the goddesses ruling over each of the five lands of the Elemental Abyss. The sisters were close—inseparable—until the Imminent Darkness, disguised as a hideous codger, came and tricked them. He gave them each a stone, and each sister thought her stone was the best one. Only in truth, each stone was the same. The stones divided the sisters, leading Raj to create each daughter her own land over which to rule. And now look at what has happened. Each sister rules her own land and slowly each land is being eaten from the inside out by the ID, but if only the sisters had banded together they'd have been so much stronger. Now they're each trapped in their respective worlds unable to help each other. Except for me. I am the link that bonds the sisters together, having been gifted with powers representing each of their Elements. Our own Elemental divisions aren't all that different from the sisters. It's not dividing us so we can better conquer our difficulties; it's just the opposite. Dividing us because being able to conquer us will be that much easier. It's a costly misinterpretation.

Li doesn't turn a glance as we pass the outskirts of the Fire Building. I remember how excited he was to become a Fire. He used to bubble over with alternating bursts of passion and indulgence. But now…now he too is like a shell of who he used to be. The dark tattooed filigree lines the side of his face, curving around his high-set cheekbone and then down his thick neck disappearing beneath the collar of his jacket. Somehow in the time I've been back and forth from the Elemental Abyss, he's seemed to have aged must faster than the rest of us. I don't know when I missed the transition of Li going from a boy into a man, but clearly he's made it. His former jaunty posture is more slouched and defensive. His thin build has begun to fill out. He turns, catching me staring at him, even though I'm unseen because of the cloaking cuff. *Just because I can't see you doesn't mean I can't feel you.* He raises a thin, black eyebrow as if to say: *Told you so.* I blush and turn away. Li is not Sloan. The two aren't even comparable, as different as Old Earth and Xon 9. But I've known Li a long time. I love him, just not in the same way that I love Sloan.

The University Complex has been indefinitely closed since the incident with the new Fire initiates. Some of the other Elemental Buildings have been open in the meanwhile, but University hasn't yet resumed. It's weird to walk by and see nobody. Even at this early hour, professors and researchers would be heading into work. All of the buildings are dark and look menacing against the red landscape. A shiver runs up the back of my spine.

We continue walking, heading down the sidewalk that leads to the Black Bazaar. This is where the Underground starts. It's an abrupt evolution from the well-kept houses and buildings of the rest of the colony, slowly becoming more broken and dilapidated as we near the Bazaar's entrance. The energy shifts and its palpable. Up until now I'd felt lonely and a bit desolate, but now I somehow feel both frightened and angry, a cacophony of dark emotions. The old, wooden sign marking the Black Bazaar's entrance is snapped in half, the sign part laying on the cracked sidewalk while the stake is still stuck into the ground. The quickest way to the other side of the Underground—to the military base where Michaela lives—is straight through. The long way around is to continue down the sidewalk.

Sloan pauses at the cobblestone entrance. "Are you sure, Ka? Remember Doran's warning?" And I think that part of his hesitation isn't so much what we will find, but what we won't find. This is where Sloan grew up in his mother's trailer where she read fortunes with her special gift of the Sight. It's where his dad was taken and wrongfully imprisoned. Sloan may have declared Water—mostly out of fear that he'd become Unbalanced like his mother—but the Underground, the Black Bazaar is his home. I remember my dream and how the Chatfield's house was ransacked. The last time Sloan and I were down here is when we visited Bina's trailer to get some ingredients—Zephyrus Seeds and Medeis Seaweed—for our trip to the Elemental Abyss. Neither of us had been back since Bina had been kidnapped by the ID's followers.

"Yes," I whisper. "If we don't, then we don't know what we're up against. I need to know how far the Imminent Darkness has spread."

Sloan sighs and heads down the alley way marking the entrance. A short passageway and two steps down and we're in the Black Bazaar. Normally, most everything would be closed at this hour anyways. The Black Bazaar is more of a nocturnal kind of place. The first thing I notice is the smell. It's putrid, filling my nostrils, making them burn. I can taste it on my tongue. Sulfur. The second thing I notice is the dark shadow that seems to rest over everything—like the fork in the road in the forest. We've entered into a part of the Underground that seems to be dying, for lack of a better word.

The shadow ebbs and flows as if it is a living and breathing thing. The normally constant breeze of Xon 9 no longer reaches here. The air is still, stagnant. All of the vendors are closed. No outside lights. Some vendors live in the trailers attached to their shops. No inside lights are on either. We pass Bina's trailer with its broken and banged up door. We pass the tattoo shop where I met Zora and got my Elemental Star. The bald man who sold Pleasure Patches is closed for business; a spray painted warning is scrolled across the gate: *Go away*. Although, I'm not sure if he's referring to people bothering him or to the Imminent Darkness. Maybe both.

Shop after shop is closed up tight. Those that don't have gates to pull down, have pieces of plywood covering their windows and doors. Some have big black Xs spray painted across their sides. "What does it mean?" I whisper to Ahna.

"I'm not sure," she replies.

But I feel like I have an idea. It's a mark. The Imminent Darkness is primitive, like an animal. And it has gone through, marking its territory. But why the Black Bazaar? Out of all of Xon 9, why would this be the first place the Imminent Darkness reveals itself?

If we went to the left, we'd head past the bar where I wrongly thought Michaela was Sloan's girlfriend before I knew she was his sister. And if we kept going we'd walk out to a small ledge where Sloan and I had many conversations, including our first argument and our first kiss. We continue to the right, leaving the Black Bazaar behind and entering into the fringes of the Underground that will take us to Michaela's and hopefully to Bina's. That's when I see it.

CHAPTER 21

Doran's house. The familiar tattered awning comes into view. How long ago was it that we were gathered beneath it? Not long. All the little trinkets—made of glass, wood, metal, and gemstones—are scattered about the small concrete pad beneath the awning. The screen door is askew, hanging from its hinge. Through the shadowy haze, I can see that the door to the trailer is open a bit. I feel compelled, drawn to go inside. Doran warned me to stay away. But I feel myself inexplicably drawn to go inside.

"I need to go inside," I tell Sloan.

"Are you sure? You said Doran's message told you not to come here."

"You don't understand. I *need* to go inside there. I don't know why. I just know that I do."

"We'll all go in then," Li says. But something tells me that's a bad idea. I have to go in alone.

I step toward the door. The energy emanating from the trailer is palpable, like a low-level hum, and I think I understand why I need to go inside alone.

"No. You guys stay out here. I won't be long." Li shrugs and Ahna doesn't object. She knows better than to do that after so many years of friendship because she knows I won't listen anyways. But Sloan furrows his brow and gives me a worried look. I know that he's thinking about how he needs to protect me—uphold his Everlasting Vow—and if I am alone inside a place that I was told not to visit, then he isn't doing a very good job.

When I move up the few steps leading inside, he doesn't try to stop me. I press the button on the cloaking cuff to render myself visible, even though I'm pretty sure the Imminent Darkness would be able to see me either way. I don't think the ID is something I could ever hide from because it would always find me as if we're somehow tethered together. I walk in. It's immediately as if I'm living the same thing twice. The couch cushions are torn and the armchair is knocked backward. Stuffing from the cushions is strewn about. The kitchen cabinets are all open, their contents knocked to the floor, the smell of rancid food. Some nutrient pills crush beneath my boots as I make my way down the hallway toward the bedrooms. *What were they trying to find here?*

The spare bedroom. I open the door. There are some clothes tossed about and a couple open drawers, but nothing else too suspicious. Zora's room, saving Doran's for last. Zora's room isn't very girlie, but neither is Zora. There's a black, silky blouse crumpled up on the floor and a pair of skinny-legged black jeans on the bed. A perfume bottle is cracked and broken, leaking sweet-smelling perfume across its surface. Nothing disturbing here really, just the feeling that someone left in a hurry. I turn back toward the hallway and pull the door shut behind me.

Doran's room is in-between. The door is open a crack. I put my hand on the knob and feel a rush of air hit my face. The hair on the back of my neck stands up. I know there's no message tube to be found here; it's snug in my pocket, pressing against my hipbone. I should turn around. Walk back down the hallway and out the front door. Get on with my friends and go find Bina. Because Bina will know what to do. She always does.

But I can't. I take a deep breath and push the door open. The window is slightly open and even though the breeze outside has stopped, the curtains move back and forth and the bedspread rustles. The room is like the shadow permeating the Black Bazaar, it seems as if it is breathing. The hum has grown louder, deep inside my eardrums, a rhythmic sound. An ancient sound. And I know that it's here. This is why I had to come inside. My heart beats in sync with the pulsing sound, instead of quickening because of the adrenaline, its slowing down. Matching heartbeats like the elves and nymphs with Nahele's Genesis Seed. The Imminent Darkness is powerful. But so am I.

There's a bedside lamp turned on and it quietly blinks off. The door slams shut behind me and there's a hissing sound as the breeze picks up inside the room. The air in front of me begins to swirl, faster and faster like a cyclone. The bedspread flips up and a small statue falls from the dresser, landing with an ominous crack. A smoke-like shadow seeps in from the window and is sucked into the whirling cyclone. Then, almost as quickly as it began, the rush of air slows down and the hissing sound reverts back to the low-level hum.

The smoky shadow has taken shape. It's a person-like shape, taller than me and wearing a long, black hooded cloak similar to the ones the human members of the Imminent Darkness wear. Although I'm pretty sure that what stands before me is anything but human. Inside the hood, where a face would be, there's nothing but blackness, except two, bright yellow eyes that peer back at me. It's always the eyes. The Imminent Darkness. Ancient and formless, or every form depending on how you look at it. It stands on the other side of the bed, near the window. I remain on the side of the bed near the door, but I have a feeling if I tried to turn and run right now, I'd find that the door is somehow locked from the outside. I'm trapped.

It says nothing, just stares at me for a long time. Then without a word, it lifts up the two arms of the robes—no hands peak out of the ends—but it has the same effect as someone raising their own arms up above their head. As the arms lift, the low-level hum becomes louder and faster. My own heartbeat begins to quicken in a matching crescendo until it feels like it will burst from my chest, then the Imminent Darkness lowers its arms and the hum becomes softer, slower. My heart beat becomes slow and even, matching the drone of the hum. Contrary to anything I may have thought, I am not in control here. If that's all this little show had to prove, I think the mission was accomplished.

The eyes blink at me and then suddenly the blackness in the hood of the cloak takes a shape. Almond-shaped eyes, a full mouth, and light olive skin look back at me. Ahna. Then the face turns blurry as it shifts again into more angular, masculine features with a tattoo down the right side of its face. Li. A blur again as the tattoo shifts to fiery filigree and the skin tone turns darker. Doran. Another blur, almost as if it's sorting through the various faces and they're just going too fast for me to see. The nose is smaller and slightly angular, the facial features are softer, and the lips thinner. The familiar silvery-green scales line the side of its face. Sloan. Then the features melt into a blur one last time and then settles on yet another familiar face. Small, round nose and round, brown eyes with a pert mouth that's slightly lopsided from biting on the bottom lip. This time it has chosen my face.

The message is clear. Not only am I not in control, but my mother is right. It can take any form at any time, even that of someone I love, even me. The Genesis Seed confirmed this when it showed me the Imminent Darkness as Sloan. I watch as my face melts back into the shadow and only yellow eyes peer back at me once again. The Imminent Darkness decides it's had enough and without a word the wind rushes in with a hiss and swirls around the cloaked form, faster and faster until just as quickly it stops. And when it does, nothing is there. I hear the door click open behind me.

...

"Are you sure?" asks Ahna.

"I know what I saw." We've left Doran's and are hurriedly walking across the Underground to the military complex. I've made myself invisible again to the outside world—a shadow just like the one drifting through the Black Bazaar.

"What do you think it means?" Sloan asks, but I think he asks more for Li's and Ahna's benefit than for his own. Because Sloan has some of his mother's gifts and I'm pretty sure he's seen things that he hasn't told me, just as I've seen things that I haven't told him about.

"I think it was a reminder. I'm growing stronger. I've got the third stone now. There's only two more left. The Imminent Darkness is probably stronger than it's ever been, but as I grow stronger it grows weaker. The only problem is that in order for it to continue to have the upper hand, it will need to start gathering its strength from outside sources. That's why it's here. It's not creating; it's recruiting."

"So what about what just happened? It traps you in a room, shows you a bunch of different faces then leaves again?" Li asks.

"It was a show of control. A reminder that I am not the one in control of the situation because it can trick me at any time. It didn't just show me random faces, it showed me my friends."

Li pauses. "Why us?"

"Isn't it obvious? My parents are safe, for the most part. At the very least they're together. But here, now, you guys are all that I have. If the Imminent Darkness takes you three, then I have nothing left."

"We won't let that happen," Ahna says. I want to believe her, but I don't think she realizes just what we're up against. She hasn't seen the things that I've seen.

"There are no guarantees, not now or ever."

"We'll destroy the Wood stone and return your powers to you."

"It still won't protect you. To me, this is my home and my friends. My life. But to the Imminent Darkness…it's just a big game, a never-ending chess match."

We reach the military complex. The bottom three floors are offices and the rest are residential commons for soldiers and other military employees. The entire building is sleek and metallic. I don't think the metals would have it any other way. Beneath the building is a state of the art prison, the same prison where Sloan's dad, Finn, is kept. The last time Sloan and I were here it was an emotional experience, what with me meeting Finn for the first time and with Sloan having rarely seen, his now blind, father. Blind or not, Finn's still sharp as a tack. I could easily see the resemblance between him and Sloan—both are intelligent and observant. Whereas I don't know when to shut up and bumble on like an idiot, Sloan is quiet and each sentence has a purpose. His dad is the same way.

We'll have to split up because three people going to visit with the new restrictions in place would probably arouse suspicion. Li and Ahna disappear around the building, heading in the direction of a small park—if you can call a couple of benches and some trees a park—on the other side of the facility. Nothing too strange about a brother and sister just hanging out. Invisibly, I follow Sloan through the open front doors to the building, but once you get inside there's a foyer with an intercom and two sets of locked doors. One set of doors leads to a lobby and the other set leads to a bank of elevators. Through the double-paned glass you can see a semi-circular counter. Today, a man about my father's age and wearing glasses sits behind it. His voice comes over the intercom: "State your business." Last time I was here with Ahna, it was a woman who was much more pleasant. I wonder if it's the situation or just the personality of the man behind the desk.

"I'm here to see my sister, Michaela Braden."

There's a long pause as the man studies Sloan. If you go through the set of doors leading to the military offices, there's a strict protocol and security check. But for visitors to the apartments it's more lax. Sometimes they ask you to state your name and will verify your identity, but I've learned that not every person behind the desk bothers with that procedure. Finally, the man presses the button behind the counter and the doors leading to the bank of elevators clicks open.

Sloan gives him a small salute as a thanks and casually walks through the doors as if this is no special visit. I follow him through and the door clicks closed behind us. Sloan doesn't need to check the list of apartment numbers and names, we head right to the elevator and he presses the button for the fourth floor, which is the first floor listed. No traveling to floors one through three from this side of the building. That means even employees have to come down and go through the same entrance we just came through. We reach the fourth floor quickly and step into the hallway. It's dimly lit with sconces made of silver metal lining the walls. The floors are black marble and each of the apartment doors is painted white with the apartment numbers painted in black. Beside each door is a small intercom. Sloan stops in front of room 411 and presses the intercom button.

A light, feminine voice responds. "Braden."

"It's me."

A pregnant pause. "Are you alone?"

I can hear the drop of hesitation mixed with a hint of fear in her voice. Michaela thinks that I'm putting her family in danger. In her mind, if the Imminent Darkness wants me then my being around is a risk. And to her, it's a risk she's not willing to take. I can't say that I blame her.

Sloan looks right at me—like I said, invisible or not, he sees me no matter where I am—and then answers Michaela.

"Yeah, I'm alone."

CHAPTER 22

Michaela unlocks the door and pulls it open. The first thing I notice is the dark circles beneath her eyes. Michaela is as pretty as Sloan is handsome. She is tall and thin with long blonde hair and deep blue eyes. She's also quite smart, but I think it's almost to a fault because there's no warmth to her.

Sloan steps inside and I follow close behind, pressing up against him to take up as little space as possible so he can push the door closed behind him. The small apartment is a mess, not up to its usual immaculate standards. The kitchen is to the right and there are two bedrooms and a bathroom down the hall to the left. The kitchen has an extended countertop that juts out into the living room which is cramped with a small sofa and an armchair, in addition to two stools near the counter.

Bina is sitting in the armchair with an afghan across her lap. Her gray hair is a rat's nest on top of her head, but that's usually how it looks. Her gray eyes are alert and beady in her frail face, but her color is better than the last time I'd seen her. Her health has definitely improved, but perhaps she'll never fully recover from the failed MindCleanse. As I've mentioned, when you try to wipe out the memories of someone with the gift of the Sight, it tends to backfire. Doesn't make it any less painful though, believe me, I've been there. Having your memories extracted like threads from your scalp via a metal crown-like device isn't exactly pleasant, in fact it's excruciating.

Sloan doesn't sit, but remains standing. Bina sets down her tea cup on a small table and looks up at him smiling. Then she glances right at me—and just like Sloan—I know that she can see me. I don't know Bina as well as I know Sloan, but I do know that she won't tell Michaela. Michaela is kind of the oddball in the family. She's a rule follower. Finn, Bina, and Sloan are more like free spirits. She reaches up her bony arms.

"Give me a hug, my boy!" It only takes Sloan two steps to close the distance from the opposite wall to the chair. He bends over and gives his mother a hug. When I first met Sloan, and having already met Bina, I didn't know they were related. Now, I often wonder how I ever missed it. Michaela folds herself up onto the couch as Sloan extracts himself from his mother's embrace. He doesn't sit. He isn't intending for this to be a long visit.

"You look like crap, Sis."

"I'm working long hours. This whole Imminent Darkness thing, or whatever they call themselves. These people are running the intelligence department ragged."

"They're not just people."

"Yeah, yeah. You sound like Mom. Listen, the military works in facts. Some, mysterious dark energy thing is not a fact. People are facts."

"I've seen it."

"Doesn't mean it's real."

"Okay, okay. That's enough from the both of yeh," Bina interrupts. "Yeh obviously visited for a reason, Sloan. Let's have it." Quick and to the point. I wouldn't expect anything less.

"I wanted to make sure you were okay. Ka received a message from Doran that the Imminent Darkness had taken over the Underground."

"She did, did she? Well, I am as whole as yeh are." She smiles her toothless smile. I don't know when her teeth fell out or why. I used to just think the Black Bazaar wasn't a fan of dentistry, but after learning Finn's story I imagine that Bina's is equally tragic.

"Ka?" Michalea's voice feigns interest. "Is she still chasing after those stones or whatever?" It's a weird question and I can only hope that Sloan picks up on it. I—we—freed an entire prison camp beneath the Council Hall and Sloan, Doran, and I are responsible for Tristen's death. Unless of course she isn't really dead.

"Those stones that will help her restore her universal gifts and allow her to destroy something that's causing chaos, death, and destruction on multiple planets? Yeah, she's still working on that." Sloan's tone is clipped and I can see the vein in his neck throbbing ever so slightly beneath his scales.

Michaela scowls at him. "You know she's on the military's Hunted list. She released people who were guilty of crimes against the Council." She says it matter-of-factly. I want to like Michaela, really, I do. I think deep down she's a good person who happens to be sorely misguided. But right now I kind of want to punch her in her pretty, little face.

"Speaking your mind about something isn't a crime. If anyone should know that, it should be this family."

Finn.

Michaela looks down at her fingernails. After a pause she looks back up and her eyes are tearful. "It wasn't her right to release them. She's also the main suspect in the murder of a former Elemental Leader, a Fire. Your girlfriend is a criminal."

"My girlfriend hasn't committed any of these acts alone. Don't make her your martyr."

Bina intervenes. "Let's not jump to conclusions, Michaela. I've told yeh, there's a lot to this that yeh don't understand. 'Tis bigger than us."

"I understand facts, Mother. Those are the facts. I've seen them in her file," Michaela retorts.

Bina shakes her head. "Sometimes seeing isn't believing. Believing is seeing."

"I'm going to get going. I just wanted to make sure Mom was okay. I'll see myself out." Sloan starts walking down the hallway and I follow.

Michaela's voice carries to us before we reach the door. "She'll be the death of you, you know." It's meant to be a warning, but instead Sloan smiles.

"I know," he whispers.

. . .

Sloan and I head toward the park where Li and Ahna are waiting for us. The doors to the military complex close behind us with an imperceptible click. Sloan glances back at the building and I can't quite describe the look on his face. Wistful? Sad? His stride is longer than mine and I hurry to keep up.

"I'm sorry about Michaela," I whisper once I'm within earshot. Even though there's no one else around—at least not that I can see—it would be weird to have a disembodied voice floating across the space between us.

He shrugs. "I'm not too worried about her, honestly. She's always been a bit of a brat. What, with me being so close to Bina and Finn...so similar. She's the odd man out. If she weren't so witchy about it, I'd feel bad for her. Which would probably just irritate her even more."

"She doesn't like pity?"

"Michaela is smart, but she has no emotional IQ. She is logical to a fault. It's the facts or nothing. There is no heart in her decision-making. And because of this she's also the most prideful person I know."

I scoff. "More than Li?"

Sloan chuckles. "Okay, maybe it's a close second."

247

The sign for the park comes into view: *Pax Park*. It's a small circular area of rocks scattered across the silvery-green grass, along with a few benches. Trees surround a sidewalk that winds its way around the circle. Once, I read that walking in circles—well, really it was walking in a labyrinth—can help ease anxiety and worry. Is it a coincidence such a park is so close to the military complex? Maybe it's a way for the workers to relax and maintain their Balance. Maybe Michaela should check it out. There are several clusters of thin trees in the center of the park's grassy circular space, so I can't see Ahna and Li from where we're standing.

Sloan pauses before the entrance. "Bina told me something."

Of course. When she called Sloan over to hug her, it wasn't just to feel his solidity in her arms, but to tell him something. Something she didn't want Michaela to hear.

He smiles. "First, she told me to tell you hello." I smile too. My feelings were right. She knew that I was there, even though she couldn't physically see me. Bina sees just like Sloan does. "And she told me to tell you, 'When the one yeh love is lost, the stone will turn to dust.'" He recites her words in a perfect imitation cadence.

I frown. "What does that mean?"

"I've no idea. I was hoping you'd have some ideas."

"Well, you're the one I love, so I hope..." I don't finish the sentence because I didn't tell Sloan about my mother's warning or of what the Genesis Seed showed me.

"Yeah, me too." He rolls back on his heels and lets out a sigh. I reach out and wrap my arms around his waist, resting my ear to his chest. Listening to the slow rhythm of his heartbeat. Never. It could never happen. The beat is too strong, his love too singular for the Imminent Darkness to get inside. The ID preys on the weak. Sloan is not weak.

"Hey, at least we know that the stone will turn to dust." He tries to smile.

"I'd rather not lose the one I love."

He turns my chin up so that I'm looking at him. And I wonder if he doesn't just sense me, but literally sees me, regardless of the cloaking cuff.

"I do," he answers my unasked question. "So does Bina. My Sight isn't nearly as strong as hers, but she told me that it will get stronger as I get older until it's as good as hers." He dips his head and kisses me. It's long, slow, and sweet, as if he's trying to savor the touch and taste of it. When he pulls away I can see the flush creeping up his neck.

"Let's not focus on the things we're losing—or might lose—okay? Let's focus on the things that we're gaining instead."

I breathlessly nod my agreement. "Okay."

"Bina's visions aren't always exact. Sometimes they're vague because she can't get a clear picture. Like she told Michaela, sometimes believing is seeing."

I unravel myself from him. "Then I believe that Bina's message isn't about you. Besides, if something's lost, it can always be found again, right?"

Sloan's smile is tight. "Let's hope."

. . .

We walk along the circular sidewalk, passing two empty park benches, before we round the corner and find Ahna. She practically jumps out of her skin when she hears us approach. She's reading a book which she abruptly closes.

"Where's Li?" I ask looking around at the scattering of rocks. There aren't many places to go in a park like this, unless he's walking on the other side of the circle.

Ahna throws up her hands in irritation. "The boy cannot sit still to save his life. As soon as I started to read my book he mumbled something and walked away." It was probably more like Ahna started to read and Li told her exactly where he was going, but Ahna was so absorbed in her book she didn't hear him. It wouldn't be the first time. "Ka, can you uncloak? It's weird talking to someone who isn't there. I don't think anyone will see us here, anyways. I haven't seen a single person this entire time. Everyone's become too frightened to go outside."

I press the button on the cloaking bracelet. "Feels good to be seen again." That's when I remember the second bracelet that I'm wearing, the thinner one that almost appears as if it's part of the cloaking cuff. The two-way communicator. "Wait. Li gave me this bracelet too, remember?" There's a small button on the side of the bracelet. I press it and hold my wrist up to my mouth. "Li? Liwald Sollomon, where are you?"

Silence answers me back. Then there's a small crackle and I can make out: "K…ah…tah…" coming from the speakers on my bracelet.

"Li? Bina's okay. Everything's fine. We need to go back. Where are you?"

"K…ah…tah…"

I look up at Ahna and her brown eyes are wide in her soft face. "Why does he keep saying your name over and over again?"

I was thinking the same thing, but I didn't want her to panic. If Ahna panics she's no good to me. I need Ahna with a clear head, not one inundated with emotions that don't make any sense.

Finally, I say, "You know how Li is. Always being stupid and messing around."

Ahna is kneeling on the bench, peering at Sloan and me over its back, her fingers gripping the back edge, her knuckles white. She nods, but I can tell her analytical side is disagreeing. Sloan says nothing behind me, but I know that all three of us are truthfully thinking the same thing. Li could be anywhere. Anywhere in the Underground, or even back at the Black Bazaar. Heck, he could even have gone home. He's been acting so strange and erratic lately that I can't say it would surprise me.

"Let's go back home. Maybe he already started that way," I say.

Ahna nods and picks up her bag, slinging it across her shoulders, and dropping the book inside. We walk back toward the entrance to the park. Just as we walk through the concrete walls of the entrance I hear a growl, coming from behind me. I pause. Sloan touches my shoulder. Ahna freezes.

I know what I'm going to see before I actually see it. The wolf from the Land of Earth. The one that tried to kill my mother. The one that tried to kill me. I turn around. I am right. The wolf is only a few steps away, on the other side of the sidewalk, standing in the grass. Its black fur is bristled along its spine and its glowing yellow eyes are hungry. It bares its fangs.

My first thought is about Li. Is that why he sounded the way that he did on the communicator? Did the wolf attack him and he's lying, dying somewhere in the park? As calmly as I can muster I say, "Ahna, you need to go back in the park."

Sloan picks up on where I'm headed. "There's a second entrance directly opposite this one, on the other side of the circle. If you go out and around you'll find it."

"Find Li." I pause. "There might be blood," I warn.

"I-I know." Her voice has an eerie sense of calm to it that I've only heard once before from my own mother as she lay dying on the floor at my knees. One word: *Key*. Ahna backs out of the entrance slowly, but the wolf doesn't care about her. It doesn't even care about Sloan. It wants me. And that's when I notice the mistake I've just made. I sent Ahna to go and find Li fearing that he's hurt. Except I think I already found him. Around the wolf's left paw is a thin, silver bracelet.

CHAPTER 23

Saliva drips from the wolf's mouth and seems to suspend in the air before dropping to the grass at its feet. It takes a step closer. Sloan moves to put himself in between us. But I shake my head.

"It's Li," I tell him. He follows my eyes to the silver bracelet.

"But how…"

"Any form, Sloan. It can be whoever it wants to be. Isn't that right?" I say louder. The wolf bends one of its ears as if it's listening to me. I know that it is. "You can take any form that you want. That's what that was about earlier. But I have to tell you I'm not happy you decided to inhabit one of my best friends."

The wolf makes a growling sound that turns into a bark and then into a laugh—a human laugh, a familiar laugh. The wolf shapeshifts before my eyes, its two hind legs become boots and a pair of jeans. The human part travels up the torso turning back into Li's beat-up, jacket with the hole in the pocket, and then up his neck, the black tattoo creeping up the side of his face. The soft lips and angular features come next followed by the too-long, shaggy black hair. However, the eyes do not change. Sensual brown eyes do not look back at me, instead the eyes remain a menacing yellow. Eyes that I've seen one too many times before.

"Ah, so nice to see you again, Ka." The voice is Li's, at least technically speaking, but it doesn't have any of him behind it—there's no warmth, no depth to it.

"Why don't you take your own form? What, are you too weak to just be yourself?" I spit, immediately angry at myself for losing my cool so quickly. I can feel the Fire pulsating beneath the surface of my skin.

Sloan puts a hand on my shoulder, but I shrug him off.

"I have no self," it replies. "I am everything and anything. I am so vast. Imagine cramming all of the Universe into a physical form. I cannot sustain the forms I take for long. That's why I must always be changing it."

"You've done enough to Li already."

"Have I?" The Imminent Darkness uses Li's hand to touch the side of his face with the burned out filigree. "I did not do this to your friend. You did this to him."

"No, I didn't." But my voice catches in my throat. I did. I did this to him. When I threw the Fire stone up against the fireballs coming from Tristen's army, it created a huge explosion that sucked the Fire from every Fire initiate tapped into the collective consciousness. I'm lucky it didn't kill them, both because it spared their lives and because I don't know how I'd live with the guilt. And although it didn't kill them, it did damage them. It drained them of their Fire and burned them up from the inside out.

The ID lowers his hand. "See? You know that you did."

"Ka, come on. Don't listen to it." Sloan's voice is soft and gentle.

I wish that I were soft and gentle.

"You ruined Li's life," the ID continues, honing in on my weakness. Helping the helpless. But I haven't yet figured out how to help Li. "You drained him of his Fire, the only thing he ever wanted. Well," the ID chuckles, "maybe not the only thing." The Imminent Darkness closes his eyes as if he's exploring inside Li's mind, opening and closing imaginary files inside his brain. "You. This boy has always wanted *you*. Well, that's quite the plot twist now isn't it?" He opens his eyes and looks over at Sloan. "Looks, like you could have some competition."

"You need a competitor to have a competition," Sloan says. His voice remains soft and even. Showing no emotion. The Imminent Darkness feeds off emotion and it feeds off negative energy. Li must be full of negative energy—he's been acting so weird and spending so much time in the Black Bazaar since everything that happened. I should have stopped him from acting like that. I should have realized that he'd be more susceptible than anybody to the Imminent Darkness. But how do you save someone from himself? You don't.

"Li knows that we're just friends," I reply. "And Li doesn't blame me for what happened. He tried to help me. He knows none of this is my fault."

"Ah, but that's where you're wrong. You think it is your fault. As you grow stronger, I grow weaker, which causes me to have to feed to regain my strength. And what do I feed on? But the energy of weakened souls, souls that have been hurt or traumatized. Souls with broken hearts."

Tears sting my eyes and the Fire pulsing in my veins begins to wane. Have I broken Li's heart? I never thought anything was there, I was positive it was just a game to him. Maybe all this time I was wrong.

"Ka, it's manipulating you. You know Li just wants whatever's best for you and for the rest of the colony. Don't let it play with your head."

"Ah, and your Protector. Does he know of Li and how he arouses a certain, shall I say Fire within you?"

"Stop it!" I yell. "Just stop it!" The words are true. I do have passion for Li, his kisses and his touch are like liquid Fire against my skin, but that's the problem. Fire and Fire only causes destruction. If the Universe needs balance, than so too do each of us and there is no better balance for me than Sloan. When I am angry, he is calm. When I am impulsive, he is well-thought out. When I want to run, he reminds me to walk. Li may love me, but he loves the old me, not the new me. Sloan loves me in all my incarnations.

"Oh, did I hit a soft spot?"

"Get out of my friend's body. Leave this place. Leave the

Underground."

"Now, you know I can't do that. You don't have all the stones yet."

"You killed Brooks." The Fire returns, searing through my body and squeezing my heart. Brooks was my friend. He helped me. He kept me safe.

"Names aren't important."

"Yes, yes they are. Names are what separates us from the likes of you."

"Now, you've gone and hurt my feelings. Oh, wait, I don't have any." The Imminent Darkness shapeshifts seamlessly back into the wolf's body. It lunges toward me and I summon my vines, but they're too slow. The Imminent Darkness knocks me onto my back, its large paws pressed against my chest. I can smell its rank breath.

"When I leave your friend's body, he will be just as I encountered him. Sad, broken, bleeding. You don't want that, now do you?"

The wolf leans over and we're nose to nose. It's breath is hot on my face. I try to move to jerk it off me but it weighs more than I do, so much so that I can feel my body sinking into the grass. *When the one you love is lost, the stone will turn to dust.* It wasn't about Sloan. It was about Li.

"Get off of her." Sloan's voice is still calm. I turn my head. He's unsheathed the jeweled dagger from Qildor.

"Sloan, no! It could kill Li too."

"What if I told you your friend was already dead?" The

Imminent Darkness whispers.

I feel a surge of fear, but it's mixed with rage. I feel the prickle against my skin. "He. Is. Not. Dead."

"That's how I can take the form. I had to kill him to inhabit the body. He was in a weakened energetic state. Wandering around the circle's sidewalk, mumbling to himself. He never saw me coming. He tried to put up a good fight though."

"ARRRGGHHH!" I roar and grab the wolf by the neck, it yelps from the current in my fingertips. We roll around on the ground and I try to get to my feet. It grabs onto my shoulder sinking its teeth deep into my skin. I let out a guttural scream and try to slap it away. That's when the dagger comes down, slashing through the shoulder of the wolf.

The Imminent Darkness lets out a human scream of agony as I roll out from beneath it. There's blood everywhere. Mine and the wolf's, coalescing on the grass beneath me. The wolf shifts back into Li. Bright, red blood is dripping from his shoulder and I can see the muscle beneath. Then it shifts back into the wolf as if it's losing its ability to stay in one form or the other.

"If you come near her again. It won't be your shoulder this time." Sloan holds the dagger and even though his voice is steady, his hand is shaking. Blood drips from the dagger's tip, matching the rubies encrusted on its handle.

The wolf lets out a howl and a puff of black smoke comes out of its mouth. As the smoke billows above it, Li's body appears on the ground before us. The smoke continues to curl out of his mouth until there's nothing left and then the smoke dissipates and disappears.

I scramble to my feet and run over to Li. His shoulder is bleeding and I can see the muscle and bone beneath. But there's also a wound on the back of his leg, one that the ID must have hid from us when it took Li's form. There's a tear in his jeans and a deep set of teeth marks on his calf where the wolf probably first grabbed him. I take off my sweatshirt and pull at the bottom of my t-shirt, ripping off the bottom hem and then trying to tie it around his shoulder to stop the flow of blood.

Ahna comes running up the grassy center circle. She sees me bandaging Li's unconscious body and Sloan standing behind me with the dagger dripping with her brother's blood. Her face goes white.

"I-I followed the trail of blood…Sloan, you didn't…"

"He did." I reply. "But not before The Imminent Darkness had already gotten to him…Li…we have to get him help." The rise and fall of his chest is slow, almost unnoticeable. "He's alive, only just barely."

Ahna falls to her knees and takes Li's hand in hers. "He's cold."

"How do we explain this to a hospital?" I ask. My own shoulder has droplets of blood seeping through my t-shirt from where the wolf bit me.

"You three, there! What are you doing?" A male voice calls to us from the entrance to the park. "Hey, wait. Is that—is that blood?" The man has metallic threads lining the side of his face and is wearing all black. Military personnel. I hear him radio into his communicator.

"We have two females and a male perpetrator. Weapon in hand. One male down." He turns back to us. "I need back-up."

Ahna stares at me, her eyes pleading. "We need to do something."

Sloan wipes the dagger on his pants and re-sheathes it. "The ring."

"My ring." My mother said whenever I need my father or to go to the Land of Earth, it will take me there. All I have to do is press my left thumb to the ring on my left index finger and think of home. Not home the place, but the feelings associated with home. "Sloan, Ahna, quick!"

I grab Li's hand and Sloan's. Sloan grabs Ahna's free hand. Mom. Dad. Family. Love. Loyalty. Caring. Help. Mom. Dad. Family. Love. Loyalty. Caring. Help. I say the words over and over. I close my eyes. I can hear the pound of boots as back-up arrives.

"What's going on here?" A voice asks.

"I don't…"

The voices grow fainter and more distant as if we are floating away from them. Then suddenly the familiar sensation of hurtling through time and space. I can feel both Li's and Sloan's hands solid in mine, my thumb still pressed against the cool turquoise of my ring. A ring made by my friend, but blessed by my mother, a goddess of the Universe and endowed with the love of my father.

I see jumbles of memories from both Li and Sloan. Li looking at me across the table in the library while I'm studying the books to find more information about my mother. Sloan diving into the water to catch my no longer breathing body as I descend to the murky bottom. Li doodling in his notebook, sketches of my face. My eyes. My lips. Sloan seeing me even though I am not really there. The memories come faster and faster until they're a blur, a mixture of the two guys I've only ever loved: one my best friend and one my Everlasting Protector.

There's a burst of blinding white light as the time-space continuum spits us out. Our hands become untwined as we tumble through. I hit the floor hard causing a searing pain in my injured shoulder. But for a moment, it doesn't matter. I feel the cool smoothness of white marble beneath me and the sun shines through the multi-colored glass representing the five Elements. Sapphire, amber, emerald, ruby and turquoise wedges of light dance across my body. The sweet flowery smell fills my nose.

I am home.

CHAPTER 24

"Ka? Ka, is that you?" In the Land of Earth my mother's voice is like a long-forgotten melody. Everything seems better here: fresher, cleaner, newer.

My mother is not how I knew her growing up. She regenerated into one of her other forms: the maiden. Novea is no more. Anuja is in her place—young with porcelain skin, light gray eyes, and long, dark brown hair. Regardless of what form she takes, she is still my mother.

"Oh, dear!" she cries and I hear her bare feet pad across the polished stone floor. I push myself to a seated position shaking my head of the lingering memories from the trip here. She grabs my shoulder, gray eyes concerned. "Are you alright?" She glances down at her hand and sees the droplets of blood. "Ka…"

"Li." I point.

It's all I need to say before she's hurrying across the floor, her cyan-colored dress flowing behind her. She drops to her knees next to Li's motionless form.

"Absalom! Absalom, come quick!"

There's no time for Ahna or Sloan to process what's just happened. Ahna rushes to Li's side and grabs his hand. Ahna, long ago, explained to me that she and Li had a very special connection.

Once, she had said, Li was riding his bike around our little community of stone houses, when he'd fallen. Ahna, who had been playing in her room, felt a jolt accompanied by a shooting pain up her right leg. Instantly, she'd recalled, she knew Li was injured. She ran out the front door until she found him on the ground beside his overturned bike, clutching his right knee in agony. It wasn't the first time she'd told me such a story, and I'm sure it won't be the last. It's hard to imagine how she must be feeling.

My father comes running into the room. He too looks younger, even though it's not the effects of a regeneration, but of living here in the Land of Earth. The brown hair and deep-set brown eyes are the same, but the creases in his face seem fewer. He takes one look at me, eyes questioning, before spotting my mother kneeling on the floor. He hurries over to her side.

"Is there a pulse?" he asks.

"Just barely," she says softly. My parents have known Li as long as I have and the twins' parents even longer. The Sollomon's are long-time family friends.

"I-I didn't know what else to do. Where else to go…" I begin to say but I choke on the words. This is all my fault. I wasn't cautious enough. I didn't listen to Li's silent cries for me to help him, to notice him. I should never have taken Ahna and Li into the Underground when I knew the Imminent Darkness was there.

"Amber." my mother says softly.

"Amber?" Ahna asks, but her voice comes out hoarse and for the first time I notice the tear stains on her cheeks.

"Ka, you've retrieved the Wood stone, yes?" my mother asks.

"Y-yes." I dig around in my messenger bag and pull out the perfectly round, orange-red sphere. I hand it to her.

"Amber preserves as well as heals. It will release the negative energy from his body."

"But how? It's just a stupid rock!" I say angrily. As I gesticulate small sparks fly from my fingertips. Sloan places a hand on my arm. Calmness. Balance.

"We need to extract its sap. Heat. We need to melt it into a resin. And then he needs to drink it." She looks down at Li. Then back up at me. "We don't have much time. The matches won't be enough."

"I-I can't," I say, feeling the tears welling up behind my eyes.

She hands the stone back to me. "Use your Fire, Kata. Save your friend. Absalom, grab a glass from the dining hall."

My father jumps to his feet and is off like a flash. I feel the stone cold in my palm. It feels heavier than before, as if it is made of lead instead of amber.

"Come on, Ka. You can do it. Don't use your anger this time. Use your Fire. Use your passion. Your life force," Sloan urges.

I close my eyes and recall Li's smiling face, the impish grin he so often used to wear. The swagger in his walk down the hallway at school. I recall his joy at pronouncing Fire, practically leaping into the black box on the stage at Pronouncement. As I think about these things a warm, tingle emanates from deep in the pit of my stomach. It doesn't feel bad, in fact it feels wonderful, as if I'm coming home after a long journey. I recall my first kiss, Li's drunken breath on my lips, leaving a bitter sweetness. I think about his eyes not meeting mine as he stood among the army of Fire, warning me to run right before he tried to kill me. And then our second kiss when I was invisible and he told me he could always feel me. How had I missed so many signs? Li's chest pressed close to mine right before I slap him…the hurt look on his face as he accuses me of treating him like he's damaged. The warmth begins to grow and I feel it flowing through me. It feels comforting and light, not blazing and angry. It feels a lot like love.

"You're doing it," Sloan whispers.

And he's right. I can feel the stone softening in my hand. My father returns with a glass and I try to squeeze the softening amber, trying to extract its rich resin from its womb. A few fiery droplets drip into the class.

"More," my mother instructs.

I continue to imagine Li's chocolatey brown eyes and slightly-lopsided smile. Why had I not seen it before? I always thought Li was a pain, just teasing me. I thought so little of myself that I couldn't even entertain the idea that Li could actually like me—even be in love with me. But that's not who I am anymore. Li is in love with a part of me that left a while ago, replaced with something bolder and perhaps more fool-hardy. He's in love with the old Ka, not the Impossible Girl. And the old Ka could never defeat the Imminent Darkness. The old Ka would never be able to save her dying best friend.

A tear rolls down my cheek as I squeeze the stone and a trickle steadily drips into the glass. Enough golden liquid coats the bottom that my dad whisks it away and hands it to my mother, leaving some remaining drops that slip through my fingertips and fall to the white floor. My mother holds it to Li's lips and tilts the glass up, allowing the elixir to flow into his mouth.

"Swallow," she whispers.

"Please, Li. Drink it," Ahna begs.

Nothing happens.

Then his long lashes begin to flutter and he groans. My mother pours the liquid down his throat and we watch in amazement as if every pore of his body seems to emanate a golden dust—like Hennie in the Land of Wood. The golden dust swirls around his body. The wound on his shoulder begins to shrink as if someone waved a magic wand and made it disappear, which in a way I guess we did. The dust dances along his body, finds the wound on his calf and begins the same miraculous healing process. After that wound is healed, the dust settles over his entire body and becomes still.

"It's working," my mother whispers.

"Is he going to live?" Ahna asks the question that we all want the answer to but are too afraid to ask.

"I can't be completely certain, but the fact that it healed his wounds so quickly is a good sign." She stands up slowly, there's a streak of blood across the skirt of her dress. "He'll need to rest. Absalom, Love, will you take him to one of the bedrooms? Ahna can tend to him while I address Ka." At home, mother was never so formal, but I guess returning back to an immortal goddess of the Universe can have that effect on someone.

My father bends over and scoops up Li as if he is nothing more than a ragdoll, cradling his head across one elbow crook and his limp legs across the other. "Come on, Ahna. I'll show you where you can rest."

Ahna turns weary eyes toward me and I nod my encouragement. I can only hope that she doesn't blame me too much for her brother's near-death. The stone has grown cold in my hands again. It's somehow reverted back to a perfect sphere. But my hand is still slick with resin. I rub it over my shoulder, where the bite marks are and feel a sting as the resin seeps into the puncture wounds. I watch curiously as each hole seems to zip up on its own, disappearing into my skin. I wipe the rest of my hand on my pants.

"Ka? You have some explaining to do. You too, Sloan." We follow my mother out into the garden. There's a long wooden table beneath a pergola covered in flowers. My mother sits at the table and gestures for us to sit too. Sloan sits on the bench across from us. I place the stone on the table in front of me.

"What happened?" My mother asks. Her tone isn't angry as much as worried.

"The Imminent Darkness is in the Underground," I say.

"And we went to check on Bina after we got back from the Elemental Abyss," Sloan jumps in.

"Ahna and Li came with us. We had to check on them too and, well, you know how they are. They insisted on coming with us."

"Ka wore a cloaking device. Ahna and Li waited in Pax Park while we were gone. Only Ka uncloaked when we met up with Ahna."

I sigh. "She said it was weird to talk to me when she couldn't see me." If I hadn't been seen, would this still have happened?

"When we asked her where Li was she said he'd wandered off."

"He's been acting so strange since everything that happened with Fire."

"Too much time in the Black Bazaar," my mother chides.

"It's all my fault. That he goes there."

"Li has his own free will, Ka. You are not responsible for his choices."

"But he was susceptible because of me. The Imminent Darkness feeds on the weak. Li was weak and it's all my fault."

"Sloan," my mother turns to him. "Thank you from the bottom of my immortal heart for protecting Ka on her journey thus far. But if you don't mind, I think I need to talk to my daughter alone."

Sloan blushes, but bows his head slightly. "Yes, ma'am." He gets up from the table but not before casting me an apologetic glance. He knows my mother isn't cross with me, but I can't help but think he feels a little guilty over stabbing Li in the shoulder.

Once he's out of earshot, my mother turns to me. "Ka, what's going on? Why didn't you use the Bloodstone?"

"Mom, it's everywhere. You don't understand. The Imminent Darkness has traveled to all the Lands. It's been in the Elemental Abyss. It—it killed the sea creatures. Brooks is dead."

She doesn't respond, but her mouth becomes pinched and there's a flicker of something in her eyes. Sadness? Anger?

I push on. "When we split up to find Li—Ahna was going to check the other side of the park—the black wolf showed up. The same one that was here. The same one that tried to kill you. But it was strange. It morphed into Li's form and it—I don't know. I guess it tried to make me feel bad for retrieving the stones, like it wouldn't even matter and that I still wouldn't be able to protect the ones that I love."

"Ka, you know that's not true."

"And then it morphed from Li's form back into the wolf and pounced on me. That's when Sloan stabbed it in the shoulder with the dagger Qildor had given him."

"Qildor?"

"A warrior elf who helped us retrieve the Wood stone."

"I see."

"Anyways, the wolf howled in pain and as it howled it turned back into Li's body and left in a plume of smoke. We saw the other wound on Li's leg…and how much blood he was losing…Soldiers saw us. I didn't know what else to do." I finger the stone in front of me and don't meet her eyes. "I'm sorry that I'm failing. I'm sorry I'm not doing a good job of saving everyone."

My mother lets out a long sigh. "Oh, Ka." She takes my chin and moves my face so that I'm forced to look at her. Tears sting at the backs of my eyes. "You are not failing. As long as you live another day to fight the good fight, you are winning. The Imminent Darkness wants you to give up. It wants you to think that you're too weak to defeat it. But we both know that's not true."

"It's my fault Li almost died."

"If it weren't for your quick thinking, surely he would have. But you brought him here and in a few days' time he'll be good as new. Moreso even."

"Moreso?"

She shrugs. "The resin has some interesting side effects besides healing."

"Such as?"

She looks up at the sky. "Possibly, maybe immortality. Why else do you think those nymphs and elves drink it like its water?"

"You made Li immortal!? Are you crazy!?" Li would be the absolute worst immortal. I can see him going through ways to risk his life just to see if he'd survive.

"I didn't say invincible. Just immortal. A small price to pay in order to save his life." I can't imagine how Ahna will respond to knowing her brother will carry on long after she's left the mortal plane. I don't think I'll tell her—or him for that matter. My mother answers as if reading my mind, but she's not. She just knows me that well. "Yes, it's probably for the best that you don't tell either of them."

She turns serious again. "Now, Ka. What's happened to Li. None of it is your fault. Or Sloan's for that matter. He was only fulfilling his vow to protect you. And Li…Li is a big boy. He makes his own decisions. It's his decision to go to the Black Bazaar and it was his decision to walk away in the park. Now, what happened to Li—and all the others—in Fire is not your fault. That was Tristen's—and the ID's—doing. And I know you're shocked to realize what I've known for a long time, Li's true feelings about you."

"You know about that?"

"I'm your mother. I've been around you two long enough to notice a few things."

"It would never have worked out."

She shrugs. "Perhaps you're right, but take this piece of advice for what you will. Does knowing change anything?" I shake my head. "Don't feel guilty over someone else's feelings toward you. What other people think and feel about you, truly it's none of your business. It's about them, not you."

I nod. It's about them not me. I shouldn't feel guilty over unrequited love. Do I love Li? Of course I do, like you love an annoying wart that's grown on your big toe and never goes away no matter what you do. But am I *in* love with him? I don't think so.

"You and Sloan, you're good for each other. I'd be worried about you and Li. You're more alike than you realize. Too much of a good thing."

I smile. She's right about that. The more I change the more I am like Li. Well, the old Li: the impulsive, adventurous one. He's but a shadow of who he once was and he's in love with the shadow of who I once was.

"There's still one thing bothering me."

"What's that?" my mother asks.

"Bina gave another prophecy to Sloan."

"What did she say?"

"She said, 'When the one you love is lost, the stone will turn to dust.' I love Li and he was almost lost to us, but now he's going to be fine. And the stone still hasn't turned to dust."

My mother smiles. "I'm sure you'll figure it out." She gets up and pats me on my now-healed shoulder before disappearing through the colorful, blooming garden and back into the castle of a house we now call home.

I roll the stone back and forth across the wood-planked surface of the table. The Land of Earth is probably my favorite. I think because it's how I imagine Old Earth to have been. Bright colors everywhere, a canvas of blue sky above and green grass below. Birds chirping all around and I can hear the chitter of other small creatures as they climb about the surrounding trees. It's about as different from Xon 9 as you can get.

I remember there's a stream nearby. I pick up the stone and wander down the cobblestone path in what I think is the direction of the stream. I quickly realize that I'm right as I hear the soft bubbling of water grow louder as I near it. The garden opens up onto a green, grassy space. The stream looks clear and inviting. There's no one around, so I slip off my boots and undress to my underwear, leaving my clothes in a pile on the grassy knoll.

I wade into the stream and it's cool, but refreshing. I walk toward the middle until I'm about chest height then bend my knees so that the water covers my shoulders. I let the stream flow around me, cleansing my bite wound that's no more, and washing away the dirt and blood that covers my arms and legs. Washing away the darkness and letting in the light. I splash my face and the water is so clear that I can see my reflection. I let out an audible gasp at what looks back at me.

A once familiar face is now a stranger. My face is slightly tanned from the suns of the Land of Wood and the Land of Earth. My cheeks are slightly rosy. A strong mouth that's filled with the words to banish darkness has replaced a soft mouth that used to mumble answers in class and make excuses. Eyes that once were skittish and blank, are now resolute and so fathomless that I could get lost in the pools of brown now regarding me. Once long brown hair that hung mousey around my face has been replaced with short, choppy brown hair that hugs around a jaunty chin.

This girl who looks back at me, she is a stranger, but I welcome her with open arms. I smile as I dunk my head back into the water, letting the cool water rush through my hair. Water trickles down the back of my neck, and I run my hand along the familiar metallic filigree and vein-like vines, except—there's a new sensation, the soft sensation of bark. Wood. I run my fingers along the ridges of the Elemental Star. How can it be? I half run-half-wade through the stream's gentle current back toward the pile of my clothes. Sitting on top of the pile, where I'd left the Wood stone, now sits a pile of amber-colored dust. A bird whistles a three-note song in one of the trees above me. Three notes. Three stones. I look up. A white bird with brown speckled feathers sits in the tree branches above me. I open my messenger bag, dripping water on its contents, as I rummage through it and pull out the sack from Bina. I pull out the speckled feather that matches the bird above me exactly.

The bird flies down and lands beside the pile of clothes. It looks at me with unblinking, black eyes. The stream babbles behind me. Cleansing. I scoop up as much of the amber-colored dust that I can into my palm, then while holding the feather, I wave it over the dust. The dust dances in my hand and, as if to aid in my ritual, a gentle breeze picks up. The breeze picks up the dust and I use the feather to smudge the dust into the wind, the amber dust swirls around me, creating a cocoon. A cocoon of new, positive energy. I continue to use the feather to fan the amber dust into the wind until my palm is empty. When I'm done I release the feather, but before it can hit the ground the small bird swoops up and catches it in its mouth and flies away with it, heading toward the purple mountains in the distance.

My mother was right. I did figure it out.

When the one you love is lost, the stone will turn to dust.

It wasn't Sloan or even Li.

All along it was me. The old Ka is lost, but the new one has been found.

CHAPTER 25

I return to the castle happy and renewed. My mother has set out clothes for me and I change into the clean pants and sweater. I make my way to the living space. There are two couches and a plush chair, all a soft purple color. There's a fire place with no fire and a wood mantle decorated with pictures of my parents and me. A large oil painting of a cyan dragonfly hangs above the fireplace and is the focal point of the room. Two walls are lined from floor to ceiling with books and the third wall has a set of fancy glass doors that lead back out to the pergola.

"You look better." My mother notices.

"I feel better. I destroyed the Wood stone."

"Really?" Sloan asks. "But how? Li is doing much better by the way—he's fast asleep, but Ahna refuses to leave his side until he's fully awake."

"That should only be a day or two," my mother interjects. "But, yes, Ka, tell us. How did you destroy the stone?"

"Well, I thought that the one I love in Bina's prophecy could be Sloan, or even Ahna or Li. Or even you, Mom. Or Dad. Anyone really, who I care about. But I was wrong. *When the one you love is lost* wasn't referring to someone else, it was referring to me." Sloan gives me a confused look. "It was the old me. The old me is the one I love that's been lost. Replaced with the Impossible Girl, who is growing stronger and more confident every day. I hadn't really noticed the change, but it's true. I'm not the same person that I was only a short while ago."

My mother smiles. "I told you, you'd figure it out."

"So what happened when the stone was destroyed?" my father asks.

"It turned to dust."

"Just like Bina's prophecy," Sloan smiles.

"Exactly."

. . .

When I make my way up the spiral staircase to one of the many guest bedrooms in the castle, I find Ahna and Li. Ahna's seated in a chair beside the elaborate four-poster bed. She's fast asleep, her head lulled back and her mouth hanging slightly open. Her face still streaked with dirt from our travels. She snores softly.

On the other side of the bed, in the corner, is another chair. I pull it across the rug and toward the bed. I watch the rise and fall of Li's chest. His breath is slow and even. The golden haze that surrounded his body earlier is all but gone now. His face is soft and relaxed. I'm sitting on the side of his body with the almost tribal-like tattoo down his cheek. It starts on his neck beneath his ear and climbs up the side of his face, past his eye, toward his temple. If things hadn't gone wrong, if Tristen had never made an army of Fire, the mark would be a beautiful silvery filigree, like the Fire of my Elemental Star tattoo.

It's not your fault, I tell myself. And surprisingly, there's no voice that replies back. My mother has draped a stark white sheet over Li's body and tucked in a plush crème-colored velvety soft blanket around him. On the night stand is a little pebble water fountain that bubbles soothingly. The mid-day sun shines through the window pane, forming a square of light across Li's legs.

I take his hand. It's warm which I take as a good sign. I rub my thumb back and forth carefully over his knuckles. Something flashes in front of me. I blink. But it's still there. I see Li up and moving. But he doesn't have his marks. We're in school. He's staring at the back of my head in Universal History class and poking me with the tip of his pencil. The vision fast forwards to a kiss on a bench in the Black Bazaar. Then fast forwards to Li standing like a soldier, noticing me in the corner. The twitch of his mouth as he tries to warn me to run. It's like I'm watching the film of Li's life. It's like the memories that flash past in the time-space continuum. Then I see Li watching me with Sloan as we stand on the ledge just pass the Black Bazaar—our spot. Sloan and I kiss. Then the vision changes to Li coming down the stairs to see Sloan, his sister, and me in his living room. And then,

Li's head down walking in Pax Park, lost in thought and not seeing the wolf lurking just nearby. I see Li well—healthy and whole. He's smiling like I haven't seen in so long and it's beautiful. I see a flash of a girl with long red hair and then the image quickly changes to Li holding a bow and arrow, a person in a hooded cloak bowed before him. I blink and the vision stops.

Li moans softly and I shush him. "Shhh. Rest."

"Ka?" he mumbles and his eyes flutter open ever so slightly.

"It's me," I whisper.

"I'm sorry for being so stupid. Shouldn't have wandered off."

"No, never sorry. Sorry serves no purpose," I tell him repeating something he once told me.

He smiles, but then winces. "I understand now."

"Understand what?"

"That you aren't the same person." The words come out slow, with deep breaths in between each one.

"You need to rest. You're not completely healed yet," I tell him.

"We aren't the same person." He sounds like he's talking crazy. Maybe it's the effects of the elixir, I know some of that first hand from my time in the Fairy Grove. "We were. But we're not anymore. I've gotten a second chance. I won't waste it." His breathing becomes slow again and his eyes slide closed.

Were Li and I ever the same person? Could it be that I was so lost in my own helplessness that I failed to see my best friend's? I always thought Li was so self-assured—almost cocky—but perhaps it was all a ruse. Maybe he was just as confused and lost as I'd been, only I didn't take the time to see. And now, he's right, we're both different. I'm slowly learning who I am and maybe now he is too. I don't bother to tell him that yeah, he got a second chance, but now my mother made him immortal so he'll probably get a whole lot more than just a second one. That kind of thing would go to his head.

. . .

I find my father on the veranda. I wrap my arms around his waist like I used to do when I was small. "I miss you," I say and it's true. Things are so different now.

"And I miss you, too." He rests his chin on top of my head. The sun is lowering on the horizon, preparing for sunset. Here the sun sets and a single moon rises. "You did the right thing you know, bringing Li here."

"I know."

"Did you figure out your new Elemental ability? Let's see, your Aunt Celosia gave you the ability to conjure Fire through your emotions—some first moon gift that was, for a child no less—and your mother gave you the vines of Earth to protect you."

"You know about those?"

"Kata, I'm your father. I know about everything." He smiles. "Well, almost everything. Okay, only the things your mother tells me."

"I think I figured it out, but I don't quite understand it."

Even though the sun hasn't completely sunk below the horizon the white moon has appeared high in the indigo sky. Stars begin to blink on like tiny night lights, one by one.

"I think I can see someone's past and future. As if I'm an outside spectator. Why would that be my gift from Aunt Constancia?" I ask.

"I am just the man to ask that." My father grins and the ridges lining the right side of his face pull up the corner of his mouth slightly. Of course. My father is a Wood. He would know better than anybody what it means. There are two pillow-like cushions on the veranda and my father gestures for me to sit. "There is a very old Wood parable about a seed that is planted in the ground. It was called the Genesis Seed"

My eyes grow wide. "Qildor is the keeper of the Genesis Seed."

"So you've heard of it? Yes, the Genesis Seed was planted. From one single seed sprouted every tree and being in the Land of Wood. Trees are unique. They put down roots and are forever tied to one spot. Because of this they see many things over the years—sometimes hundreds of years. They watch the world change around them, observing its past, present, and future. As they grow, so too does the world grow: starting out as a sapling, aging into a mature tree, and eventually becoming what's known as *radix sapientiae*, or to put it simply, wisdom of the roots. In other words an old tree."

"So the gift of Wood is the ability to see the change"

"Yes, I think that's the gist of it."

"Will it happen every time I touch someone?" That would be horrible. I'm not sure I'd ever want to touch anyone ever again for fear of what I'd see.

But my father shakes his head. "I don't think so. Just like the other gifts it has to be summoned."

"I didn't summon it with Li."

"Perhaps, you did without realizing it."

I realize then that he's right. I did summon it. I wanted—no, needed—to know if Li was going to be okay. And now I know that he is and that he will be, thanks to the wisdom of the roots.

. . .

With the moon high in the sky, Sloan and I make our way toward the beach. The beach is beautiful pink sand and the water clear turquoise here, unlike anything I've ever seen. We sit together in the soft sand, Sloan behind me, my back pressed against his chest, my elbows resting on his knees. The dark water blends into the horizon, making it impossible to tell where water ends and sky begins.

"I've never seen so many stars," Sloan says softly.

"Me neither. Not until I came here for the first time."

"Do you think there could be other Xon 9s out there"?

I practically laugh. "Given the things we've seen, I'm pretty sure there's another hundred Xon 9s out there."

"Where to next, Impossible Girl?" He nuzzles my neck.

"The Land of Water."

"Sounds like my kind of adventure."

"It's the one I fear the most," I admit.

"More than Metal?"

"I can't swim. My track record's not that great. I've nearly drowned more than once."

"I can teach you."

"I'm afraid."

"I thought you weren't afraid of anything anymore."

He jumps to his feet, kicking off his shoes. He pulls his shirt over his head. Like, Xon 9, the temperature here is warm and constant. And I have the feeling the sea will be the perfect temperature too, unlike the frigid lake in the Land of Wood. He pulls at my hand and I kick off my shoes. He holds my hand tight as we wade into the dark water, soaking our clothes. Only the moon reflects in the ripples around us.

"This is crazy."

"Of all the things we've said and done in the last few days—you think this is crazy?" he smiles.

"It's so vast, not like the tiny stream," I object.

"When a human baby is born, its body is made up of almost eighty percent water. Being in the water is as natural as us breathing air. We are the water. It's the most natural Element of any of them to a human."

I try one last time. "It's dark out here. I can't see a thing,"

"Don't see. Just feel. Close your eyes."

I obey and close my eyes.

"Feel the water caressing your skin. Feel how it responds to the movements of your body. We are water. Water is us. Feel the silkiness of its texture." And I do. I feel its cool smoothness and how it responds if I drag my fingers over the surface or dip my hand into its depths to scoop a palm full. Then the gentle resistance I feel as I bring my hand back up and out of the water. The sea is alive. And it's as if we're dancing. I make a move and the water responds. The water makes a move and my body responds in turn. I spin and twirl, feeling the tiny currents around my body. My toes sinking into the sea's sandy bottom.

I am a ballerina in the white light of the moon.

Seeing isn't always believing. Sometimes we see what we don't want to believe.

Believing isn't always seeing. Sometimes we refuse to believe what it is we see.

Don't see.

Just feel.

ABOUT THE AUTHOR

Jennifer L. Kelly is a middle childhood educator. She resides in Cleveland, Ohio. When she isn't writing, she can be found fangirling over *Doctor Who*, doing yoga, spending time with her dog, taking photos for her #bookstagram, or making candles for her Etsy shop: TheBookishFlame. This is her second series for young adults. Her first novel, *The Prophecy: The Lucia Chronicles Book 1,* was published in January 2014. Visit her website **Skim.Scheme.Scribble:** **www.jenniferlkelly.com** Or say *HI!* :

info@jenniferlkelly.com

JenniferLKelly3

AuthorJenniferLKelly

AuthorJenniferLKelly

ACKNOWLEDGEMENTS

There are so many people who have supported me on this journey. First, I'd like to thank my Dad because he is the second set of eyes on all of my books. Second, I'd like to thank my Advanced Readers in the #bookstagram community. Thank you for being so kind and supportive! And for sticking with me through five books! I know that's a commitment, and I appreciate it! Third, I'd like to thank the artists that have worked on this series with me. The beautiful Elemental Star that was created by Joshua Jadon and for the map on which Rebecca Solow worked so hard to match my vision to her artistic talent! Thank you!

Turn the page for the beginning of …

THE WATER QUEEN

The Elementals Book 4

06.13.17

I am afraid.

I have a mission.

I am not prepared. But I have no choice.

I am the Impossible Girl. A myth, a legend, a story told to Xon 9 children before they go to sleep at night. A bed time story. Only I'm not. I am very, very real. I didn't ask for this. I didn't ask people to take risks for me. I didn't ask—never would ask—people to *die* for me.

But they do.

And they will continue to do so. Because truthfully, it isn't for me. And it doesn't matter if I asked for it.

Long ago a girl was born to an immortal woman who fell in love with a mortal man. The girl was bequeathed with many gifts from her mother's immortal sisters: The Elemental Goddesses.

Passion like the flickering flames of a roaring fire.

Compassion like the fertile soil giving birth to the most delicate of flowers.

Wisdom like the oldest of trees that have silently watched the passage of centuries.

Intuition like the bottomless depths of the vast sea.

And—

Strength like the strongest of metals.

These were the gifts given to the girl and these were the gifts that the Imminent Darkness wanted to take away. The Universe needed balance and this girl was an anomaly. Mortals and Immortals don't fall in love. She shouldn't exist. But they did. And I do.

In order to protect me, my mother traveled to the mountains of our home planet and to a mystical place called the Elemental Abyss. There she threw in five stones—one for each of Xon 9's Elements: Fire, Earth, Wood, Water, and Metal. With each stone went a piece of my personality, thus fracturing it, so that there was very little semblance of the true Ka Waylon left. Good-bye courage. Good-bye intuition. And forget wisdom. Buh-bye. Except the day came that I had to choose. Which Element did I want to be affiliated with for the rest of my life? I chose Fire. Big mistake.

Soon the truth began to emerge, secrets that had been kept from me for the eighteen years of my life and that could only begin to be revealed on the hundredth solar alignment. Secrets that involved my true identity—the missing parts of who I am—oh, and the whole half-immortal thing. (Very cool.)

Turns out I represent all the possibilities of Xon 9's people. The

Imminent Darkness has spent hundreds of years trying to divide us, separating us by our differences. But no more. We no longer need to choose. We are not only passionate like Fire or merely wise like Wood. We are everything: strong like Metal, intuitive like Water, and compassionate like Earth. We can be all of these things. So I say to the Imminent Darkness (because I know that you're listening, you're always listening, behind every whisper or shadow you are waiting): No. More.

So you see, I am afraid. I am afraid I will somehow mess up the entire future of my planet. I am afraid that the Imminent Darkness will win. And I am afraid that the most difficult tasks still lay before me.

Luckily, I am not the only one afraid.

Because the Imminent Darkness is afraid of me too.

CHAPTER 1

The coolness of the sea laps at my ankles. I toss a small pebble into the cerulean blue water and listen for the satisfying *plop!* as it breaks the stillness of the surface. Birds chirp in the distance and a soft breeze rustles the shorn hair at the back of my neck, tickling the Elemental Star tattoo that marks my skin. I run my fingers over it, feeling the green vines of Earth that have sprung to life at the tip of the star, and then moving my fingers to the smoothness of the filigree that makes Fire, before lastly running my fingers over my newest addition: the rough ridges of bark. Wood. Three stones retrieved. My fingers find the flat smoothness that is Metal and Water, the two stones I have yet to retrieve. Because those Elements have not been returned to me, those portions of my Elemental Star remain dormant, just regular inked skin.

I close my eyes, allowing the colors of the sunset to dance across my eyelids. This is Earth. Well, not really. Not even Old Earth if we're being technical. But Earth as my mother imagines it. A Land created by Raj and Katayun, the father and mother of the entire Universe, to placate their feuding daughters. Five sisters. Five goddesses. Five lands. Five elements. Simple math. I was never much good at math though.

Someone sits beside me. I feel the ever-so-slight shift in the pink sand beneath me. I've been heightened. I can feel—and see—things that I've never in my entire life. The smell of soap, leather, and salty sea drift over to me and I smile. I open my eyes and Sloan puts an arm around my waist, scooting me closer to him. Sloan is my boyfriend. He was my teacher, but before you get all weird about it, he is only four years older than me, making him twenty-two. On Xon 9 we only attend two years of University. Well, that's how it used to be before the whole operation got shut down. Thanks or no thanks to me.

Sloan is my protector, quite literally. He took an oath many years ago when his mother, Bina, had a vision of the Impossible Girl arriving on Xon 9. In order to fulfill his oath he took a teaching position until I came along. And that's when things changed. A lot. At first I thought it was creepy how he was always watching me and encouraging me to stand up for myself. Actually, I realize now he was encouraging me to be myself. Period. Only I didn't understand at the time. Now, I know better. Poor guy not only took an Everlasting Vow, he even went and fell in love with the very girl he was meant to protect. Luckily for me.

I take in his shaggy brown hair that is in sore need of a cutting. It hangs into his brilliant green eyes, which are framed by long dark lashes. The right side of his face is lined with silvery-green scales that fade away into the collar of his black t-shirt. Gills mark either side of his neck, which is convenient since he's a Water. Funny, that he represents the very thing I am afraid of most. Besides the Imminent Darkness.

"I don't want to leave." I rest my head on his shoulder.

"I know." He tilts my cheek so that we're face to face and kisses me gently as if I was some fragile, breakable thing. Which we both know I am not. I am not only each of my Elements that has been returned to me, but I am each of my Elements at an exponential level. I guess that's what happens when a group of Immortals get in on the gift-giving. Go big or go home.

He pulls away carefully, but our hipbones are still pressed against one another. The sea laps softly in front of us. Who would want to leave this? He turns so that the smooth, angular side of his face is in my direction and stares at the sea. I know he loves it too. This place—unlike the red barrenness of Xon 9—is a bountiful world of color, sound, and mystery. But it won't be long before the Imminent Darkness returns here. It tried once. And it will try again. One by one, the ID seems to ruin everything that I've come to love. Or that I try to love.

The sun eases itself down past the horizon leaving a line of golden-white light across the sky, caressing against the indigo of the night sky. Tiny pinpricks of light begin popping out across the vastness above our heads, billions of stars seeming to blink on, come to bid us good-night. You'd think it was impossible there could be so many stars. But you may have figured out how I feel about impossible things.

"We should go." And I know he means that we should return to the castle, where my mother and father are, and where Ahna and Li are waiting for us. I nod and Sloan helps me to my feet, pulling me up from the sand, which now coats the seat of my shorts and the backs of my legs. When he pulls me up, he doesn't let go. "You don't have to do this," he whispers.

I sigh. "You know that I do."

"No. I want to be clear. You get a choice in this, Ka. No matter what anyone else says or wants you to do. It's your choice. It always has been."

"What choice is there when there isn't one?"

"Not doing is a choice too."

I turn into his arms so that my forehead is even with his chin. "That's the coward's way."

"Your Metal hasn't been restored yet," he says, referring to the Element that is both the strongest and most feared of Xon 9. Not to mention the most misunderstood. And I can feel him smile from the movement of his chin. "Or is there something you want to tell me?"

"Trust me. No Metal yet. I'd think if I had it, I wouldn't feel so afraid."

"Maybe. But fear is good. I know plenty of Metals who experience fear. Luckily, fear can help keep us from making irrational decisions, if we acknowledge it. Being afraid and still being willing to go forward, that right there is called courage."

I pull back slightly so that I can see his eyes. The Land of Earth's single moon reflects a sliver of light in the green pools that gaze down at me.

"You think I'm courageous?"

He grins. "More than anyone I know." He kisses my forehead then takes my hand leading me away from the beach and back toward the castle, which from here looms large and pristine above us, golden warmth emitting from its windows, beckoning us back. "And Ka, I think you've made your choice quite clear."

I intertwine my fingers with his, a tether that always reminds me of who I am and what matters most. "I don't follow."

"Fear is a choice too."

. . .

I never used to be afraid. Not like this. But I've seen things and once you've seen things, you can't unseen them. The Imminent Darkness is as old as the Universe itself, the same Universe that birthed my mother, the immortal Earth Goddess with three faces: Anuja, Novea, and Kesara. The ID is all about power and uses the fear that it creates to manipulate people and bend them to its will. It is ancient and formless, feeding on the negative energy of the devastation left in its wake, which only makes it grow stronger. And its appetite is ravenous because with each retrieval of a stone, I grow stronger and the Imminent Darkness becomes weaker. My mom said it's all about balance. Unfortunately, I'm what is causing the

Imbalance.

The castle appears stark on the outside with its white stone walls, but what it lacks in ambience on the outside, it makes up for on the inside. In the backyard is a lush garden with a pergola and a long table for outdoor dinners. It rarely rains here—only for short periods of time to keep everything thriving—after all, this is my mother's world. Inside the main doors is a purple runner atop the polished, white stone floor that leads to a wooden throne upholstered in amethyst-colored velvet. There are many nooks and crannies in the castle, including a winding staircase with an elaborate banister that leads to six spacious bedrooms and six bathrooms. Why anyone would ever need six bathrooms is beyond me, especially since our family only consists of me, Mom, and Dad, but I suspect it has something to do with Mom holding out the hope that she and her sisters can someday reconcile.

I have four aunts: Celosia, Isa, Constancia, and Tullia. The rulers of the lands of Fire, Metal, Wood, and Water respectively. I've only met the two and let's just say I could see maybe why Celosia and Mom didn't get along. The Land of Fire is all fire and brimstone, quite literally. My aunt Constancia I've only met in avian form, but she was very kind as far as birds go. Many moons ago, my mom and her sisters were each given their own land after a codger tricked them. He gave them each a stone and the sisters fought over whose stone was more special, until Raj and Katayun could no longer bear it and created a land for each of their daughters to rule over. Separately. The codger, of course, was the Imminent Darkness looking to divide the sisters who had once loved one another so dearly, in order to cause chaos. Like Mom said, balance and all that junk. And yet, despite everything, my aunts were overjoyed with my birth, much to the ID's disappointment. They gifted me the very stones that were later used to protect me, and which I am now retrieving. If that's not a peace offering, I'm not sure what is.

We make our way to the den with its large stone fireplace with wood mantle, decorated in pictures of yours truly and above which is an oil painting of a brilliant cyan-colored dragonfly, a homage to another one of my mother's many forms. Two walls are lined floor-to-ceiling with books and the third wall, across from the entrance, is a set of glass doors that lead out to the garden. My father has started a fire and he sits on one of the soft purple couches beside my mother. Both of them are reading. Ahna sits in the plush violet armchair and she too is engrossed in a book about as thick as a tree trunk. The only one not reading is Ahna's twin brother, Li, who is sprawled across the remaining couch, his lanky form taking up all three cushions in their entirety.

I feel a pang of guilt at Li's presence. His too long black hair that falls carelessly into his almond-shaped eyes, the wide nose, and perfectly arched lips. Perfect, if not for the black tribal-looking tattoo that now runs down the right side of his face, curling down his neck and into the collar of his t-shirt. Li and I were never a *thing* exactly. I've known him forever and he's one of my best friends, but he was my first kiss. And the only kiss I'd ever experienced before Sloan. Li was the forbidden fruit, taking me to the Black Bazaar and making me feel things I probably shouldn't be feeling. But he's always been there for me, even when he was unwillingly turned into a soldier to be used against me—against the Leadership Council of Xon 9—in the name of the Imminent Darkness. And yet, his love for me was strong enough to break the bonds of collective consciousness, if even for the briefest of moments, to warn me. That kind of loyalty and that kind of love is what makes my stomach now twist up in a knot. *We are not the same people.* I remind myself of his words. We've both changed. And Li doesn't even know the half of it.

Not only did he lose his Fire because of my actions, but the Imminent Darkness took his form in order to attack me, using Li as if he were nothing more than a pawn in some sort of sick game. It almost—I almost—killed him for a second time, but luckily was quick thinking enough to use my ring to bring us here. My ring was made by my friend Doran using the pieces of the destroyed Earth stone. It has a living memory which can return me home whenever I want it. Or need it. My mother used the nectar of the Wood stone to save Li and now, you'd never know he was on the brink of death only several days ago. The part that he doesn't know is my mother happened to make him immortal in the process. Not just half-immortal like me, but full-on totally immortal. That would just go straight to his head.

Li looks up at the sound of our arrival. "Hey, Kata," he says and winks at me. Like I said straight to his head. He's fiddling with something in his hands, but I can't tell what it is.

"You take up the entire couch like you own the place. Move

over," I order. He obliges, sitting up and moving over to make enough room for both Sloan and myself. I can see now that the object is some kind of wooden puzzle cube with sliding pieces. Each piece a different color. It must belong to my mom. She loves puzzles and riddles. "A little primitive for your tastes, isn't it?"

Li scoffs. "Actually, I'm finding it quite challenging. You see I have to align each piece so an entire side of the cube is all the same color."

Mother closes her book. "Your father made that for me. It's modeled after some Old Earth toy." She smiles warmly at Dad, who is oblivious, still engrossed in his own book.

"Here, let me see it." Ahna reaches across the space between the chair and sofa, snatching the cube from Li. She flips her thick braid over her shoulder and bites her bottom lip as she slides and moves about the pieces. In a matter of minutes she's solved the puzzle, each side now made up of a single color.

"Well done!" Mom claps which finally causes Dad to look up. My father is a Wood and was a liege to the Council before he came to the Land of Earth. The Leadership Council is the governing body of Xon 9 and is made up of five Woods, four males and one female. Wood is considered unyielding and steadfast. They have a reputation for making the best leaders. The lines between Council and Imminent Darkness are too blurred for my taste, as the Imminent Darkness has its share of followers on Xon 9. Only, they're none the wiser to the fact that the ID is using them to feed, not the other way around, and in the process breeding aggression, paranoia, and corruption with its negative energy.

Li scowls. "You take the fun out of everything."

I feel Sloan laugh silently beside me. Ahna was always an excellent student, especially in Earth Science and Universal History, her two favorite subjects.

"So," my father says setting his book on the arm of the couch, "are you kids ready to return home?"

Ahna nods anxiously. "Yes. I'm worried about Mom and Dad." Mr. and Mrs. Solloman, Li, and Ahna, were our neighbors. Now our house sits vacant next to theirs. There's no reason for us to go back. But Li and Ahna need to go back.

"I'm sure they're fine. They're no fun just like you," Li says.

Ahna sticks her tongue out. "Well, some of us follow the rules so we don't get ourselves into trouble like you." Li definitely is the black sheep of the Solloman family. He's all fiery passion and impulsivity. Or at least he was. For a long time after the army of Fire incident, he didn't seem like himself. This back and forth banter reminds me of the old Li.

"I agree with Li," I say. "I'm sure they're fine, Ahna. Your Mom and Dad obey all the rules and don't draw attention to themselves. If anything, they're probably just worried sick about you guys." There was no way of telling Mr. and Mrs. Solloman what happened or where we went when we left Xon 9. The Imminent Darkness's presence was growing stronger, curfews were being implemented, among other rules to try and keep the colonists safe…or out of the way. If we tried to contact them, the Imminent Darkness could have followed us. Or worse, tried to hurt Mr. or Mrs. Solloman.

Ahna's brown eyes fall on me. They used to be warm and inviting, sometimes chastising at my procrastinating ways in school, but now there's something different there that looks back at me. A bit of iciness mixed with wariness. I almost killed her twin. I can understand the chill beneath her gaze, but surely she knows I love Li as much as she does. Right?

"Yes, I suppose so." Her tone is clipped, but then she shakes her head and smiles as if willing herself to not let that small sliver of hatred show. "Tomorrow then?"

"I think it would be best," my mother agrees.

"Ka and I think it's time we go too," Sloan says looking at me sideways.

"Yeah, I don't think I can put it off any longer. The longer I wait, the more damage the Imminent Darkness is doing." I glance at Li who is still scowling down at the solved puzzle in his hands. "And now that Li's better, I guess we don't have a reason to continue to stay."

"Don't be silly. This is your home," Mom says, but her gray eyes betray her worry.

"Kata's right," Dad says. "There are two stones left and each moment she isn't looking for them, is a moment the Imminent Darkness grows stronger. Tomorrow, Sloan and Ka can head to Tullia's Land, and I'll take Li and Ahna back to the colony."

The only thing is now that the ID has infiltrated the Elemental Abyss, where the portals to the five lands are located, and destroyed the magical creatures that protect it, I'm not sure how we're going anywhere.

Mom shakes her head. "Are you sure that's a good idea Absalom?"

"I'll pop in and out and be back before you're even up for breakfast," Dad grins.

"You'll be taking the watch then?"

Dad holds up his wrist and taps the sapphire watch face. "You bet."

Li looks up. "That looks like an ordinary watch to me." Li wasn't conscious when we used my ring to come here.

"It has a living memory." I hold up my index finger. "Like my ring. It can return to the last place that it was or, in my case, Mom made it so I can come home when I need to. It's how we brought you here."

"Huh. That's crazy." Li shakes his head in disbelief then glances up, a sly smile spreading across his angular face. And I know exactly what he's thinking before even says it. Because this is the Li I know. The lover of cloaking cuffs and Pleasure patches. Mischievous. Entrepreneurial. And a little bit brazen. "I bet there's a huge market for something like that back home. Because you know, I happen to know a guy."

THE WATER QUEEN

The Elementals Book 4

06.13.17

www.ingramcontent.com/pod-product-compliance
Lightning Source LLC
Chambersburg PA
CBHW022138170626

46807CB00005B/1986